POE STREET

POE
STREET

MICHAEL RALEIGH

For Katherine

What Reviewers and Authors Have Said About Michael Raleigh's books

DEATH IN UPTOWN:

"Michael Raleigh's *Death in Uptown* is perhaps the finest debut of a P.I. since that of John Francis Cuddy in the first Jeremiah Healy novel…Paul Whelan and Uptown are an unbeatable team, guided by the hand of a fine writer."—Author Robert Randisi, *Orlando Sentinel*

"Credible and earthy…tautly written, full of muscular action."—Edward Gilbreth, *Chicago Sun-Times*

"The vividly realized setting of this impressive first mystery is Uptown…A promising debut."—*Publisher's Weekly*

"Michael Raleigh's *Death in Uptown* is one fine first novel. It has what too many private eye novels lack, a heart."—Stuart Kaminsky, Edgar-winning author

"The mystery is beautifully done with a can't-miss plot twist at the end. I highly recommend it."—Author Mark Richard Zubro

A BODY IN BELMONT HARBOR

"Sleek plotting and an abundance of small diversions brighten Raleigh's second tour of Chicago's ethnically mixed Uptown area. Raleigh, who delivered the goods in his debut novel, *Death in Uptown*, shows no signs of faltering."—*Publisher's Weekly*

"For hard-boiled mystery fans who like their detectives on the gritty side… Whelan will hit all the right notes. This is only Whelan's second outing, but already he's established his bona fides alongside Robert Ray's Matt Murdock, Jeremiah Healy's John Cuddy, Jonathan Valin's Harry Stoner…"—Bill Ott, *Booklist*

"En route to a neat solution, Whelan finds time to protect a hooker from a conventioneering pharmacist, break up a cross -burning on his neighbor's lawn, mix it up in a bar brawl with his loose cannon police buddy Al Bauman, make cautious time with a smiling waitress… a Shaggy satisfying Valentine to Chicago's seedy Uptown."—*Kirkus Reviews*

THE MAXWELL STREET BLUES:

"With his flair for vivid prose and his vesting of dignity in the humblest of characters, Raleigh renders a superlative work on another of Chicago's darker recesses."—Edward Gilbreth, *The Chicago Sun-Times*

"The third Whelan mystery…possesses the same attributes as its predecessor: an agreeably low-key protagonist, plenty of vivid Chicago atmosphere; and a well-rounded portrayal of mean streets and the often very decent people forced to inhabit them."—Wes Lukowsky, *Booklist*

KILLER ON ARGYLE STREET

"Like his hero, Mr. Raleigh has a thing for losers, characterizing them with compassionate care that spills over into affectionate studies of bartenders, waitresses and the owners of a slew of delis, bodegas, and restaurants on Whelan's ethnically mixed turf."—Marilyn Stasio, *The New York Times*

THE RIVERVIEW MURDERS

"An old-fashioned knight at the hard-boiled round table, Whelan honors the dignity of the poor, respects the social integrity of the neighborhoods and goes nuts for ethnic food."—Marilyn Stasio, *The New York Times*

"Raleigh's Paul Whelan series brings to mind the late Ross McDonald's Lew Archer novels...This series is a small treasure. It's like finding a tasty little combo that can be enjoyed in a small club for a while but will certainly move on to bigger venues."—Wes Lukowsky, *Booklist*

"Replete with an engaging supporting cast, Raleigh's latest tale demonstrates his knack for fashioning living, breathing characters out of his tough urban settings. The mystery fiction that Sara Paretsky fashions from Chicago's South Side is full matched in Raleigh's gritty North Side tales."—*Publisher's Weekly*

IN THE CASTLE OF THE FLYNNS

"One of the warmest and funniest novels I've ever read."—*Irish News*

"An amazing book, a troika of laughter, love, and loss. There is wonderful and hilarious writing in this man's book and if you escape without shaking with mirth or silently weeping, then check into the nearest morgue, for it's dead you are."—Malachy McCourt.

"The McCourt brothers can move over. The Chicago branch of the Irish mafia weighs in with a hilarious rendition of an Irish Catholic childhood circa 1955."—*Booklist*

"A hymn to the love, nourishment, and the healing of a wonderful extended family."—Peter Sheridan, award-winning Irish playwright

THE BLUE MOON CIRCUS

"Hilarious and tragic and very, very American—it's as if both Huck Finn and Tom Sawyer had run off to join the circus."—Henry Kisor, *Chicago Sun-Times.*

"Beguiling, wise, and wonderful."—*Kirkus Reviews* (starred review).

"Full of remarkably engaging characters and fascinating circus lore. This warm, slyly humorous novel from the author of *In the Castle Of The Flynns* is highly recommended for all reading tastes and all fiction collections. An absolute charmer."—*Library Journal* (starred review).

THE CONJURER'S BOY

"Raleigh's tale of outsiders looking for a way in examines the resilience of the soul by way of a tour through the catastrophes of the twentieth century."—Sam Reaves, author of *Mean Town Blues*

PEERLESS DETECTIVE

"Clever and surprising, a pleasure of a read."—Michael Allen Dymmoch, award-winning mystery writer

Prologue

The statue stood on a corner shelf in the long living room. It was a bit under eighteen inches high: a woman caught in mid-step, her head to one side as though averting her eyes. Her hair was red, and she wore a diaphanous gown that clung to her like a silken skin, a study in green and pink pastels. The silver-haired man named Morrison took her down from her niche in the wall, one of many. Indeed, she herself was but one of many statues and works of art along the far wall of the great parlor. From a visitor's vantage point, there was little about the statue other than a certain charm to indicate her worth. In truth, there was nothing in Morrison's improbably bedizened home, not his original works of art nor his painstakingly collected jewelry and silver, that was as valuable as the statue. Men would kill for this statue, and more than one had tried.

Morrison turned the plaster figure over and unscrewed the base of the statue. From within, he withdrew a long paper cylinder. For a moment, he examined the other contents of the hollow statue. Then he unrolled the cylinder, a ruled sheet filled with names and figures, dollar amounts, and notations in shorthand comprehensible only to him. The code was a matter of no small pride, as were the sums listed on the sheet and the encrypted information. Names and dollar amounts were clear, but their significance was apparent only to Morrison. Flattening the paper with a bronze ashtray, he uncapped a pen and wrote a name on a new line, followed by a figure and then a notation in his odd encryption. He blew on the ink to dry it, then glanced at the list of names. Half of these people would be known at least by reputation to most of the general public. All of them would be well-known in certain circles. All of them had this in common, that they had come in time of difficulty to Morrison, and all of them were now on his list. In his debt, for years to come.

He put the paper back in its compartment, pushing aside the several other documents that already occupied the space, then replaced the bottom and put the red-haired woman back in her spot. Morrison took one last look at the Greek woman on the shelf, then allowed himself his nightly moment of indulgence, gazing with pride at the accumulated art on these shelves. He then moved out of the room to his dining room, the drawing room, and the great odd feature of the house, the long, narrow, ornate ballroom. The great old houses of Chicago's original gentry on Indiana and Prairie Avenues boasted this outlandish feature, a ballroom. In this room, Morrison entertained his guests two or three times a year.

As it had from its creation in 1889, the mansion dominated the neighborhood, so different from most of its neighbors that it might as well have been in a jungle. Just a few yards from the fine house on Seminary Street were places on Maud and Poe Street that had been carved into six and even eight flats to accommodate those in more precarious economic straits.

There were other houses like this just south of the Loop and along the Gold Coast. But the red brick mansion, with its gold and white trim, its black turrets and immense windows, was the only one of its kind in its neighborhood. In certain light, you could study the fine red house and imagine that it had been here all along while these lesser homes grew up around it like the second growth of an old forest.

It pleased Morrison that little was actually known about him. Upon arrival in Chicago, he had dropped hints of a fortune made, in lumber and coal in the American West and Canada though other stories clung to him like a second shadow. He was short and handsome, impeccably groomed, perfectly dressed. A persistent rumor had Morrison making vast sums of money during Prohibition running Hiram Walker's finest from Canada through Detroit and to the saloons of half the country. Another suggested that he had bilked several men out of their holdings by brilliant but questionable means, and still another that Mr. Morrison was a gambler of high skill and improbable luck. Some who claimed to know of him from the old days suggested that all these tales might be true. Accounts persisted of Cary Morrison bankrolling Chicago mobsters and politicians, cementing his importance and guaranteeing his security—if such things are ever perfectly secure.

What was known to be true was that somewhere along the line, Morrison had divested himself of almost all of his holdings elsewhere and used the resultant pile of cash to insinuate himself into the highest levels of Chicago society, showing up fully formed, like someone out of a Scott Fitzgerald novel, with mansion, staff, and limousines. For good measure he bought a trucking company and a local brewery, telling anyone who asked that a man needed hobbies.

A wag wondered in a column in the pages of the *Chicago Sun* why a man with such aspirations to quality would settle for Chicago. Two days later he apologized publicly and there were no further questions and jibes at the expense of Mr. Morrison.

The gossip columnists were fond of Morrison, recording his comings and goings, his visits to the Blackhawk and the Chez Paree and the Pump Room, noting his companions—he was said to be fond of dark-haired women—and engaging in the most circuitous speculation about his mysterious past.

A reporter trying to get Morrison to speak of his past had visited the mansion on Seminary Street and been turned away by a young man in a suit. The reporter was making his way back to his car when Morrison himself appeared in the doorway. The reporter said it was a little like seeing a movie star in person. Morrison was wearing a dark red silk smoking jacket and puffing on a long slender cigar. He was dapper and tanned, and he smiled at the reporter.

"No hard feelings, Chum," he said to the reporter. "You come up with something interesting for us to talk about, something that has nothing to do with my past life, and I'll talk to you. Good evening."

Then Morrison nodded, and the young man shut the door on the reporter.

Among his friends, Morrison counted politicians, show business types, and what the papers delighted in calling "reputed mobsters and captains of industry." And although the rumors remained vague and devoid of detail, it was bruited about that most if not all of these people were in some way in the debt of the man called Morrison.

Still, unlike most men of wealth or influence, he lived an oddly restrained life, with a small household staff, and his tall, silent chauffeur, said to be deadly. There was an occasional bodyguard, a dark-haired man with a shuffling walk. Since Morrison went out infrequently these days, the services of the bodyguard were seldom required. The driver was usually sufficient.

As he passed in front of a full-length mirror, he glanced at his reflection and told himself that there was little about this person that people of his past would recognize: From a combination of surgery and the scars from a fire, it was no longer the same face. The premature silver of his hair had been a gift from nature. Morrison had simply reinvented himself.

He stood at the window and now the wind from the south brought him the smells of his neighborhood: the harsh, acidic odors of the tanneries along the river, the gritty smoke of the coal yards not half a mile from his home. The whole neighborhood smelled like a hobo camp. He was no stranger to these smells, they put him in mind of times he would just as soon forget.

He noticed now a new smell in the air—somewhere the city was burning. He heard sirens approaching from several directions. A fire worthy of the name, then. He looked out his window and shook his head. The city was always burning, the air frequently ripe with the smell of smoke, smoke from the city's decrepit wooden housing stock, smoke from trash burning in the alleys. A city of smoke, surrounding his house, his unlikely house among its poorer cousins.

He peered out the window and saw a single plume of smoke to the east, very close. Poe

Street, then. A little more than two hundred yards or so away but worlds apart from Morrison's fine home: another of Chicago's innumerable geographic ironies, a dark, tough little street hardly a block long. A man had been mugged on Poe Street a few months earlier, and just a few days ago, a woman with three children had been evicted.

But Morrison understood that any trouble in his life was unlikely to come from Poe Street and its hardscrabble denizens. Trouble might come from any of a number of his murky business dealings, or from those who viewed him as a rival or as a superior competitor.

He took one more look up and down his street, vaguely troubled now by a sense that he was watched. A few feet away on the far side of his street was a small park, closed now, but just the other night, Morrison had stood at his window looking out at the street and seen the glow of a cigarette in the darkness of the little park. Perhaps someone stood there now, watching his house.

Morrison sniffed at the acrid air, shut his window and went upstairs to bed.

He woke, startled and disoriented. A sudden street noise in the night—no, a woman's voice. For a moment he thought he had imagined the voice. Then he heard her again, the voice loud and harsh and rich with rancor. He sat unmoving in his bed and acknowledged his shock. He knew her, of course, recognized not only this voice but the anger in it. The old anger, and alcohol, of course. The voice faded and he thought perhaps she had moved off. Then he heard her again. Morrison crept to a window at the far end of his wide bedroom and peered out at the street from behind the heavy curtain, and for a moment he felt that the room was spinning.

If asked, Morrison would have said her presence here was improbable, the fact that she still lived flew in the face of all logic. But there she was. The woman was standing on the sidewalk facing the main stairs of the house. She had aged, of course, dyed her hair, but it was unmistakably her. Her head was thrust forward, arms at her sides, face dark with fury. In the pale light of a street lamp he could see the cords of her neck from the strain of her shouting. She wobbled slightly, and the liquor muffled her speech, so that he could make out only a few words, but he'd heard the speech before and knew its contents well enough. She raged in the night and bellowed his name, not *Morrison* but the name she'd known him by. It struck him that perhaps his neighbors would assume the drunken woman had no idea where she was, shouting the name of a man they'd never heard of. This reassured Morrison but he was nonetheless taken aback by her appearance outside his home. He had no idea how this woman from another time and place, a closed chapter of his life, had tracked him here.

As if reading his thoughts, she yelled out, "Yeah, I found you, you bastard. I knew I would."

A new voice bit into the night, an irritated neighbor shouting at the woman to go away. A man's voice from the apartment building just north of Morrison's home. The woman turned, reeling slightly, and trained her anger on this new foe. She screamed at him and the neighbor told her that she was drunk and he was calling the cops. Morrison watched as the woman staggered over to the apartment building and went up the steps. He saw her peering at the names and then poking the doorbells, one after another. Then she left. After a few paces she seemed to recollect her purpose and she stopped, turned, and pointed at Morrison's house, and Morrison could almost imagine that she saw him behind the curtain. He stepped back suddenly.

"I'm not finished with you yet," she called out. "You phony son of a bitch," she added, and then he heard the *thunk* of something thrown at his house. Then she was gone.

At some point he decided she would not come back. He turned on the lights, shook his head, lit a cigarette with trembling fingers. He forced a smile, told himself it was all ridiculous. But he was shaken: for the first time in years the world he'd so meticulously constructed around himself had been breached. It was not that he feared this woman, nor any individual, for that matter. It was the encroachment of the past that unsettled him. He looked around at the fine furnishings of his great house and told himself that this was his reality now, this was the world he had created for himself piece by meticulous piece even as he put together the persona that he now went by. This was his life, and he would brook no encroachment from his past. He would not allow it. If the woman came back, and he believed she would, he would kill her. He had killed no one in many years, but the man who called himself Morrison would have no compunction about killing this person. There were people who could perform this task for him, but he would do this himself. Old habits die hard.

Across the street, a man stood in the shadows between two houses and watched the mansion. He was dressed entirely in black, nearly invisible from the street. From his vantage point, he had watched the small, raucous drama outside the mansion, watched Morrison in his window. He was no less surprised by the woman's appearance than Morrison had been, but he was single-minded, not to be diverted from his purpose. He watched as the woman stomped off, still spewing profanities into the otherwise quiet night, and after a while, he lit a cigarette and moved off in the general direction she'd gone, although without haste.

* * *

In the harsh light of morning, a man in a rumpled brown suit and a black fedora crouched behind a trash can in the alley behind the red mansion. The smell of the garbage on a hot morning was, he would have said, a small price to pay for this vantage point, for he had learned that he could see a surprising amount of the activity of the house from just this spot, this angle. And at certain serendipitous moments—such as this one—he could actually glimpse Morrison himself engaged in the varied and nefarious activities that had created the man's reputation. Mornings in particular were fruitful for surveillance. Just now he'd seen Morrison sitting at his great desk as a red-faced man in a dark suit stood before him, literally hat in hand, and made his case. Successfully, it had to be assumed, for as the man in the cap watched, Morrison called out and a slender, well-dressed young blond man appeared with a strong box which he placed on the desk. Morrison used a key on this box and withdrew a tightly bound stack of cash which he handed to the red-faced man. The other man made fervent gestures and spoke earnestly, until Morrison cut him off, then dismissed him with a little motion of his fingers, as though he were shooing away his cat. The man in the alley took out a small camera and took several quick shots. These would find their way into a folder with other, much older photographs of the man in the house.

The man in the alley smiled at the tableau inside the mansion. A bit more this time than he'd expected: Morrison handing out his money and a well-heeled customer signing away some portion of his freedom or his security. The second man's identity was irrelevant. A bonus that might or might not prove financially rewarding. Now the watcher moved quickly up the alley, hoping to cut through the gangway between two smaller houses.

He stumbled slightly—many of these Chicago alleys were still paved in the old red brick cobbles, and it was an easy thing to catch the toe of one's shoe. He righted himself with a hand on a fence, and then became aware of someone behind him. He feigned nonchalance, then turned quickly to catch the man off guard.

He saw the knife too late to do anything about it, understood a moment later that he'd been stabbed. He stared at the knife, then looked his assailant in the face. He did not know this face, an odd face, he would have said, an ambiguity to it. But then he was stabbed again, and now there was no time.

Chapter One

Ray Foley stood on the corner of the narrow lane called Poe Street and studied the place where he had lived before the War with his mother. The windows of all three floors were boarded up, but the front window of the basement flat where they'd lived had been pushed in. He thought of peering in but decided against it. He knew what it looked like: three small rooms heated by a tiny gas stove along one wall. Still, his mother had made it work, for a time. She had died when he was in Sicily. He was never sure she had gotten his last letter. He glanced at the pushed-in window: a squatter lived there now perhaps, or kids hiding out.

Ray shifted the canvas bag from one shoulder to the other. It contained all his worldly possessions. He was hatless, tall and rangy, and deeply sun- and wind-burned from his time in Europe. For a couple of minutes he stood there, gazing at the length and breadth of Poe Street and observing that this was not much to come home to.

His mother had always said that if you blinked, you missed Poe Street. A short, blunt dogleg of a street, less than eighty yards long and bent in the middle, an afterthought. One end opened onto Maud Street and the other onto Kenmore. Even the Great Chicago Fire had missed Poe Street as it scorched its way across the City from south to north but never crossing back this side of Halsted, keeping just to the east. And so it was that on Poe Street one might find houses that predated the Fire, rattling, rotting frame buildings with sunken front yards that showed the City's old level before they'd raised the street grade in the long slow fight to pull the town out of the swamp and stop cholera. Anywhere else this street might have been called an alley. But it had Poe's name on it, so it was a street. All around it, other writers like Schiller and Dickens, Goethe and Shakespeare had their own streets that went on for miles. But for Poe, the short-lived writer, there was just this glorified alleyway to show for his meteoric but brief career. People who had lived their whole lives in Chicago would tell you they had never heard of Poe Street. But it was there, nonetheless, a small islet of anonymity.

Halfway up the block was the vacant lot where old Mrs. Gray had been forced to sell her house for back taxes. Someone had bought it and torn it down, leaving a dark gap like a pulled tooth. Two streetlights were out so that it seemed an elemental darkness had descended onto the middle of the block.

For four years Ray had believed that it would be enough just to be home and in one piece, having survived the landings at in North Africa, at Sicily and Omaha Beach, and that last year of unrelenting combat in the pursuit of the German Army. Now, a month back, he understood that just escaping with his life was not going to be enough. He'd come back to a city where he no longer had a living relative, where he might as well have been a stranger, new in town, trying to make it.

There was nothing to come back to, nowhere to make a start.

Dusk and the cool air came in from the lake and brought with it a smell he recalled from the old days, of fish, sand, the lake itself, and overhead he saw a pair of nighthawks wheeling about. On nights like this, they had sometimes gone down to the river, close enough to Riverview that they could smell the smoke from the cigars and cigarettes and the hamburgers frying on the flat grills, and they'd watched bats fluttering just overhead.

Up the street, a cab pulled over to the curb, and a woman emerged. A blond nurse, a small girl. She glanced back his way, did a second take, then she frowned slightly, and he found himself looking away, but not before he realized he knew her, or at least remembered her from the days before the War. A blonde now but a brunette when he'd last seen her. She'd lived in a rooming house at the east end of Poe Street, and Ray had made the effort to learn her name. McCoy, he thought. Georgia. Or Gladys.

They had even spoken once, a perfectly chance meeting on the street, the two of them watching as a small dog ran in frenzied circles trying to stay away from its owner, a heavy-set man in a suit. The dog scampered and barked, clearly enjoying itself.

"I hope it gets away," Ray said.

"Me, too," she'd said.

He looked her in the eye and hesitated, knowing this was the moment to say something but caught without words. She'd smiled and said she had to go to work.

Now Ray watched her cross the street and head toward a small apartment building on Seminary down the street from the mansion. So no longer on Poe Street but still in the neighborhood. McCoy, yeah. Gladys McCoy, he would have said. He saw her pause at the door to her building and then she turned. He raised one hand in a shy wave. She gave him the slightest of nods and then went inside. Ray thought of following her and immediately felt foolish. The girl already had her own place, and she would have no interest in an out-of-work GI who was staying in a rented room and looking for work. He turned away, wondering if he was the sole returning serviceman in Chicago who didn't know any women.

*** * ***

The young nurse stopped just inside the street door to her building and glanced across the street. After watching her, the young guy had moved on. But she'd caught the look and the stiff attempt at a wave, and then his sudden embarrassment when their eyes met. A soldier just returned, she would have bet. She knew him, this soldier, remembered him as a shy boy who lived before the War in a basement flat with his mother. Good-looking kid, serious, she'd seen him leaving for his job with a paper bag for his lunch and she'd seen him once or twice in the small hours of the morning returning, climbing down from the streetcar.

In the end, it had been a photograph that showed her how to change her life, a photo on the cover of *Life Magazine* of an Army nurse. The photo identified her as Lt. Catherine Hines, and she seemed self-possessed, smart, purposeful. And content. There was trouble coming and people were saying that the U.S. would get into it and fight the Germans, maybe the Japanese as well. They would need nurses. Gladys McCoy studied the confident-looking young woman in the photograph and decided this was how she would change her life.

But her name was not Gladys McCoy, not anymore. That girl was dead. Somewhere between Poe Street in Chicago and a field hospital on Guadalcanal she had disappeared and in her stead appeared another girl, Hannah Marcel. If asked how this change had taken place, Hannah Marcel might have mentioned the photograph of the Army nurse, but more likely she would have pointed to a moment in a darkened wing of the long hospital building when a nurse from Chicago stood at the foot of the bed of a dying marine who had survived numerous wounds only to succumb to sepsis. A 20-year-old from Austin, Texas who had not yet lived, not really. When death came she stood near him and studied the youthful features in repose. She noted the sparse hair over his lip where he'd been attempting to grow an Errol Flynn moustache, the small scar from boyhood on his chin, a boyhood just barely finished before the war took him. The nurse shook her head at the waste, the utter lack of fulfillment of youthful promise and swore this would not happen to her. She would take over her life from that point on.

Later that week the former Gladys McCoy got hold of a bottle of peroxide and with the help of two other nurses dyed her hair. The catcalls and whistles she received from the recovering soldiers, sailors, and marines told her she'd made an interesting choice. The name she worked out later, from a list compiled as a pastime. Now Gladys realized she had been looking to make this change for years.

In the coming months, the years of the War, Gladys came to understand that for all of her life she had been who people said she was, or what they told her she could be. She would put an end to all of that now.

The war convinced her that she could survive anything. She emerged with her new name, the platinum hair, and a new way of looking at the world. Still in uniform, she visited her aunt and grandmother in Flint, Michigan and then returned to take on Chicago. For a week she roamed the city, allowing herself to see it as a tourist might—museums, the Boul Mich. On the beach at Oak Street a man whistled at her, and on Michigan Boulevard a sailor followed her for half a mile until she told him she was spoken for. In her first month back home, four men asked her out. She went out with two of them, but only once each.

They needed nurses and so the hospital gladly took her back, new name and all, and she found a flat, a small furnished apartment near the church and less than a block from her old Poe Street place. It amused her to think that she would start her new life just around the corner from her old one.

Close enough to be comfortable, to know her way around. But just far enough from Poe Street.

* * *

Late the next night, Ray was heading for his rooming house when he caught a sudden, furtive movement in the shadows on Poe Street. Ray paused and scanned the street. Then he saw him: barely visible in the uneven light from the street lamps, a man in a dark shirt watched the street, then crouched down beside the door of a car, trying to pick the lock. He was tall and wiry with short gray hair, and Ray knew him immediately.

Willie Foy. Burglar, thief, in and out of jail half his life.

You want to stay away from that one, Roy heard his mother's voice. *Willie Foy's nothing but trouble.*

And here he was at his chosen profession, trying to break into a car.

As if he'd heard Ray's thought, Willie Foy looked up suddenly, saw Ray watching him and froze for a moment. They watched each other and Willie Foy seemed to give him a short, sharp nod, and then he was gone, scuttering quickly up the street and disappearing in the gangway between two old frame houses.

I heard you were dead, Ray thought. It struck Ray then that more than once he'd heard of the death of Willie Foy.

No, he's still here.

Ray stared up the street in the direction Willie Foy had gone, momentarily unsettled. He would have admitted that, notwithstanding his mother's clear opinion about Willie Foy, the man was a link to Ray's past. In an odd way, Willie Foy made him think of his mother.

* * *

As he moved away from his window, Morrison turned and gave a final glance at the dark street behind him. Once more he had the odd sensation that he was watched. Not the woman this time—she could not be silent. He moved back to the window, and now he saw his watcher. No, watchers. A cabbie across the street in front of the tiny playground, leaning on his vehicle. And inside the playground itself, almost hidden in the shadows, another man putting a match to a cigarette. As he watched, the cabbie got into his car and drove away. When Morrison looked again, the man in the playground was gone as well.

Still, of late Morrison had come to sense trouble. He had learned over the course of a

crowded life with no small amount of peril to trust his instincts, and his sense of trouble had proved in the past to be reliable. Morrison believed he was well-prepared for trouble of nearly every stripe: there were men on whom he could rely to handle certain types of difficulty. But prepared or no, on this warm June night Morrison experienced the uncommon and uncomfortable feeling that some sort of trouble was coming and, more critical, that he was for once not in perfect control of his world.

Showing my age, he thought. Then he told himself not to be swayed by foolish notions.

* * *

Ray had seen the man who lived in the mansion many times before the war. So many people and places from that time had changed, but here was one constant, the rich man in the red mansion.

Another world, Ray told himself. He lives in another world.

He started to walk away and then became aware of another young guy like himself, leaning against a Checker cab and staring in wonder at the Morrison house.

As they passed each other they exchanged nods.

"Some place, huh?" Ray said.

"Can't believe how some guys have it," the cabbie said.

Yeah, Ray thought. How some guys have it.

As he turned to walk away, he became aware that the other man was watching him. He turned to face the cabbie.

"What?"

The man shook his head.

"I thought I knew you, that's all. Maybe you just look like somebody else."

Ray nodded.

"I used to live around here."

"That must be it," the cabbie said, and then climbed into his car.

Ray began walking, more or less making a circuit of the old neighborhood. Not much had changed. On Clybourn he watched a streetcar crawl by, one of the old red ones. New cars, painted a bright blue, had appeared just before the war but the old ones were still on the streets—they hadn't built streetcars during the war, just as automobile production had come to halt. From here he thought he could smell the mud reek of the river, just a couple hundred yards away, further up Clybourn the sweet malt aroma from the Meister Brau brewery, and as he drew abreast of the great lumber yard, he could smell the high piles of new lumber soaked in the rain, and beyond that, the heavy odor of the coal yard. In the stillness a few noises carried—a dog barking, a radio somewhere down a side street. A car went by without its lights, the tires hissing against the wet pavement.

And now a new sound asserting itself over the night. A fight. Up ahead, two men were pummeling a third man. Ray watched as this man slid down against a brick wall, covering his head with both arms. The men pounded him, and when he was on the pavement, one of them began kicking him.

Not my fight, Ray thought.

But this was no fight, two on one, and you couldn't just watch and let it happen. Besides, he'd fought the German army and he wasn't afraid of a couple of street punks. He began moving toward the fighters, about to yell something. Then one of the men moved slightly and Ray caught just a glimpse of the recipient of their violence. A small man, dark-haired trying to protect his head.

Eddy Walsh.

For Christ's sake, Eddy Walsh.

Now Ray called out.

"Hey, you, punk!"

One of the men paused, looked over his shoulder, squinted in the dark at Ray, and Ray recognized him: Butch Turner, a local hood. Ray broke into a run, bearing down on the two men. The second man now turned to peer up the street at him, and Eddy Walsh chose that moment to kick out, catching this second man in the back of his knee. The man fell on his side and Eddy crawled on top of him.

Butch Turner faced Ray, fists up. A big man, fleshy, with a gut that sagged over his belt.

"You want some?" he said, but Ray saw the uncertain look in his eye and bore down on him.

"Sure," Ray said, and waded in.

He took a grazing blow over the top of his head but landed punches, struck the other man in the side of his mouth and his ribs, then a solid punch that caught nothing but jaw and Butch grunted and fell backward. He rolled over and climbed awkwardly to his feet, and then he was lurching up the street, hitching up his pants as he went. His companion was already a few yards ahead of him. When he was halfway up the block, Butch turned and pointed a finger at Ray.

"I'll see you again, you punk. We'll settle this."

"Rematch, Butch? Set it up, pal."

Ray watched them for a moment, and then turned to face Eddy Walsh.

Eddy was up on one knee, gasping for breath.

"What's up, Foley?"

"What's up? My old pal Eddy Walsh is getting his ass kicked on Clybourn Avenue. That means it's just like old times."

Eddy Walsh gave him a sheepish look and Ray found himself laughing. Then they were hugging. A squad car slowed down and two cops peered at them. Ray shook his head and waved them off, and they drove away.

He held Eddy out at arm's length. The two men had done some damage—Eddy had a cut across the bridge of his nose and his left eye was swollen. Eddy leaned over and spat blood on the pavement.

"So what's going on, Eddy? What was that about?"

"Oh, you know how it is, Ray. A misunderstanding."

"No, I don't know how it is. I don't have anybody beating my ass on the street."

"It's money. Ain't it always? I owe Butch a few bucks, he's in a hurry for his money."

"He probably owes somebody else."

"I'll take care of it, Ray."

"You sure?"

"Oh, yeah. I got something going, Ray. Something good. What about you, Ray?"

"I've got nothing going yet. I need a job and a girl. I'm not even sure if I'll be staying. So you've got something good?"

"Yeah, I'd say so. Me and some guys I know. You know, all you need is one score, one time, Ray. Set yourself up." Eddy gave him an appraising look. "Maybe you should come in with us, Ray."

"Everybody thinks they're gonna make one big score. Sounds like snake oil to me, Eddy."

"No." Eddy pointed a finger in Ray's face. "I thought this through."

"You and who else?"

"Some guys. Jimmy Seeger—you remember Jimmy. And a couple older guys. Floyd

Hennessey, that old fighter, Barney Donlan. And that Willie Foy. Actually, he's the one putting it together."

Ray shook his head. "Oh, for Christ's sake, Willie Foy's been in jail half his life, Eddy."

"Yeah, but he knows his way around. And he's got his eye on a place."

"And—what? You're going to rob somebody?"

"No strong-arm stuff, Ray. We're gonna hit this place. Nobody gets hurt, we make some dough."

"Sounds like trouble, Eddy."

Eddy looked away for a moment, as though he'd lost the thread of the argument.

"I been through a lot of stuff, Ray, just like you. And now I think I deserve something for it."

"Sure you do, Eddy. We all do, but—"

"Yeah, but I'm gonna do something about it. And maybe when I've pulled this off, maybe then I'll take off. Go someplace. California. Hollywood!" His face brightened. "Always wanted to go to Hollywood, see those dames. Best looking women in the world."

"You know, Eddy, last time I saw you, you didn't look so cocky. Paris, this was. You were riding in the back of a jeep. With two MPs."

Eddy gave him a surprised look. "You were there?" Then he looked away, annoyed. "Yeah, that time, well—"

"What did you do—punch an officer or go AWOL?"

"I just slipped away for the night, went to a club, looking for this Frenchie."

Ray nodded and recollected the scene: a sullen Eddy Walsh sitting cuffed in the back of an Army jeep, two MPs in the front seat.

"You know why I remember that time so well, Eddy? It was two surprises. One, I was seeing my old friend Eddy Walsh, so I knew you'd made it through the landings and everything else. And that was good. And the other thing was the MP in the front seat, driver's side. I'd seen him before."

"That prick."

"Maybe, but I saw him on Omaha Beach. He saved my bacon when I was just standing there, scared frozen, those German gunners shooting up the beach and all of us, and that MP knocked me down and half-dragged me over to a hump of sand and told me to keep my head down. A minute later I watched him get shot. And he got up again and started pulling kids out of the line of fire. All those Navy beach masters and MPs were getting shot that day. Never saw anybody like him before or since. I didn't know what happened to him until I saw him in that jeep keeping company with my pal Eddy."

"He's from here, you know that? That sonofabitch," Eddy snarled. Then he added, "Tough guy, I'll give him that. I got to go, Ray. And thanks for bailing me out, pal. I owe you."

"You don't owe me a thing. Maybe we'll grab a beer some night."

"Sure thing, Ray. Maybe I'll track down Jimmy and drag him along."

"Good. I haven't seen him since before the War."

Eddy took out a pack of Luckies, shook out a couple of smokes and handed one to Ray. Then he produced a small silver lighter and put fire to both of them. Eddy inhaled, blew smoke out through his nostrils and grinned. He clapped Ray on the shoulder.

"Take it easy, Foley. Hey, that fight's coming up—Joe Louis and Billy Conn. I'm gonna lay a few bucks on Conn. He nearly took him last time."

Ray smiled. "That was then, Eddy."

"I think the Brown Bomber is through, Ray."

"We'll go someplace, have a couple drinks and listen to it. I like that joint on Racine."

"Peg's."

"That's the place."

"I'll look for you there."

Eddy made a little wave, fluttering his fingers daintily, said "toodle-oo" and they both laughed again. Eddy winked then, his face suffused with the old cockiness and just the trace of contempt, a certainty that he was a half-step ahead of every other guy on the street, even his old friend Ray Foley.

Over the years he'd managed to avoid getting involved in Eddy's schemes, but it was clear that the War had done nothing to change Eddy. He was looking to make a score. And he was putting his money on Billy Conn to beat the great Joe Louis. Perfect: one cocky Irishman backing another. Ray shook his head.

Ray watched him go, and wondered what Eddy was planning, with his Big Score.

There's no such thing as the Big Score because they always want another one.

Chapter Two

A party was in raucous progress at the Morrison mansion, and Ray Foley slowed down to take it all in. Lights were on in every room, he could make out women laughing, a man's deep guffaw. As he watched, a taxi pulled up and three women in summer dresses emerged and scampered up the stairs. He heard one of them call out, "Wait for us! We're here!"

He remembered this man's parties before the war, an unexpected slice of a fantasy life. Other people were converging on the mansion, cabs pulling up and disgorging their passengers. Some of them looked his way, and Ray realized how he must look: a hatless young guy in a wrinkled shirt rolled up to his elbows. At the top of the stairs, a young blond man in a dark suit ushered some of the guests in and shot Ray a quick look.

Right, I'm not even as well-dressed as the help.

A well-dressed older couple passed him and the silver-haired man gave Ray's clothes a quick once-over. Ray stepped back now and tried to get a clear view of the dancers in Morrison's first floor ballroom.

A ballroom, for God's sake.

He was not alone in watching the party inside. A man in a suit and wide-brimmed fedora leaned against a tree a few houses down. Closer to him, a young guy in a filthy shirt and ball cap glanced at the mansion while pursuing his more critical task: peering into the gutter along the parked cars. He walked, limping, in a half crouch. As Ray watched, the kid bent down, ran his fingers along the curb and came up with his prize. He held it up to Ray. A bent cigarette. He straightened it and smoothed it out.

"That's a whole smoke," he said, and stuck it into his shirt pocket. "Second one tonight," he added.

Ray nodded and looked back at the mansion.

"The guy that lives here is a millionaire," the boy said.

"I imagine so."

"You ever been in there?"

Ray turned to him, amused. An odd-looking boy. The face of a happy child, arms like a stevedore. One arm, he noted, bore a long scar, whitish against the boy's tan skin.

"Do I look like somebody that would be invited in there?"

"No. You look regular, like me. I never been in there, either."

The boy cast a final look at the mansion and announced that he had to go.

"Okay," Ray said, and decided to make his own long way back to his room at the YMCA. As he walked, he had the strong sensation that someone was watching him. He turned. The kid was gone, as was the man in the dark suit and hat. But there had been someone there, someone else, he was certain of it. He'd learned these things in the War.

Later, he lay in his small, hard bed and listened to the street sounds. He understood that it would take him some time to get used to the noise of the city—the first time he heard a car backfire he froze, it sounded like a shell. His sleep was still troubled: by dreams of the men bobbing lifeless in the waves off Normandy, and by the image of a young German soldier in a French town, lying on his back in the sun, brought down by a shot from Ray. He had no doubt he had been responsible for other deaths in the War, but this was the only one he had clearly seen go down from a shot from his weapon. A German corporal with the face of a young boy. Ray's nights were getting better, though, these two dreams appearing less and less frequently.

The war, or rather the surprising fact of his surviving it, had wrought two other changes in him: one was a determination that no one, nothing, was going to keep him from putting together a decent life. The other change was a new habit: like two million returning servicemen he smoked. The Allies may have won the war, but the tobacco companies had come out undefeated.

The next day he bought the papers, all of them: the *Times*, the *Herald American*, the *Daily News*, the *Tribune*, a new paper called the *Sun*. He read them over meat loaf and mashed potatoes in the Y cafeteria and in his room, far into the night. He read them all, desperate to learn about the city he'd left, how life here had continued, prospered, failed, all if it, he wanted to know everything. If you wanted to start a life, you needed to know things, all kinds of things.

They shared cover stories, all of them fascinated with a killer named Heirens, who'd murdered a young girl and two women. Tojo's war crimes trial had begun and the Huks were in revolt in the Philippines. Clark Gable was in town to promote a picture and a church group was protesting a new movie, "*The Outlaw,*" starring Jane Russell, and Ray told himself he would have to see this picture. The new cars were coming out soon, the first ones made in America since early in the war. A Clark Street saloon had been shut down for serving minors and employing a 16-year-old "dice girl." In sports, they were still talking about the passing of Lou Gehrig, but Joe Louis and Billy Conn were the big story, preparing for their long-anticipated rematch in a fight that seemed to reassure people that the old days could indeed come back. The most startling story of all concerned the latest test of the atomic bomb: at Bikini Atoll they'd dropped one on an entire fleet of mothballed warships, 73 in all, and one bomb had pulverized all of them. He wondered if this meant the days of sending foot soldiers slogging through sand and mud and jungle were finished.

There were rooms to be had: sleeping rooms and furnished rooms, and rooms with particular conditions: rooms for "couples only" and rooms for "colored." Over the next two days he looked at rooms that might have been fit for a guy on the run but just barely. Eventually he settled on a room in a transient hotel on Armitage, not far from the old place on Poe Street. It was small and clean, a bed and a table and chair, with a bathroom just up the hall and a phone on the wall a few feet from his door. And a window, a window onto Bissell, a window that peered directly into the upper branches of a maple tree. Just up the street there was a small church, and when he leaned out the window he could see the steeple. He found it oddly reassuring, given the fact that he would never go inside it.

The next day he began to reacquaint himself with the city, first on foot and then on streetcars and the new trolley buses. The fare was still a dime but the trolley buses had begun to take over from the streetcars, still using the great black tangle of overhead wires that could occasionally snarl traffic for blocks, just as their predecessors could.

His wandering reminded him that the streets had changed just before the War: Center Street was now Armitage, Custer Street was Shakespeare. They did this in Chicago from time to time and he never understood why. The Foleys had lived for a time on Alaska Street, and that was gone as well—Weed Street now. He wondered what was wrong with a street named after Alaska.

A couple of nights later he made his way home from a tavern where he'd had a beer and listened to a pair of old fighters explaining to the common folk why Billy Conn was about to have his head handed to him by the aging Joe Louis.

Near his room, he spotted three men standing in a darkened doorway across the street, heads together, conspiratorial. Ray smiled. He knew all of them, and it was plain what they were discussing.

You guys might as well be wearing a sign.

As he drew abreast of them, they moved into the narrow gangway between the buildings. Jimmy Seeger and Eddy Walsh, and the gray-haired Willie Foy, managing to look disheveled and clever at the same time. Ray took a final look their way and walked on, thinking of the wary look Eddy Walsh had shot his way.

Not sure who your friends are anymore, Eddy?

Ray told himself this was a logical result if you were spending your nights in dark places, making shady plans with Willie Foy.

* * *

There were five of them, a ball and a bat and two gloves between them, and they were setting up in the alley behind Poe Street because it was hot and the nearest park was all the way over on Wrightwood. They were formalizing what were to be the bases: Home plate was a scrap of cardboard, first and third were fence posts, and second was a piece of plywood they'd carted with them just for this purpose. They were deciding on the teams when the youngest pointed out that they weren't alone.

His companions all looked where he pointed and saw the man sitting on the alley floor.

"He's sleeping," the boy said.

"Drunk," the eldest said, for the lessons of his own household had made him wary of sleeping drunks. Wary and in this case hopeful, for it seemed to him that a drunk was not likely to be bothered by five kids playing ball twenty feet away. They would move home plate twenty feet back and the drunk would be out of their line of play.

They crept forward now and one of them said, "Oh, look."

And that stopped them, for it was clear what their companion had seen. The man in the alley was blood-soaked, his white shirt thick with it. His fedora was slightly askew, but they could see most of his face and saw that one of his eyes was open, staring blankly at the alley pavement. And the face was gray, the cheeks sunken.

One of the boys said, "Oh, geez," and the youngest started gasping, and then all five were running out of the alley. At the mouth of the alley they encountered a man in a suit and told him there was a dead man covered with blood just a few yards away.

* * *

There were already two squad cars and an ambulance in the alley when the black Ford sedan pulled up and two men in suits emerged. One was big and bulky, and he walked favoring one leg they way one nurses an old injury. The other was thin and pale and frowning. He shook his head and screwed up his face against the alley smells.

His partner looked at him.

"Your delicate nose doesn't like the alley, huh?"

The thin one peered into the nearest trash can and grimaced.

"Maggots," he said in an aggrieved tone. "There's maggots in here."

"Well, this guy," the big one said, nodding in the direction of the dead man, "He's not worried about maggots anymore."

The uniformed officers made way for the two newcomers. The heavy-set man nodded at one of the uniforms.

"Hello, Patrick."

"Joe." To his partner the cop said, "This is Joe Carmody, Detective Sergeant Carmody, that is, and that's Detective…—" He looked at the other man in question.

"Kessel," the second man said, and made a show of putting a handkerchief to his nose.

The big man called Carmody nodded toward him and said, "He's delicate." Then he looked at the body.

"So what do we have?"

"Knife wounds, two of them."

Carmody stood for a moment, scanning the alley. He squinted, frowned as though something were missing. Then he went down on one knee and peered at the dead man. He pointed to the wound in the middle of the man's stomach.

"Lotta blood. So we know this wound here," he said, pointing to a wound high in the man's chest, "wasn't first. That's the heart, that's what killed him. But if it had been first—"

"It would have killed him instantly. Wouldn't have been much blood."

Carmody nodded.

"So where's the rest of the blood? There's none on the pavement."

He looked around expectantly. Eventually his partner spoke through the handkerchief.

"He wasn't killed here."

"That's right. Body's been moved."

The second officer now spoke up. "Why? I mean, a guy in an alley, maybe he's just a bum, why would somebody kill a bum and then move him?"

Carmody moved closer, squinted at the wrinkled suit, touched the dead man's hair, the skin, studied his face.

"First of all, this is not a bum. If this is a guy living in alleys, he'd have dirty hair, greasy. And he's shaved recently. Sometime in the last twenty-four24 hours before he died, I bet."

The detective picked up the man's limp hand, looked at the fingernails.

"Nails are clean. Nah, this is no bum. As for the other thing? You move a body when you don't what it to be found, which is obviously not the case here, or when you don't want people to see where it happened. Because the location would tell us something about why this guy got himself killed. Been dead a while, that's for sure. Let's see what's in his pockets."

The detective fished around in the dead man pants pockets and came up with a wallet. There was cash in the wallet, and a photograph of an older couple, and a white card that Carmody studied for a moment and then held up.

"It's a business card. His name is Frederick Webb." He peered at the card again, squinting in the sun.

"What do you know? He is or was a private detective. From Seattle." Carmody showed the card to his partner.

"*Frederick Webb Investigations*," Kessel read. He made a face. "Like that Jew. Silver. Wonder if he knew this guy."

Carmody looked at the two officers.

"This Silver, he's a guy we know."

"Yeah," Kessel said. "The Kike with the fancy suits."

Carmody looked at him for a moment, amused. To the two uniforms, he said, "My guy here, he's got a name for everybody, every kind of people. You're German, he calls you a Kraut. You're from Georgia, you're a stump-jumper. A *stump-jumper*," he said, slightly incredulous.

He pointed a finger at his partner. "Someday, you're gonna call the wrong guy the wrong thing and get your bell rung."

Kessel shook his head. "I've got no use for that Jew."

"Fuss about him later," Carmody said, irritated. "Right now, we've got a dead man a long, long way from home." He looked down at the dead man.

"What are you doing so far from home, Frederick? And what got you killed in my town?"

Ray was headed back to his room, approaching Armitage when he saw the squad car blocking the alley. Beyond it a few yards away, cops and commotion. At least three cop cars and an ambulance, and they were loading a body.

A body, Ray thought. Too soon to be seeing another body.

Two men in dark suits emerged from a black Ford, a big man with a red face and his partner, a thin, dyspeptic-looking man who squinted at the covered body as though expecting trouble from it. Detectives, Ray had no doubt, and the big red-faced one seemed to be in charge. They spoke to the uniformed cops and then began talking to a third man, an elegant looking man in a gray summer suit. There was something familiar about the one in the gray suit. And then Ray had it, he knew him. He'd seen this man driving a jeep in Paris with a handcuffed Eddy Walsh in the back seat, and he'd seen him before that, on Omaha Beach.

A uniformed cop approached Ray, jutted his chin out at him. Young cop, blue eyes, baby face.

"Know anything about this?"

"No. What happened?"

"It's police business. Doesn't concern you unless you've got something to say."

"I was just looking."

"Okay, you looked, now move on."

Ray met the cop's eyes and, for just a half-second, thought it might be interesting to give this cop some lip. Then he reflected that it was a bit early to be getting into confrontations with the police. A guy living in a rented room, soldier or no, was little more than a drifter.

"Okay. I'm leaving."

He shot one last look up the alley and saw that the big detective had noticed him. The detective said something to his partner and then held up his hand. He called out to the cop at the mouth of the alley.

"Hold that guy. I need to talk to him."

The cop reached for Ray. Ray stepped back and said, "I heard him."

Ray waited as the big cop huffed and puffed his way up the alley, followed at some distance by his partner.

The detective removed his hat and wiped his sweating forehead with a damp-looking handkerchief. His tie was askew and the top button of his shirt was undone, his jacket was wrinkled. This was a man who would never quite look well -dressed. The thin detective stayed back a couple of paces and squinted at Ray as though he couldn't quite make him out.

"What's your name, son?"

"Ray Foley."

"I'm Carmody." He shot a thumb over his shoulder. "That's Detective Kessel. I've seen you before. You live around here?"

"I've got a room about a block away."

"Where?"

"Over by the El tracks on Armitage."

"The rooming house. Okay. So we've got a dead man here, Foley. I'm pretty sure I've seen you roaming the streets. You seem to get around. Know anything about this?"

"No. I was just walking by. What happened to him?"

"Somebody knifed him."

"Robbery?"

"Who knows? Have you seen anything unusual?"

"I don't know what's usual yet."

The one called Kessel grimaced but Carmody just looked at Ray.

"Anybody hanging around that you haven't seen before?"

"No, not really. Like I said, I don't know who belongs here and who doesn't. There's an old guy who sharpens knives, I keep seeing him. And there's a guy I see up on Armitage, just standing there all the time outside the drugstore."

"By the fire hydrant? Raggedy-looking guy in a ball cap? That's Bob the Book."

"So he's a bookie."

"That's right. And if he gives you a tip on a horse at Hawthorne, don't bet on it. If Bob knew anything, he wouldn't look like he does."

"Good thing to know."

"So you're just back from overseas? Is that it?"

"Yeah."

"Where?"

"North Africa, Sicily, France, Germany. World tour."

Carmody nodded. Ray looked past them, where the elegant man in the gray suit was watching all of them with interest. The other detective noticed and stepped forward.

"What? You see something?"

"That guy there in the gray suit, I know him."

"From where?"

"Over there. I saw him overseas. Saw him on the beach. Normandy. He was an MP, directing guys where they could find cover."

Kessel looked annoyed.

"Nowhere else?"

"No."

Carmody gave him an interested look, then shot a quick glance over his shoulder at the man in the gray suit.

"So you know our man Max Silver."

"More or less."

"Then you know he's a private detective. Like in the movies. You know, Sam Spade, Bulldog Drummond."

"No. I don't know anything about that. Or about him."

"You never talked to each other?"

"Like I said. Omaha beach, he pushed me down behind a sand dune and told me to keep my head down."

And saved my life.

All the Navy beachmasters on Omaha beach were dead, and the MPs had taken over, and this man Silver had stayed there, directing men to cover, heedless of his own safety. As Ray watched, he saw the MP hit twice before finally crawling over to find cover next to Ray.

Ray looked up the alley at the man in the gray suit and could see him frowning, could almost read the man's thoughts.

He's trying to remember where he met me.

Ray smiled, amused, remembering their last, fraught meeting.

Now the man in the gray suit raised a hand in recognition, and Ray nodded.

Kessel looked from Ray to the private detective and back.

"So you and the Jew are buddies, huh?"

"No. Like I said. I met him in the War." Ray looked at Kessel and understood that this was one of those moments, frequent since his first day under fire, when he felt his forbearance giving way.

He met Kessel's gaze.

"So where'd you serve?"

"I got a bad foot."

"Is that right? *The Jew's* got a couple of Purple Hearts. You have anything like that?"

"I said I got a bad foot."

Kessel glared at him, his face red. Ray tilted his head and tried on a small smile.

Detective Carmody moved toward him, put a cautionary hand on Ray's chest.

"Your jaw's too tight, Kid. Take a deep breath. My partner, he doesn't like a lot of people."

Carmody smiled at his partner's expense and Ray caught the look they exchanged.

Not blood brothers, Ray thought.

"Be on your way, Foley."

Ray indulged a last look at Detective Kessel and then left.

Chapter Three

A tramp had found the body. The woman lay on a pile of rags beneath the single functioning light bulb in the basement of an abandoned building on Maud Street. She had been stabbed once, most likely as she slept.

Detective Kessel frowned.

"You don't expect to find a woman on the bum. What a place to die."

Carmody looked at him. "Country's full of women down on their luck. We just don't see them."

He bent over and picked up a battered black purse with a broken strap. For a moment he went through the contents. Then he held up an envelope.

"Addressed to Mrs. Opal Fremont. Address Livingston, Montana."

Then he held up a card.

"She's got a social security card. This says 'Opal Raines.'" He shook his head. "Long way to come, Montana to Chicago, just to die in a basement."

Kessel indicated a gin bottle on the basement floor.

"Probably a boozer."

Carmody gave him a look. "Wouldn't you be?"

He went down on one knee and looked at the dead woman. Then he looked around at the basement.

"What was the point of this? She had nothing to steal." He peered at the stab wound. "Stabbed once. Just once."

"So what?"

"So somebody who knew what he was doing wanted her dead. But why? What harm could she cause anybody?"

The detective got slowly to his feet. To the dead woman, he said, "All right, Opal. We're gonna get you out of this place."

* * *

In the morning Ray rose early. When he emerged from the rooming house the sun was still climbing to the east and the streets were cool. A dark blue LaSalle was parked in front and a well-dressed man was leaning against it, and Ray understood without looking at him that the man was waiting for him. He turned and began walking toward Sheffield and the man followed.

"It's Foley, isn't it?"

Ray stopped and turned. The man's wide-brim fedora kept part of his face in shadow but he'd now seen this man twice in the last few days.

"We know each other. We've met."

"Right."

"Max Silver."

"I remember. Omaha Beach."

"Glad to see you made it back."

"You, too."

Up close, the detective was shorter than Ray but wider across the shoulders. Dark eyes, a handsome face , an uneven lump on the bridge of the nose where it had been broken.

Ray looked back at the car.

"Is that your car? The LaSalle?"

"Yeah. I had it in storage while I was overseas. Collector's item now, I guess."

"I heard they stopped making them. So what can I do for you?"

"Let me buy you a cup of coffee."

Silver nodded toward the small restaurant across the street and Ray said, "Why not?"

Over a cup of coffee, Max Silver asked Ray casual questions occasionally mixed with more pointed inquiries, and Ray was amused to see how this detective compiled his information.

"So I guess you're looking for work."

"Yeah. Before the War I worked at the Borden Dairy. I thought I'd go over there and see if they're hiring."

The conversation lost steam, and Ray was signaling the waitress for a refill when Max Silver leaned forward.

"I was interested to see you talking to the police. What did they want with you?"

"Asking about that dead guy. They were just asking if I'd seen anything unusual. The big one—Carmody—said he'd seen me roaming around."

"So have I."

"Well, I didn't have anything to tell him. So what's this to you?"

Silver made a little half shrug, looked away, and Ray had the sense that the detective was about to lie to him. He decided to play a hunch.

"You knew him. The guy—the man who was killed."

"Not really. I'd heard of him. He sent me a letter once. He was looking for someone and he thought I might be able to tell him something about this person. We were in the same line of work."

"So the dead man was a detective. Like you."

"Carmody told you that, I assume. Yes, he was a private investigator from Seattle."

"Seattle. What's a guy from Seattle doing here?"

Silver looked past Ray and for a moment seemed to have become distracted. Then he met Ray's eyes.

"Working, I assume. On a case."

"That's tough. All the way from Seattle to get killed in that alley."

"He wasn't killed where they found him," Silver said, and Ray caught the faint snarl in his voice.

"You know that?"

"Yeah. I know there was no blood where they found him." A moment later the detective said, "So you didn't see anything odd? Anybody out of place?"

"I'll tell you what I told that Carmody. I haven't been back long enough to know what's normal. I don't even think I understand this town anymore."

"It'll all come back to you."

"Maybe. Maybe I won't stick around long enough to see. But in answer to your question, I haven't seen anything strange, nobody."

The detective tossed a business card across the table.

"Hang onto that. Give me a call if you see or hear anything about this. Or if you see somebody out of place."

"I already told you, I wouldn't know—"

"I think you would."

Silver tossed a bill on the table, nodded to Ray and left. He looked at the card and tucked it into his shirt pocket.

For a while after Silver left, Ray nursed his coffee and thought about the dead man in the alley less than a block from where he now sat, a death by violence. He saw the irony, that he'd somehow thought he was leaving violence far behind him on the far side of the Atlantic Ocean.

On the way back to his room, he heard someone calling his name.

Across the street he saw Jimmy Seeger waving.

"Jimmy!"

"Hey, Ray."

Jimmy Seeger grinned and showed his improbable set of buck teeth. Even from across the street, Ray could see Jimmy's unmanageable cowlick. To Ray he would always look like a boy who'd just moved to the Big Town from a farm. Jimmy waved again and was gone.

Ray thought about what Eddy had told him, about the two of them throwing in with a trio of guys in their fifties to make "a score." He shook his head.

"You should come in with us, Ray."

Not likely, Eddy.

* * *

He wasn't ready to join whatever craziness Eddy and Willie Foy were involved in, but Ray had to admit that he wasn't quite home yet. He was not settled, that was it. It struck him that he'd fought all the way through

Europe and gotten shot and had the shit scared out of him two dozen times, to come back to nothing?

* * *

I ought to be able to do something here. This ought to be my town, he thought. *I'm five years older and thirty pounds heavier than when I left, and I've been in combat. I've seen the ocean, I've seen mountains, I've seen Africa and France and Germany—for Christ's sake, I've been to Paris. I read books and learned a few words in French and German, and everywhere I went, I felt like I belonged and I didn't much care whether people agreed with me or not.*

Time to take Chicago.

He wasn't sure what he'd do for a living but he had time to decide that. He had money left, unspent pay with no one to send it to, and his winnings in the two greatest poker games of his Army career, and the few bucks he'd put away before he left town.

I won't starve.

All right then. What do I do first?

He watched a couple of men walking by, well-dressed, confident.

A hat. I need a hat to separate me from the schoolboys. A hat and a suit and a sportcoat. Shoes. Time to dress like a grownup.

* * *

The next morning he went up to the Wieboldt's at Lincoln and Belmont and bought a cheap gray fedora, a sportcoat, slacks, and a tie. In the late afternoon he rode a streetcar to the cemetery. His mother's grave was on the far side of the cemetery, within a few yards of the El tracks. And, like many of the others, it was slightly overgrown with grass and small weeds, and he went down on his knees to clear it. When he was done he stood beside her narrow headstone and rested his hand upon it.

"I'm back, Ma. Sorry to leave you all alone all this time. Couldn't help it. But I'm back."

It seemed wrong just to leave, so he sat down on the grass and had a smoke, then another, and began speaking to her, telling her about the War and the things he'd seen and done. He told her how the town seemed to have changed and what he'd noticed of their old street. Then it was time to leave her.

Maybe it was better you died before all of it, he thought. It would have made you crazy, wondering what was happening to me over there. You missed that, and I'm glad.

He patted the top of the headstone and turned away.

* * *

In his second week he began to feel more comfortable. One morning he decided to get up at six as he had so many times on his way to the dairy, and he wandered simply to see if this part of the city life was unchanged. He passed a few men and some women hurrying to catch a streetcar, and sights that he remembered from before the War: delivery trucks and vans. He saw a Borden dairy man setting down bottles of milk on a doorstep, taking back the empties. Just ahead of him a muscular white guy wielding huge tongs carried a block of ice around to the back door of an apartment building. Ray thought it might have been the same iceman who delivered chunks of ice to their flat, for his mother to place in the lined compartment above their old icebox—they'd never had a refrigerator.

On Halsted he encountered a produce wagon, a weary-looking black man holding the reins as a thick-legged gray horse pulled the wagon. The wagon had come all the way north from the great produce markets along Randolph Street or even further away on South Racine. It was loaded with crates of fruit and vegetables, and loose piles of melons. The scant traffic at that hour moved around the old man on his wagon and he seemed impervious to them all. Ray followed the produce wagon for blocks, until it turned up an alley to unload part of its load at a small grocery store.

He made his way back to the rooming house on Armitage. When he reached the doorway, he paused and turned, oddly sure that he was being followed. He stood there for a moment watching the street in both directions. A cab went by, slowly. Ray watched it, then took one more look up and down the street before going inside.

Chapter Four

The party in the red mansion drew two crowds. The first was the obvious, the crowd that thronged the lower rooms of the mansion, crowded the narrow staircases and stumbled drunk and giddy from one bedroom to another on the second floor until guided firmly but politely by Morrison's maid and housekeeper. They seemed not to mind the heat, this crowd, eating and drinking and dancing to the mixed quartet of musicians playing jazz in the long ballroom that ran the length of the house from front to back.

The second crowd was the one that gathered on both sides of the street, sat on porches, leaned on cars, and envied the dancers seen intermittently through the front windows. A few simply stood on the sidewalk in front of the mansion and stared up at the revelers.

Ray Foley leaned against a tree in the small playground and watched the party.

When he returned to his neighborhood, he heard music, laughter, loud voices: a party was in full swing in the big house on Seminary. It seemed every light in the mansion was on and Ray could see people inside, well-dressed people talking, drinking, dancing. To a band, not records. From this angle he could see the band and he recognized the song: *"Frenesi,"* Artie Shaw's song. Ray slowed down and watched the party. Some of the guests had spilled out onto the front steps and a few stood near the high wrought iron fence, glasses in their hands, smoking and talking. Up the street, Ray could see neighbors at their windows, watching—in the second-floor window of one house he saw a man with binoculars.

I don't blame you, Ray thought.

A long green Packard pulled up in front of the Morrison house and three women spilled out of the back seat, one of them chanting "We're late, we're late."

One of her companions called out, "Hold the party!"

Ray watched them prance up the steps of the mansion. The third one turned and gave him a slow look and a half-smile. Her dress might have been painted on.

Ray looked around and saw that a small crowd had gathered, most of them hanging back a respectful distance but all of them fascinated by the lights and music and the beautiful people in the windows and out on the lawn. Ray saw a couple of girls huddled together under a streetlamp, watching. In the glow he could see the wistful looks on their faces. A few feet away, a man in a dark fedora leaned against a tree and stared at the Morrison party. He was overdressed for the warm night in a worn leather bomber jacket. Ray couldn't see his face but he looked young, and there was something in the way he stared at the party in the big house that Ray understood.

Yeah, you want that to be your life. We both want to be in there. Who wouldn't?

Ray took a step back. The guy in the hat gave him a sudden look, seemed to study Ray for a moment, and then focused back on the party.

For a few more minutes Ray watched the silhouetted dancers and listened to the music. Dancing to live music with a girl. The last time he'd done that had been in a dancehall for GIs in Paris. His partner was a nurse named Betsy, from Oregon and they'd shared a beer and danced to a couple of numbers and then she had left with her friends.

Ray wondered about Betsy from Oregon.

* * *

When the party was over there was still much to do. Morrison had his maid open most of the windows and turn on fans to push out the cigarette smoke and stale air. A drunken guest had fallen on the front stairs, and Morrison told a maid to get the man a taxi.

Then they were gone, all of them, guests and staff.

Morrison went to the window and saw a police car making its casual progress up the street. The car slowed in front of Morrison's home, then moved on.

Ironic, Morrison thought, that a man who surrounded himself with staff at most times felt most comfortable when alone. In truth he'd spent much of his adult life alone, some of it on the run in a long series of rented rooms and flophouses, or moving from one place and one identity to another life and a new name.

As he prepared himself for bed, Morrison thought about his staff: Bennie, the slow-witted young houseboy, Lucas, his driver, the Irish girls Annie the maid and Mary, his cook and housekeeper. Morrison told himself that with both Annie and Mary out of the house, this meant none of his possessions would be lost for at least one day: small articles tended to go missing under his household staff's unsteady watch—whether from incompetence or larceny, he did not know. He had his reservations about the Irish as household staff. Still, Mary was an excellent cook and Annie, though somewhat prone to sulking, learned fast and did as she was told, and Morrison had thus far been reluctant to fire her. She was, after all, an attractive girl. He would not consort with his household staff, but watching her provided a pleasant diversion. And Passeau, his personal assistant, was ill and had missed the party. Frequently ill, it seemed, a handsome young man with a delicate constitution. But competent and clever, even if a common cold could lay him up for the better part of a week. There was no question of his loyalty, only of his health.

Benjie and Mary were recent additions: in the past year Morrison had been forced to fire their predecessors, the sullen maid Sophie, whom he had caught going furtively through his pockets, Hatch, the shifty houseboy, and just recently, a young and utterly incompetent cook's assistant named Estelle. He was unsure how long the current batch would last.

Of all his staff, Morrison was most comfortable with Lucas, a decorated veteran of the Great War, taciturn, unflappable, and quite dangerous. As for Passeau, he had begun to make Morrison uneasy. For the length of their relationship, Morrison had sensed a certain circumspection in Passeau, a guardedness that did not diminish his effectiveness as companion or staff but kept Morrison slightly on edge. On several occasions Morrison caught the dark-eyed young man watching him with what Morrison would have called wariness. In public Passeau was beyond reproach in the performance of his duties, running interference for his employer on crowded streets, performing errands, making discreet arrangements. Passeau kept Morrison's calendar, arranged his schedule. Morrison sensed Passeau's fascination with him, with his life. About Passeau's life, Morrison knew very little. A circumspect young man, guarded about his past.

Passeau's murky background made him think about Hatch—the late Hatch, found dead in the river. Like Passeau, Hatch had been competent, intelligent, discreet, and possessed of a cleverness and resourcefulness lacking in Passeau. But a man who has spent much of his life looking over his shoulder will recognize another, and Morrison gradually came to recognize Hatch as a young fellow awaiting life's next main chance. Once while putting cash into one of his three safes, Morrison had chanced to see Hatch reflected in the high polished gleam of a sideboard, watching him. Morrison spun round and met Hatch's gaze.

"Busy yourself, Hatch."

A short time after that, Morrison had fired young Hatch, giving him a month's salary and a reference. Several months later Passeau showed him an article in the *Daily News*, about a dead transient found floating in the river, identified as James Hatch. Beaten to death and robbed. Just the sort of end, Morrison reflected, that he might have predicted for the shady Hatch. Indeed, Morrison had no doubt that Hatch wasn't even the poor lad's real name. He was experienced enough to know that there was at least the chance that the furtive Hatch had planted himself in the house as a sort of spy. A spy for whom? It was an interesting question. A dead spy now, and whoever had sent him would doubtless be working on a new stratagem.

In contrast, Passeau, it had to be admitted, had never given cause for mistrust. Indeed, Passeau had developed the classic English butler's ability to gaze off into space, seeing nothing he was not meant to see. Morrison reflected on the odd nature of a wealthy man's existence: surrounded more often than not by strangers whom one entrusted with one's schedule, one's safety, one's belongings. Even, in some cases—though not in Morrison's—with one's secrets. An idiosyncratic sort of existence.

A different sort of problem, if there was one, was Mackal, a former police officer hired on occasion to provide an additional layer of security for those times when Morrison wasn't sure the presence of Lucas sent a forbidding enough message. Mackal was big, hard-drinking, and sullen, but fearless and armed to his yellowing teeth. And now he had become a cause for irritation: he'd been expected to provide security for the party and had not shown up.

Morrison read for a time, listened to a little music on the radio, and closed his eyes.

He woke with a start and realized he had nodded off. He lit a cigarette and sat there smoking for a time, thinking of the next day's appointments and concerns. A man of influence would be waiting for Morrison at a certain restaurant on Oak Street, hat in hand, hoping to change the terms of a financial transaction, and desperate to keep their business concealed from his public. In the afternoon, he would meet an ambitious but small-time hoodlum for a drink, and listen to a proposal. He also expected to hear from the office of a member of Congress who would express his concern over the possibility of a financial transaction with Morrison becoming public knowledge. At some point after these duties were addressed, Morrison would have Lucas drive him to Marshal Field's, where he would purchase half a dozen ties and some shirts.

Morrison thought again of the woman. After showing up twice the previous week, there had been no sign of her for several days. Just the night before, he'd had Mackal drive him around the neighborhood to see if he could spot her. He had no doubt she would reappear, probably when he least expected it. But he would do what was necessary. He had long since determined to do whatever was necessary to repel the encroachment of the past. His past was dead.

From somewhere in the back of the house he heard a noise. He froze and forced himself with the patience of a man who has been in straits before to remain still, noiseless. Morrison held his breath and then hoisted himself in silence from the bed. He stood, listened, heard nothing. He told himself it might have been a cat on the back stairs. And it might have been a footstep. He went to the back window and saw movement, someone in the alley behind the house. A woman in dark clothing. He thought of the woman who had stood outside his house, screaming, but this was someone different, taller and, he was certain, younger. As he peered into the dark alley, he had the odd sense that there was something vaguely familiar about this woman. Then the woman slipped into the yard of a house on the opposite side of the alley. Now he heard the sound again, movement, someone on the back stairs. Morrison moved to a small side table and opened the drawer, taking out the small pistol. He moved carefully toward the back of the house, and now he heard them, moving, muttering, whispering. More than one, then. Something closer now, in another part of the house.

He thought of calling the police but felt that his safety would be compromised as he stood there on the phone. No, the gun and surprise gave him the advantage. He was moving steadily toward the sound of these intruders and had just entered the kitchen when a figure emerged from the darkness to his left. He turned, heard himself gasp and felt the blade in his stomach. Then he was stabbed again and he was sinking to the floor, conscious now of the pain in his chest, vaguely aware of familiar odors, stale smoke, and perfume, he thought. And somewhere in the back of the house, movement, movement and someone speaking in a low voice. As he hit the floor, he squinted to see the face hovering over him. He knew this face.

* * *

Ray woke to the sirens. Three, four of them. He heard voices in the street outside, someone shouting, the sounds of people running. He squinted at the small clock on his side table: 2:17. He got out of bed and staggered to the window where he caught just a glimpse of a fire truck moving west on Armitage. A cop car and a fire chief's car followed, and now he saw people, some of them half-dressed, turning that corner on the dead run.

He pulled on pants and a shirt, put on shoes without socks and dashed out to see what was happening.

At the corner he stopped and tried to make sense of the chaos. He saw a hook-and-ladder making the slow, stiff turn onto Seminary. Two men emerged from the liquor store on the corner and ran toward the action, and he found himself running along with them. Then he saw it: the red mansion was burning. All of Seminary Street was lit a garish orange from the flames, and sparks climbed high in the night sky. Half a dozen fire department vehicles lined both sides of the street, and uniformed police officers kept the onlookers back. The fire trucks pounded the flames with high-pressure streams of water but the fire seemed unaffected. On both sides of the Morrison house Ray could see people in pajamas and robes staring at the fire. He moved closer, only to be stopped by a long-faced cop who told him to stay back.

"Whole thing's gonna go, fella, you don't want to be any closer."

As Ray watched, the cop moved people back and another cop now ran a rope across the street and secured it around a light post.

A few feet away a thin man in a battered fedora stood with a lunch pail, caught on his way to or from work by the excitement and the size of the flames.

"That big house," he said, catching Ray's eye.

Just as the man spoke, there was a great cracking sound, a deep splintering noise, and a staircase to the upper floor caved in with a whoosh and crashed down. For a time the flames continued unabated but the firefighters managed to confine it to a part of the main floor. An hour later the fire had been reduced to small patches of flame that sprouted here and there as a new piece of furniture or a rug caught fire and was then put out.

Ray found a place to stand, at the entrance to the playground on the far side of the street from the mansion. He was chilled and exhausted but unable to look away from the fire. Around the mansion, some of the onlookers had given in to their fatigue and the crowd thinned. The night sky bled out and dawn took over, and Ray realized how long he'd been here. The street was dense with smoke but a new smell took over, the heavy odor of burnt wood and cloth soaked with thousands of gallons of water. A fireman emerged from the Morrison house, pointing behind him as he spoke to a fire chief. The chief turned and motioned to a pair of men in dark suits, and Ray recognized them as the detectives he'd spoken to. Ray got up from the stairs and moved closer to the street.

"It's out," someone said.

The big one, Carmody, listened to the fire chief and then mounted the stairs. His partner said something, shook his head. Ray caught part of it.

"—can't go in there."

The big detective waved him off. He beckoned to a fireman, who came up and handed him a flashlight. Then Carmody disappeared inside. A moment later he emerged, said something to the fire chief and motioned to the uniformed officers and the ambulance crew. Then he crossed to where his partner was still waiting. He jerked his head in the direction of the Morrison house.

"There's a body in there."

"Who?"

"I think it's him. C'mon, something else I want you to see."

Ray saw Detective Kessel give a slow shake of his head, but he followed his partner back across the street and they entered the house followed by a firefighter.

As Ray watched them, he became aware of someone moving behind him. He turned and saw a young guy hanging back near a doorway and watching the unfolding scene. Ray thought he recognized him now—a young guy with an absent look in his eye that Ray had seen rooting around in the gutters for cigarettes. Now the kid noticed Ray looking at him and nodded toward the big house.

"You hear that? There's a dead body in there. The rich guy in that house, somebody killed him."

Ray nodded.

Yeah, Ray thought, *it's a big deal. Something happened on your street.*

But he had to admit, when it was a guy you'd seen, a neighbor, even if he remained a stranger, there was something shocking as well. A neighbor was dead, by violence. Ray's father had always referred to death as "The Guy in the Black Hat."

Don't look so excited, kid. It means the Guy in the Black Hat found his way to your neighborhood.

The ambulance moved up the street and pulled up in front of the mansion, and a moment later they brought out a body on a stretcher, the face covered. A nurse bent over the body, touched the throat, then said something to the detective and shook her head. Ray recognized the nurse he'd seen a couple of days earlier.

"That's him," the kid said, nodding to himself. "They killed that guy. Stabbed him in the heart."

"Says who?"

"A guy up there," the kid said, and pointed to a man in a suit a few feet away. The man stood with his mouth open, a vacant look on his face.

"How would he know?"

The kid gave him a puzzled look, then shrugged, embarrassed. Ray studied him for a moment and realized now what it was about the kid that was different. He took in the wide-eyed look, the distracted smile. As if he'd heard Ray thinking out loud, the kid turned to him and grinned.

"He was a millionaire. And they killed him. Gangsters, I bet. Musta been gangsters."

"I guess so."

He looked into the bright blue eyes of this boy and remembered another boy with that look, in the final push into Germany, a kid who just couldn't stand the terrors anymore. A disturbed boy like this one.

He looked away but the kid was speaking to him.

"I seen guys killed, lots of guys. I was in the Pacific."

Ray met his gaze. The kid held up his arm, the sleeve rolled high on his biceps. Ray saw the long scar that he'd noticed before. Now he saw that it ran most of the kid's forearm and up across his bicep.

Yeah, Ray thought. Combat, the Pacific, and he'd come back with his mind scrambled.

"I got that at Peleliu. I got a purple heart."

"Peleliu. I heard that was tough. I was at Omaha Beach."

The kid gave him an odd look now, a soft smile, and then he moved away. Ray closed in on the scene in front of the house. New faces were arriving, it was morning. New onlookers and a different group as well, and Ray understood that these people were Morrison's staff.

"Oh, God," a red-faced older woman called out. "They've killed 'im!"

Then she burst into tears and was being consoled by a uniformed officer. A few feet away a younger woman in a black maid's uniform stared at the building with her hand to her mouth. A taller girl moved up beside her and said something. The tall one was both tough-looking and attractive. The maid looked at her, surprised, and nodded, pointing toward the body. Off to one side, a bulky man in a white busboy's uniform, a boyish face, stood alone, his face white with shock. In the midst of them all, Ray saw the bulky form of Detective Carmody, wiping his face with a handkerchief and peering around at the onlookers. Then the older woman collapsed on the sidewalk. The young nurse ran to her aid and Ray recognized her as the blond girl he'd been watching just a couple of nights earlier.

Carmody approached her and Ray was amused to see the young nurse giving him orders. Carmody said something to the uniformed cops and one came over with a blanket. The nurse folded it into a pillow and put it under the older woman's head, then gestured for another blanket. This one she folded into a higher bundle and put it under the woman's feet, raising her legs.

Shock, Ray told himself. The older lady's had a shock.

A second ambulance arrived and the nurse watched them take away the woman in the black dress. Then the nurse was finished. Ray watched her walk quickly toward Armitage, serious and self-possessed, and then she broke into a brisk trot. Late for work, perhaps. As he stared after her, he noticed a man watching the action from several houses away and puffing at a cigarette. A big man, Ray would have said, and this man wore a dark suit and hat, and he watched the action while leaning against a tree. There were perhaps a hundred people staring and gossiping, gesturing, but something about this man had caught Ray's eye. It was something in his posture, a tension, as though at any second he might bolt. Another squad car came up the street and the man stepped quickly back. Then he seemed to notice Ray. Ray met his gaze and the man tossed his cigarette out onto the street and walked away quickly, without a backward glance.

A second woman in a maid's uniform, this one much younger, arrived and spoke with people in the crowd and then just stood there drained of color, her hand to her mouth.

A bystander broke off from the crowd and passed Ray. He met Ray's eyes and shook his head.

"They got that guy that lived there. The rich one."

"He's dead?"

"Yeah. And robbed. That's what they're sayin'. Jesus, a rich guy like that, in his own home. And it looks like they torched the place. And I live right up the street," the man said, and hurried away.

More people arrived, including a pair of official-looking men, one carrying a satchel. Some kind of doctor. A cab pulled up and a young man emerged, in a suit but no tie. He was tall and slender, with close-cropped blond hair and striking eyes, large brown eyes, a woman's eyes, Ray would have said. A scuffle ensued as the young man with the strange eyes attempted to push his way through the police cordon and into the house. He was forced back by two of the uniforms. Ray moved closer.

"I have to see him!" the newcomer shouted. "You have to let me by!"

He lowered his head and tried to squeeze between the two officers and one of them pushed him against a squad car.

Carmody stepped up to the young man and asked him something Ray couldn't hear.

"My name is Geoffrey Passeau. I'm Mr. Morrison's personal assistant. I need to see him," the young man said. "I need to see him," he repeated in a tremulous voice. He appeared distraught, but there was, Ray thought, just the hint of performance in all of it, a young man finding himself on a grand stage for just a moment.

Ray saw the detective move closer. He put a big hand on the young man's shoulder and said something in a quiet voice, and led the young man over to the stretcher. A policeman pulled back the sheet covering the stretcher and the young man stiffened for a moment and then pulled back as though trying to escape what he saw. his shoulders slumped, all the fight gone out of him. The big detective patted him on the shoulder and then led him away. As they moved away from the ambulance, Detective Carmody looked around at the remaining bystanders.

"You folks can go on about your business now," he said, and as his eyes moved from face to face he seemed to stop when he got to Ray Foley. He hesitated, let his gaze rest on Ray for just a moment, then moved on.

It struck Ray that he'd seen Morrison just two days earlier, driving by in his chauffeured car, a two-toned Bentley. Ray watched them, the sleek car and its sleek inhabitant, and a phrase came to him from a poem read in school, a poem about another well-heeled man who was a mystery to his neighbors: *Imperially slim*. And like the subject of that poem, the shadowy figure known as Morrison was dead before his time.

In the street light he could see the young blond man sitting in the back seat of the squad car. He seemed to be studying the faces in the street.

A black Hudson Super Six pulled up a few feet from the Morrison house and a man unfolded himself from the front seat. Ray recognized this man: the chauffeur. Tall and well-built, gray-haired like his employer, a hard-faced man who studied the crowd and the police presence, and it seemed to Ray that he already knew what had happened. The chauffeur stood there beside his car and watched the house but came no closer. Then he began to scan the crowd. His eyes fell for a moment on Ray and then he turned and looked up the street, toward Armitage. He seemed to find something of interest there. Ray followed the man's gaze and saw a figure just turning the corner out of sight. He noted that the man in the dark fedora was gone. Perhaps this was the man the chauffeur was watching. Several more cars turned up Seminary from Armitage, a couple of dark sedans and a cab, a Checker cab that pulled over and came to a stop.

The young man called Passeau emerged from a squad car now, mopping his forehead with a handkerchief as he spoke to Carmody. Ray watched him and then looked back up the street. He forced himself to stand there across from the mansion for another minute or so. The flames were finally out, the worst damage confined to the very front of the building. Ray looked around and saw that perhaps half of the onlookers had heeded the policeman's directive to disperse. The rest were watching the house. At the edge of the crowd, the goofy kid was still there, telling any newcomer what had happened in the big house. Up the street, the chauffeur closed his car door and moved slowly toward the house. He did not look Ray's way but seemed to be watching Passeau. Carmody was speaking to Passeau but managed to scan the crowd one more time. When his gaze fell on Ray Foley, Ray decided it was time to leave.

"See anything interesting?"

Ray turned to find Detective Kessel watching him.

He flanked me, Ray thought.

The detective managed to look amused and hostile at the same time.

"I see what you see. A guy's dead and somebody set fire to his house."

"Yeah, another dead guy and here you are."

"Half the neighborhood is here."

"Is that right?"

Carmody came shuffling across the street, puffing on a cigarette.

"Foley, right? We meet again."

"I guess so."

"You keep turning up where there's been a killing."

"I live right up the street."

"Is that so. You know anything about this? Seen anything?"

"No, I never knew that guy."

"But you're from around here, you knew who this man was."

"I knew him to see him. He's been around here as long as I can remember. But I already told you I haven't seen anything. I mean, I saw guys watching them bring out the body just now."

"What guys?"

"A guy in a black suit, black fedora. He was kind of hanging back behind the tree over there. And there was a young guy, a baby-faced guy, he was all excited about this."

Carmody was nodding, and Ray had the odd sense that the cop wasn't even paying attention to what he said. He looked up the street for a moment and then met Ray's eyes.

"Yeah, we saw him. He lives around here, I've seen him going through the garbage."

"He's got a couple of screws loose," Kessel added.

"So that's all you've got, huh?" Carmody said.

"That's all. I didn't know this guy."

Carmody eyed him for a moment and then held up two fingers.

"There's two of them in there."

"Two bodies?"

"That's right. The owner of the house and another guy. About your age."

Ray looked away.

"You got something, Foley?"

"No. I don't know anything about this, except what you tell me. So who's the second guy?"

"We don't know. Like I said, a young guy," Carmody said, watching Ray.

"Maybe the guy that killed Morrison."

"So they killed each other? Is that your idea?"

"Maybe. Why not?"

"Because they were found in different parts of the house." After a moment, Carmody said, "Tell you what, Foley. You show up at another crime scene like this one, we'll bring you in."

"Like I told you, I'm just back in town, I've got nothing to do with any of this."

"So you say," Kessel said.

Carmody was already walking away. Then he slowed down, shot Ray a look over his shoulder. He seemed on the verge of saying something else. Then he shook his head and walked on.

New blood had fed the crowd of spectators once more, but Ray had lost his taste for all of this. As he made his way back to his room, he thought of the second body in Morrison's house—*about your age*, Carmody had said.

Ray thought of Eddy Walsh and a knot grew in his stomach.

45

Chapter Five

For two nights Barney Donlan had slept on a bench at North Avenue Beach. Now, tired and filthy, he made his way back toward Poe Street. He needed clothes and something to eat, and then he'd pack a bag and leave for a while, go up north to Waukegan, where he had a cousin who would put him up for a while until things cooled off. None of this had worked the way it was supposed to, and he still didn't have a nickel to show for it. Willie Foy's fault, all of it. Word on the street was that the guy Morrison was dead, and Barney understood none of it. But he was on the move, he'd lie low for a few days and then find Foy and get his share of the money, whatever that was.

He had gone a few blocks when he realized he'd picked up a tail. Twice Barney slowed down and nearly caught him. At Halsted he stopped and turned slightly, lighting a smoke with the match cupped between his hands while he scanned the dark street behind him. Barney's pursuer was still there, and this time Barney had gotten a look. Slender and dark and moving in stealth, keeping to the shadows. Barney shook the match and tossed it, looked around with studied nonchalance and moved on. He turned abruptly up Dayton and noted that a couple of street lights were out, making this block darker than the others.

That was all right. He wasn't afraid of the dark. If it made this man behind him a bit more confident, so be it. Barney was after all a fighter, a fighter all his life, in the streets and in the ring. As a younger man he'd had notions of making his name in the prize ring, but an early bout with another Chicago Barney, the great Barney Ross on his way to fame and three world titles, had convinced him that his future was not in the prize ring. Still, Barney Donlan knew he was a match for most men he was likely to encounter on the street, and this creep somewhere behind him would be no different.

He swung back toward North Avenue and made for the far end of the block. A few yards from the corner he stopped suddenly and spun round. He saw nothing. He stood there, his fists cocked and legs spread wide for balance, and then he had an odd sensation.

He got behind me.

Barney Donlan turned, scanned both sides of the street and saw no one. He wondered if his pursuer had given up, or simply lost him. Then, with a small shock Barney saw him. He squinted to get a focus on what he was seeing, and then he understood. The other man was moving on all fours to stay low, out of Barney's line of vision, and Barney had to hand it to him, that was a smart move on a dark street. So he prepared to face him and the other man came at him, moving fast and, to Barney's confusion, staying low, in that crouch, like some kind of animal. Scrambling fast and closing the distance between them.

Quick and wiry, a good little welterweight, Barney thought.

Barney Donlan cocked his right hand back and held his left out, and he was in mid-punch when this figure of the shadows was on him. Fast, Barney would have said, very fast. He felt the blade enter his chest. The other man met his eyes and Barney felt the blade go in again, but he knew the second strike wasn't even necessary. He gasped, he tried to protest. *Wait*, he wanted to say. His legs went weak and his vision clouded, and then he was falling against a fence. Barney Donlan slid down the fence and died in a sitting position. The tannery worker who found him six hours later on his way to work thought he was a drunk who had not quite made it home, until he saw the blood on Barney Donlan's shirtfront.

* * *

Midnight and a soft rain, and Ray headed home after sitting by himself in the window of a diner and nursing a cup of coffee. He was nearing his room when a man slipped out from a doorway and began matching him step for step.

Eddy Walsh.

Eddy Walsh, soaked and big-eyed, casting a nervous glance behind him as he walked.

"Eddy? What's up? Somebody following you?"

"Maybe. Ray, can you put me up?"

"It's just a room, Eddy."

"I'm in Dutch, Ray. I need a flop. I can't be out on the street and I can't go back where I'm staying."

"All right."

In Ray's room, Eddy went directly to the window. Ray sat at the small table and watched him. Eddy peered down at the street, then shook his head.

"You can't see shit from here."

"I didn't take the room for the view, Eddy. It's just a place to sleep. What's going on?"

Eddy stepped back from the window.

"We hit a guy's house, rich guy, and things happened, it got out of control."

"Morrison. That was you. Jesus, Eddy."

"It wasn't supposed to go like that. It got out of control."

"What got out of control?"

"The guy got killed. That wasn't supposed to happen."

Eddy took a smoke out of a crumpled pack of Luckies and lit it.

"Who killed him, Eddy? And who the hell is *we*?"

"We didn't kill the guy, we didn't kill anybody. It was me and Jimmy and those guys I told you about, Barney Donlan, Floyd Hennessey, Willie Foy."

"Morrison, Eddy. Morrison? You hit his house and now he's dead and his house burned down. I was there, Eddy, the cops were all over the place. That was you guys. You're saying you had nothing to do with him getting killed?"

"No, Ray, we just wanted the cash and a couple things we could pawn. That was all. That wasn't us, Ray. It should have gone smooth. He wasn't supposed to be home."

"Says who?"

"It's what we heard. Willie cased the place. He knew this guy's habits and his, you know, schedule."

"So much for what Willie Foy knows. And they found another dead guy in there, Eddy. A younger guy, the cops told me. So two killings."

Eddy blinked, looked away suddenly, but Ray had seen the look that came into his eyes.

"You know something."

"No, Ray, I don't know anything about that. I'm telling you, there was somebody else there. And that guy Morrison. He heard us and he came downstairs, and there was somebody else there, waiting for him. That's who killed him."

"Did you see it happen?"

"No. But I think Willie did. He just said, 'That guy's dead, there's somebody else in there. We were already outside the place and Willie went back in."

"Did he see the guy?"

"No. But he heard him moving around. He didn't see the guy." Eddy looked down for a moment and then said, "He saw us, I guess."

"You think that's what happened?"

"I don't know what I think." Eddy took a long pull on his cigarette and blew out smoke. "But okay, here's the other thing I'm wondering. About Willie. I mean, he said there was this other guy there, that this guy killed Morrison. But I didn't see it. I didn't see anybody but us. So—suppose there was no other guy. See what I mean?"

"Sure, it means Willie did it."

"I don't know. But he went back in, Ray. We were already out of that building with some cash and other stuff and Willie went back in."

"For what? Money?"

"See, we got some money that was in a drawer, but we couldn't open his safe. Willie went back in and he came out with nothing. So we got a few bucks, some silver, a couple of rings. And some goddamn statue that Willie grabbed as we were getting out."

"A statue?"

"Yeah. Willie kept that. He said it was old."

"What did it look like?"

"A girl. You know, a woman, like a Greek woman in the pictures. Red hair, a long green gown kind of thing, and a little green wreath on her head. I told him to leave it, it was just one more thing to carry, but he wanted to go back, said he thought he could get a few bucks for it. Like all of a sudden Willie Foy is an expert on statues."

"Not likely. I don't think Willie Foy is an expert on anything. So he went back in."

"Yeah. He said he'd look around for cash, too. But he came out with nothing but that statue. And he looked pretty scared when he came out. His face was all pale."

"What about the other guys, Eddy?"

"We all just ran. The two old guys ran through a yard and I just took off, fast."

"And Jimmy?"

"I lost track of him. It was pretty crazy, Ray."

Eddy looked off into space, frowning, and Ray could see the idea forming: you lost track of him because he never made it out.

"You pretty sure Jimmy made it out?"

"Why wouldn't he? The rest of us did."

Ray said nothing to that.

"You have to lay low, Eddy."

For a moment Eddy Walsh puffed on his cigarette, not even really inhaling, and said nothing. He looked off into space, rocking slightly. All the color had drained from his face. Then he looked at Ray and forced a smile

"I'll be all right. Things are starting to come together for me. I'll get my dough from Willie when we meet up and I'll be all right." He smiled now for the first time. "I got my eye on a girl."

"Somebody you just saw on the street or somebody you've actually talked to."

"Oh, I've talked to her, Ray. She's from the neighborhood. Works up at

Woolworth's. And it turns out she knew Morrison. She used to work for him. She told me he was a real prick. Always firing people. He fired her, he fired one of his house guys, he fired a cook who pissed him off."

"So what's this girl's name?"

"Sophie. She's Irish. Red hair, green eyes, big girl—almost my size, Ray. What a dish."

Ray remembered the tall red-haired girl at Morrison's house.

"They'll make you crazy, Eddy."

"Good, that kind of crazy, I need."

* * *

In the morning, Ray was unsurprised to see that Eddy had slipped away. He shaved and washed and went out for breakfast. Outside, he found that he had more company. Detective Carmody was leaning against his car and smoking. His partner stood by the hood of the car and stared at the passing traffic.

For Christ's sake.

"Already? Aw, c'mon," Ray said.

Carmody took a puff, blew out smoke.

"Yeah, already. Some people been up for hours. I've got something else to ask you. Names, actually, I've got names for you."

"Okay."

"Jimmy Seeger," the detective said, watching Ray's eyes, "Barney Donlan, Floyd Hennessey." He paused, waited a beat until Ray began to answer, then said, "Eddy Walsh."

Ray looked away to compose himself. He pursed his lips, shrugged.

"Yeah, those are all guys from the neighborhood. Barney Donlan and Floyd Hennessey, those are a couple of the old guys I used to see around the neighborhood, they knew my old man. Jimmy Seeger I knew from playing ball over at Hamlin Park. Gym rat, always playing ball."

Carmody waited, saying nothing.

"And Eddy Walsh is a friend of mine. We grew up together."

Now Carmody was nodding as though Ray's answers were sufficient. He looked behind him at his partner, took a puff on his cigarette, and then looked back at Ray.

"How about Willie Foy?"

"He's nothing to me. My folks knew him. My Ma always told me he's no good. Just a con man."

Carmody watched him again, then said, "Here's the thing, Foley. Word is out on the street that these guys pulled a job at the late Cary Morrison's place the night he was killed. They robbed the house."

"Says who?"

"We have witnesses who saw these guys running from the place. And at least two of them have tried to sell things from Morrison's house. And we know you were pretty tight with this Walsh kid, he's your friend. One way of looking at it is your pal would let you know about it."

"He never said anything to me. And I don't know how he'd wind up pulling something like this with Willie Foy or these other old guys. I don't see it."

"So you never heard that these guys were planning a job."

"No. And I've only seen Eddy once since I got back. We shot the breeze over a beer and talked about trying to make some money. He seemed to think he was in pretty good shape."

"And he didn't invite you in on any kind of burglary job?"

"No. But he knows me. There's no way I'd be getting into that. I'm not a thief. Besides, I have money. I'm all right for a while."

Carmody gave him an interested look.

"Money from what?"

"Do I ask you where your money comes from?"

"Answer the question."

"I put some away just before I went into the service in a Postal Savings Account. And for three years I've been getting paid by Uncle Sam without anyplace to spend it. So I'm all right for a few weeks. Maybe a couple, three months if I go easy on it."

"And then what?"

"Then I better hope I find a job."

Kessel looked at Carmody.

"You going to tell him, or what?"

Carmody looked from Kessel to Ray.

"Two of your friends are dead."

"What?"

Ray thought immediately of Eddy.

"Who's dead?"

"Barney Donlan. Jimmy Seeger. They found Donlan about half a mile from here. The Seeger kid was the other body we found in the house."

"In the house?"

"See, your friend never made it out."

Both detectives watched Ray's reaction.

"Jesus."

"You didn't know, huh?" Carmody asked.

"No. What happened? I mean—how?"

"Stabbed. Like our boy Morrison. And like this Frederick Webb we found in the alley a couple blocks from here—remember him? If I had to come up with a theory, I'd say the same guy did all of it."

"What about—?"

Ray was about to ask about Eddy and caught himself.

"The other ones? Maybe they're dead, too, and we just haven't found the bodies."

Kessel shrugged and looked up the street. "He didn't know."

"I see that," Carmody said. "So it looks like your friends bit off a little more than they could chew, Foley. I sure hope you're not in this."

"I'm not. I've got nothing to do with any of this."

"All right, Foley. But if you see any of these guys, you give me a call. I think you know where to find me."

"Yeah. Sheffield Street Station."

"So I'll be waiting on your call."

"I don't think I'll hear from anybody."

Carmody shrugged, already walking away. In the car, Ray saw Detective Kessel give him a look of distaste.

He headed up toward the paper stand at the El station and thought about Carmody's news. The news about Jimmy Seeger had shaken him. Poor Jimmy Seeger, hapless Jimmy who'd always thought there had to be an easy way to make a lot of money and was now dead because of it. Barney Donlan he'd never known well—a man in his forties. But a tough son of a bitch, a former fighter. A guy had gotten close enough to Barney to kill him with a knife and get away with it. Ray thought about Eddy Walsh and wondered where he was.

Chapter Six

Up ahead, a woman emerged from a Clark Street cocktail lounge, and right behind her a man, and they were both talking at the same time, her voice low, his getting louder as she walked away from him. She was small and blond, and now Ray recognized her, the little nurse from Poe Street. She was moving fast, and the man, a big man, reached out for her but she was faster and he got nothing but air. When she paused for traffic at the curb, he caught up with her and grabbed her by her sweater. She shook it off and turned around and put a finger in his face, and said something Ray couldn't hear. The man grabbed her by the arm and shook her.

"Let go my arm, you," she said, and he shook her again. and said "Where do you think you're going?"

She tried to pull away but he yanked her by the arm until their faces were almost touching. The big man took her by the wrist and twisted it until she was forced to stand on her toes. She swung at him with her other arm but he blocked the blow.

"Hey," Ray called out. "What're you doing to this lady?"

The man squinted at Ray—nearsighted, maybe. "Mind your business."

"Let go of her."

"Who the hell are you—– Sergeant York?"

"Let her go."

"Or what?"

"Let's find out," Ray said.

He walked faster and as he closed the distance between them, he calculated the big man's reach and hoped he had no hand speed.

The man turned, managing to look both irritated and confused, and when he took his eyes from the woman, she slapped his face.

Oh, lady, Ray thought. *You're making this very hard.*

Her companion made a growling sound and cocked his fist.

"Oh, you bitch."

Ray saw the woman duck. He lunged at the man in time to catch his arm in mid-flight. He stepped behind the big man and flipped him over his leg. The man got up, red-faced and sweating and furious, and as he righted himself the blond snuck in and kicked him in the shin.

He roared and turned to her, slightly off balance, and Ray bounced a right hand off his jaw. He fell back against a lamppost. When he regained his feet, he faced Ray.

Ray backed up a step, slipped into his stance, left hand extended and right fist close to his chin. The big man moved to his left and brought his fists up. He threw a punch that Ray saw coming and easily slipped. Ray threw a straight left that caught the other man in the mouth.

The big guy lurched back, stopped, put his hand to his mouth. It came away bloody. He stared at it, glared at Ray, then said, "Screw this shit. Screw you. And screw her."

And then he left.

The blonde was standing a few feet away, and when her companion started walking in the other direction, she took off one of her shoes and went after him, awkwardly running in one high heel.

"Here, you bastard," she said, and tossed her shoe at him.

Ray blinked. It was a perfect shot, the heel bouncing off the back of the big man's head. He half-turned and glared at her, but she reached down and slipped off the other shoe and reared back, and he had second thoughts.

What a little fighter, Ray thought.

When he was gone, she retrieved her shoes and managed to slip them on again without missing a step as she walked toward Ray.

A small crowd had gathered and Ray grew self-conscious.

It was the woman who saved the moment.

"Thank you. That mug was gonna rough me up."

She managed to look both mortified and furious at the same time, her cheeks bright red.

"Don't mention it. Is that guy your husband?"

"Him? Don't be ridiculous."

"Are you all right?"

"Sure. If he'd have hit me, I would have scratched his eyes out."

Somehow Ray had no doubt of this. "Okay," he said, and turned to leave.

"Well, thanks again," she said, a tentative note in her voice.

He glanced at her. Good-looking and very tough. Maybe she was what he'd been waiting for, blind luck sending a girl his way. But he'd seen things like this before, a couple get into a fight and a guy gets involved and all of a sudden they're in love again and they both turn on the good Samaritan. Tomorrow this girl and her boyfriend might be back together—until their next fight. Still.

How many chances like this would he get? Ray was about to say something to make conversation and couldn't think of anything.

"Well, I've got to go," she said. She hesitated a moment and then said, "Thanks again."

"Don't mention it," Ray said. He held up one hand, and then he went on his way because he didn't know what else to do.

When he'd gone a few feet, Ray heard the woman call out.

"My name is Hannah."

He turned, smiled, and slapped himself on his chest. "Ray. Ray Foley," and the girl nodded and smiled.

Hannah, huh? Changed your name and your hair. Okay.

He remembered how she'd seemed at the scene of the Morrison killing. Calm and smart and self-possessed.

Maybe out of my league.

He recalled the blonde looking his way in the Marquis Lunch cafe a few days earlier.

Was that you?

He took a quick look and saw her turning a corner.

Interesting. That's some girl.

* * *

Hannah Marcel thought about this Ray Foley. Wearing the evidence of his War. She'd noted the deeply sun-burnt face and what looked like a scar on his neck, just below the bottom of his ear. A cute kid—No, not a kid anymore, none of them were. This one was probably twenty-two, twenty-three going on thirty. On the other hand you had to be careful with these returning GIs. A lot of them had been gone three years, even four, and they came back desperate. Desperate for sex, worse yet, desperate to fall in love and have the life they'd been daydreaming about while suffering overseas. All around her Hannah knew girls who were getting married to men just back from the War, in some cases girls marrying boys they'd been seeing just a few weeks or a couple of months when the War came. But after four years of falling in love through the mail they were all convinced that this was the great romance of their lives. And some of them, of course, were just desperate to climb into bed with a warm body. And then, knocked up, knocked up and married before they could even blink.

Hannah shook her head.

Not for this girl.

All the trouble in her life could be chalked up to men. It just wasn't worth it. She had come back from the war feeling in control of who she was, and now she would take control of her life. She turned on the lights in her living room and for a moment stood in the middle of the floor, looking around at the place she'd been able to put together. She was proud of the place—three rooms for one person, rugs on all the floors, a new refrigerator and an old stove that still worked. Most of the girls she knew lived either with their parents or alone, in rented rooms. Several of them lived in "sleeping rooms" in the homes of strangers.

Not for her.

She reflected that this little flat on a dark, quiet street was palatial compared to every place she'd ever lived before, and she wondered what her mother would have made of it. She'd be saying, "You need to find a good man," that was her mother's idea of a successful life. But Hannah knew her mother would have been impressed. And proud.

She'd have been proud of me anyway, Hannah thought. She raised me tough. And that's what I am.

Now she sighed, thinking of the scene she'd just created in the street, a guy taking a whack at her right there in the street, a fight, people gathering, their eyes on her.

To hell with all of them. And him.

All she could think of was that she needed to smack the big creep in the mouth and be done with him.

The gentleman's name was Ralph and she realized she could not have misjudged him more. A big man—she'd always liked big men, not having learned from her mother's mistake in this regard—big-boned and red-faced, quick to laugh and good for a story when he was sober. He smelled of Wildroot and Four Roses and he chewed Sen-Sen in the common but mistaken belief that little gray candies could hide whiskey breath. And when he had been drinking enough, he changed, did Ralph, just as her father had: the red face grew a little darker, the hair started hanging across his sweaty forehead, his breathing grew audible, and his eyes—she remembered this from her father most of all—the eyes bulged a little bit, giving him a menacing aspect that seemed to come from nowhere. A different face.

Yes, old Ralph was a drinker of that worst kind, who turned into another person after a few too many drinks.

The incident on the street had been the second time he'd shown this side. The first time he'd seen the look in her eye and caught himself. He would be back, she knew. He'd call her, he'd come and lean on her doorbell late at night, and if he was really feeling remorse, he'd show up at the hospital. The prospect of a man tearful and blubbering, coming to beg in front of her co-workers for one more chance had its appeal. But he'd tried to hit her, and no matter what he said he would do it again. She was through with him.

She thought about Ray Foley.

* * *

It was the lead story in the *Daily News* and all Eddy Walsh could do was gape open-mouthed at it. Barney Donlan had been found stabbed to death, and his murder was linked to the Morrison killing. The story went on to say that a second body found in the Morrison house had been identified as James Seeger, like the others stabbed to death.

Jesus, he never made it out of that place.

A police spokesman said that they were seeking at least three other members of what he called "the gang." The story did not name them, and Eddy wondered if this were at least a small bit of luck. The best thing, he knew, was to stay out of sight for a while, say nothing to anyone until this all blew over. But he needed to find Willie Foy, he needed his share, then he'd be on his way.

He thought about his conversation with Ray Foley.

I said too much. Shouldn't have said anything. You opened your mouth, sometimes you called down your own bad luck — an idea of his mother's, and Eddy thought there was something to it.

At his more candid moments Eddy admitted that he was terrified. It was hard to keep quiet about something this big, harder still to lie low. By day he kept himself out of sight, by night he looked for Willie Foy in the usual places. That was the most frustrating thing, that they'd never gotten together to split the haul from Morrison's place.

And so he spent his nights roaming the streets and looking over his shoulder. But he'd gone to see the girl. He'd spoken to her in veiled terms about what was going on in his life, about the element of danger, the fact that he would have some money in his pocket soon enough. Eddy had to admit he'd deeply enjoyed the girl's reaction: she'd gone wide-eyed and white, and he was certain that for a moment she'd stopped breathing.

He did his best to create the impression that he was that kind of guy, a guy who lived a dangerous life. A dangerous fellow, in fact.

By the middle of the next day he understood that he was being watched. No, followed. A face in a small knot of people waiting to cross North Avenue, heading to the subway station, one face turned toward him. When Eddy focused on them, all those faces were turned toward the street.

So for the time being, until he was ready to make his play, he headed back to his rooming house. He stayed in there and listened to the noise of the traffic outside on Clark Street, and the snoring of the guys on either side of him.

A few nights after he spoke to Ray, Eddy slipped out and made his way to a small grill up the street from his rooming house. It was a long narrow room wedged improbably between two stores, brightly lit with walls painted white, the place fairly glowed. Eddy found a stool near the back and ordered bacon and eggs. He ate quickly but lingered over a second cup of coffee. A few stools away, a young guy got up, tucked a paper under his arm and tossed a dime on the counter next to his cup. Something made Eddy look up. The young guy seemed to notice him. For a moment it seemed the guy would speak. Then he thought better of it. He nodded, raised one hesitant hand.

Yeah, I know you, too, Eddy thought. *CYO ball, maybe.*

Eddy nodded and raised his cup in greeting. The other man smiled, clearly unable to recall where they'd met.

Eddy watched the young guy leave the grill. He sipped his coffee and lit up a cigarette. Then he froze. Just to his right, at one of the small tables along the wall, a man had lowered his paper and was watching him. Eddy stuck the smoke in his mouth, fished out some change and laid it on the counter. He winked at the waitress and left.

Outside, he turned and watched the man at the back table. He was perhaps in his thirties, with sallow skin, in a black porkpie hat that he hadn't removed.

And now Eddy folded his arms and gave the man the opportunity to meet his eyes. Nothing.

Made you nervous, Pal?

He watched the man in the porkpie hat a moment longer, then went on his way. It was a warm clear night, not a night to lie on a gut-shot mattress in a rented room and stare at a ceiling. He thought of going to see the girl at Woolworth's but it was late, she'd already be gone. Eddy cut onto Diversey and made for the lake.

He'd gone three or four blocks when he realized he was being followed. Without turning, he understood that the man in the porkpie hat had merely given him a head start. Eddy turned quickly into the long narrow gangway between two apartment buildings. He made his way nearly to the alley that ran behind the buildings, then turned to face his pursuer.

Yeah, you and me right here.

Outside in the faint light of the street he saw the other man's shadow, saw that he'd paused, hesitant. He saw the very tip of the man's head as he leaned forward to peer into the dense dark of the gangway. Eddy slipped his hand into his pocket and gripped the taped-up roll of nickels.

"I'm back here, champ," Eddy called out.

Then the other man filled the entrance of the gangway. He paused there for a moment, then came forward. Eddy squinted at him. There was no porkpie hat. Another guy?

Eddy planted himself and brought up his fists. The other man came at him quickly, and now Eddy recognized him: the earnest young guy in the diner. And as this man came at him, Eddy tried to place him, tried to imagine him in a fedora, in uniform, in a baseball cap, anything. The other man kept coming and Eddy took a step back, cocked his right hand.

"I'll lay you out, Pal," he said.

Then he saw that this man held a knife, carried it low, casually, a man used to handling a knife, and Eddy took a swing, threw two punches in combination, thought he'd landed one, and then he felt the blade. He looked into this man's face and saw that they were eye-to-eye. Eddy tried to make sense of the look in the man's eyes. He felt his legs go, felt the pavement under him.

Chapter Seven

Three days later, Ray stopped at a news stand at Fullerton and Halsted, where an old newsie hawking the *Daily News* reminded him and the rest of the passersby that the big fight was tonight, the rematch between the great Joe Louis and the handsome, reckless Billy Conn—every guy's favorite long shot.

That night Ray wandered, looking for a place to listen to the radio broadcast of the fight. He found a tavern on Armitage with a hand-lettered sign taped to the diamond-shaped window in the front door:

FIGHT TONIGHT LOUIS-CONN TELEVISION

"Television!" Ray said aloud. "This I've gotta see."

Ray pushed his way in and found a mass of men in suits or sport shirts crowding along the length of the bar. In the very middle of his back bar, in pride of place, the owner had positioned his television.

Ray had seen a television set only on display in Goldblatt's but here was the genuine article. It was a squat wooden box with a speaker on one side and the screen, small and gray, on the other. It looked like a radio with a big glass eye. He tried to move closer but a wall of customers kept him five feet from the bar. Ray tried to insert himself between two of the other drinkers but succeeded only in annoying the biggest pair of shoulders in the place. The man turned, frowned, then smiled.

"Hey, it's the Foley kid."

The shoulders belonged to a pipefitter named Keely, built like a tackle, an old acquaintance of his parents. Ray nodded.

"You were in the service. Glad you're back."

"Me, too."

"I heard you did good. Come here. Hey, you, let young Foley squeeze in here. He's just back from the service. Bronze star, wasn't it?"

And a couple of purple hearts, Ray wanted to say but of course none of that mattered. He had made it home.

Keely leaned over the bar and yelled to a bartender. "Hey, how about a glass of beer for this soldier here" and it wasn't a question.

A beer came sliding up the bar and stopped in front of Ray, spilling foam on the bar.

"Drink up, Foley," Keely commanded.

They made small talk for a couple of minutes and then the owner hit the lights. It was fight time.

Bodies pressed up against the bar, pushing Ray into the wood. Behind him he saw enterprising patrons standing on chairs and tables and the bottom rung of the barstool, and you could have walked in and lifted wallets from half of them without anyone noticing, because this was Louis and Conn and they'd waited for it for five years.

The ceiling fans were outclassed by the heat from 50 bodies and the air had gone blue with tobacco smoke, and you could smell sweat and old clothes and hair cream and beer breath, and Ray wanted to laugh, for this steamy room was at least one familiar part of the old life, it hadn't changed.

The fight did not live up to five years of build-up. Both fighters were older and slower, but Conn had aged faster. Joe Louis stalked him patiently for the first rounds and let Conn dance. The images on the gray screen were small and distant and beset by sudden flashes of static.

In round eight, Louis ended the five-year debate with a sudden combination that laid Billy Conn onto the canvas. And that was it.

The press of bodies relaxed, men stepped back, grumbling, arguing. A guy who had lost ten bucks on Conn proclaimed that the fix was in.

Keely laughed. "Right, he let himself get hit like that as part of his grand plan."

He looked at Ray.

"Not much of a battle, huh?"

"No. After the first couple rounds I was just waiting for Louis to lower the boom."

Keely nodded and sipped his beer. Then he turned, remembering something. "Oh, I heard about that other poor kid. Gives the best years of his life, decorated soldier. Comes home and gets killed in his own neighborhood, in his hometown."

Ray tensed, felt a sudden foreboding.

"Who was that?"

"You know, that kid, Eddy Walsh. They just wrote him up in the paper, just this week."

Ray drained his beer just to be doing something. His stomach tightened and he wondered if he would be sick.

When he did not respond, Keely leaned toward him.

"You knew him, right? Oh, sure you did, and I don't mean to, you know, bring up something—Jesus, you're probably cut up plenty about this. I just—"

"It's okay. I didn't know."

"Oh, Jesus. I'm sorry. It was in the papers."

He was stabbed to death, you're going to say. He was stabbed to death.

"I guess somebody knifed him."

Ray forced himself to look at Keely, to respond, a nod here, something to hide the shock he was feeling.

"Oh, I'm real sorry, kid. I thought you knew about it."

"No. But thanks, I needed to hear about it."

Ray finished his beer, thanked Keely and threaded his way through the maze of drinkers, dazed.

I guess somebody knifed him.

Ray told himself there was no reason to think this was anything but a random killing, a robbery gone very wrong. But no matter how he looked at it, he could not convince himself.

No, it's the same guy.

* * *

The funeral home was on North Avenue near the El tracks and Eddy would have enjoyed the crowd he'd drawn. A dozen or more men stood outside the building smoking and talking.

Some of them paused to watch Ray as he entered.

It seemed that half the neighborhood had forced its way into the small parlor of the funeral home. Ray put his head down and made his way to the casket. A knot of people had gathered at the casket so that he could barely make out the figure in their midst. On the far side of the room, Eddy's uncle tried to console Mrs. Walsh. He spotted Ray and nodded. Ray shook his head. Eventually he made it to the front of the room and dropped onto the narrow kneeler there. He looked down at Eddy, heavily powdered, his face looking somehow swollen but otherwise unmarked. For just a moment Ray felt a sudden wave of dizziness, so that he had to clutch the top of the kneeler. He stared at the folded flag on Eddy's casket and fought to steady himself. He felt that he should pray, that was what you did here, you dropped down next to the casket and said some prayers, but he was taken instead by a sudden impulse to talk to Eddy.

I'm so sorry, Eddy. This is too soon. A guy who survives combat ought to have a chance at life when he gets home.

He spoke wordlessly, intent on the youthful face in the casket. He shook his head and said, "These guys got you killed, Eddy," and then realized he had spoken aloud. When he looked around, he saw people watching him. And in the very back row, trying with not much success to minimize his bulk, was Detective Sergeant Carmody.

As Ray left the funeral parlor, he told himself he would find out who did this. And then? Who knew?

A large hand rested itself on his shoulder. Carmody.

"Hello again, Kid."

"We have to stop meeting like this. People are gonna talk."

"You still got that smart lip, that's good. I'm sorry about this Walsh kid. I know he was your friend. That's tough."

Ray nodded but said nothing.

"So—anything you can tell me? Anything you heard? Maybe from your friend?"

"No."

"But you've talked to him, you've seen him."

"Watching me?"

Carmody gave him a sardonic look. "Lucky guess."

"I saw him just once. He seemed nervous."

"But he didn't have anything to say to you about this Morrison thing?"

"Yeah. He said he had nothing to do with any killing."

"Did you believe him?"

Ray looked Carmody in the eye.

"About that, yeah. Eddy could spin tales, but he was no killer."

"Here's a thing to think about, Foley. This kid was your friend and you knew these other guys. There's at least a chance that you're in this—"

Ray held up both hands. "I told you I—"

"—*whether you had anything to do with it or not*," Carmody said, with heat. "Maybe this guy knows you were Walsh's pal. That puts you in it. So watch your back. All I'm saying to you."

"Yeah."

Carmody eyed him.

"Floyd Hennessey. Know him?"

"Yeah. Old Navy guy, knew my father. He was in this, too. Why?"

"We fished him out of the river a few nights back. Been in the water a while, I'd say."

"How do you know it was Floyd?"

"He had his discharge papers on him. A lot of these old guys carry their papers around."

"Yeah. So do I. Stabbed?"

"No. Drowned, we think."

"That leaves one, Foley. So what do you know about Willie Foy?"

"He caused all this. I hope he's dead, too."

Carmody squinted up at the setting sun and seemed to consider this. "Maybe he is."

Carmody gave him an odd look now, a sly look, Ray would have said.

"I don't think he's dead. I think he's out there. I think maybe he left town for a little while and he's back, or if he's not, he'll be back someday. And one of us will see him. And if it's you, Kid, I hope you give me a jingle."

"Maybe I'll break his arms for him first."

"No, you get on the horn and let me know. I'd appreciate it."

Carmody patted Ray on the shoulder.

"In the meantime, have some fun in the Big Town, Foley. Don't be like this poor kid." He nodded toward the casket

Ray smiled. "That's what my uncle always called it. 'The Big Town.'"

Carmody gave him the little squint again. "You look like a guy that knows how to have a good time. Your first day back you probably went out and got hammered."

"My first day back I went to the cemetery."

"The cemetery?"

"Yeah. It's the only place I knew somebody. My Ma's there."

Carmody nodded slowly. "Fair enough. All right, Foley. You hear things, you give me a jingle. Bittersweet 0676."

"Right."

"Take it easy, Foley."

Ray watched Carmody walk up the block and disappear around a corner. For a moment he stood outside the funeral parlor and lit up a smoke. Up the street, a car pulled out into traffic. A blue Lasalle.

In his room, Ray pulled a chair over to the window and watched the street traffic. The sun had set and he could hear a pair of nighthawks overhead. He opened the screen and stuck his head out to watch them circle. Here was a city noise from his childhood, the nighthawks coming out to feed on the insects of the evening sky.

He tried to focus on himself, his own situation, what he'd do with himself to turn a dollar, how to find a girl. That was, of course, the big one, finding a girl. He thought of the blond nurse. But he could not keep his mind on these things for long. Carmody had given him too much to think about.

If the old cop was right, it wasn't over yet, none of it.

He thought about that, Eddy's senseless death. He remembered the moment when Keely had told him about Eddy, right there after the Louis-Conn fight. And now Ray saw a pattern: a fight postponed five years by the war, like so many other things, jobs, school, marriages. Plans for life. The war had frozen life in 1941, held it in suspended animation for five years and finally released it.

Ray thought about Eddy Walsh. In almost every memory of his childhood, Ray saw Eddy. Even as kids, Eddy had been a little bit crazy. His father drank, his mother seemed to be sick most of the time, and this left Eddy with a degree of freedom that none of the other boys had. An adventurer among them, it seemed, with no end of stories about the things he'd seen and done as he wandered around the city for half the night. More than once the cops had brought him home, and there was talk of sending Eddy out to "the Home" at Roosevelt and Ogden. In fact, it was difficult for Ray to think of a time in his childhood or his teens when Eddy hadn't been a part of his life.

Now Ray recalled a moment when he'd intervened when an older kid was manhandling Eddy in an alley behind a schoolyard. The older boy was a genuine street boy, said to be sleeping in boxcars and vacant lots. He was filthy and ragged, and smelled of smoke. He was also quick and long-armed, fought like a feral cat, and Ray had been no match for him, but at least he'd pulled the kid off Eddy.

The first of many such occasions. Ray's mother had once warned Ray about Eddy.

That kid will get you killed, sure enough.

But more than once his mother had been the one to tell Ray to bring Eddy home with him, so she could put hot food in him.

And now he was gone, and although Ray knew he'd had nothing to do with it, he could not shake the feeling that somehow, on some level, he should have been able to prevent Eddy's senseless death.

When people die, his mother had once said, *you feel responsible, even if there was nothing you could have done. You feel like you should have done more for them.*

I feel responsible, all right.

He thought about the Morrison killing, and Jimmy, and Detective Carmody, and understood that what he was now planning would doubtless land him in the soup. But he saw himself as a guy just back from the Service with nothing else going on in his life, a guy with a few bucks and fewer prospects, and nothing to hold him back from getting at the truth about the Morrison killing. It was obvious that the person who'd killed Morrison and Jimmy had also killed Eddy Walsh. Counting old Barney Donlan, four murders.

If you're still out there, I'll find you.

But the first thing would be to look for Willie Foy, the one who had caused all this. Eddy had mentioned a statue, Willie had gone back in and come out with a statue. If Ray could find something about the statue, it would be a start. And if he could find Willie Foy.

On the far side of the street a dark figure moved off in the growing dusk and Ray recalled Carmody's warning, that Ray himself might be in it anyway, whether he had been involved or not.

Okay, then, I'm in it.

Chapter Eight

'm in it, Ray had told himself, and it seemed as logical a choice as any other. And where to begin? With a certain gentleman whose place of business was the street.

The man Ray needed to see was standing on the corner of Armitage and Sheffield trying hard to attract attention. He was medium height and skeletally thin, and wore a straw panama hat and a flashy blue suit that would have shamed a peacock. He was variously known as Slick Bob, Bookie Bob and Bob the Book, and if you wanted to lay five bucks on a horse in the fifth race at Washington Park, Bob was the man to see. The War had been hard on horse racing but Bob had clearly prospered. At the moment he was leaning on a bright green Packard that clashed with his suit and fanning himself with the straw hat. Bob the Book looked up theatrically as Ray approached though Ray knew Bob had been watching him for several minutes.

"The Foley kid, ain't it? You made it home. Good for you."

"Hello, Bob. Still in business?"

"Oh, I do all right." Bob grinned. "Want some action? Put a nickel on a horse? Cubs, maybe? I hear things."

"Like what?"

"Like three o'clock this morning I'm heading home and a guy stumbles out of a saloon on Clark Street and pukes in the street. And this gentleman is supposed to pitch today for our Cubs. In this heat? This is a free one, Foley. In acknowledgement of your service to our country."

"So I should put a couple bucks on the Giants."

"Who am I to say? But they're starting a rookie pitcher. I can get you three-to-one."

"What I really need is a little information. Remember the rich guy they found dead in his house? That Morrison?"

Bob gave him a wary look. "So what if I do?"

"I heard from a pretty good source that somebody I know might have been involved."

"Yeah? Who's that?"

"Willie Foy."

"Willie Foy's an asshole. I've got nothing to do with him. Can't back up his bets, for one."

"And I heard there was some trouble about something Willie Foy took. A statue. Know anything about that?"

Bob shrugged. "Statues I don't know about. They're beyond me. And that thing, that Morrison thing, I wouldn't know anything about that, nothing at all. Complete ignorance."

Bob gave Ray an owlish look to see if Ray bought the story.

"I wonder where a guy would go to get rid of a thing like that. A statue."

"Well, an item like that, you'd want to go to a specialist. It's complicated finding the right buyer for a particular item, or vice versa, the appropriate article for a special client."

"You mean a fence."

"That term has negative, what-do-you-call-them, connotations. I think of this person as a go-between. I myself have acted in this capacity. But I don't do statues. You want to get rid of a statue, you need to talk to Oscar Leroux."

"That's his name?"

"He made it up. He's got a flair for the romantic."

"You think he'll talk to me?"

"He's a pretty candid guy. My half-brother, in point of fact."

"I'll use your name."

"No. He'll just tell you I'm an asshole. We don't get on. Families." Bob shook his head. "But he runs a pawn on Belmont."

* * *

Oscar Leroux leaned against a counter in his shop watching the street for new blood while he listened with one ear as a short pale man tried to build up the value of a set of silverware. He was just over six feet tall and weighed perhaps 270. Unlike most pawnbrokers, he did not do his business through a grate or a security window. Nor did Oscar keep a gun unless one counted the magnificent reproduction of a Winchester 76 made for him by a down-on-his-luck sculptor from a long slab of cedar.

Now a figure appeared across the street, a young guy with a deep sunburn and a GI's gait, a serious-looking kid, and empty-handed so he wasn't coming to sell something. A guy who came carrying nothing might be trouble and this one had an odd look. A copper? Oscar wondered. No, too young for plainclothes.

Oscar glanced at the man with the silver. "Three."

"But it's worth—"

"It's worth nothing while you're lugging it around the street. Take it to a couple other places and see what they offer. Then come back and take the three bucks. Right now, I'm busy. I believe this young gentleman," he said with a nod at Ray, "has something to ask me about."

The man nodded. Oscar pulled out a drawer beneath his counter and handed three dollars and a pawn ticket to the man, who took it without a word.

"Yes, sir?" Oscar said, lifting his chin to Ray. "What can I do for you?" He spoke in a deadpan voice, looked Ray over and wasn't impressed by what he saw.

"Bob the Book said you might be able to help me out."

"That asshole."

"He said you'd say that, too. I need to know about something that somebody might have pawned. A statue."

Oscar shrugged. "Statues, I got. This one's bronze, nice piece. Art Deco." He nodded at a small metal angel on a shelf behind him.

"No, this is a particular statue. It's connected with the Morrison killing."

Oscar Leroux held up a hand.

"I don't know what kind of business you think I run, son."

"I think there's at least a chance that somebody came in with a statue to sell you."

Oscar gave him a pained look. "Maybe they did, maybe they didn't. What's it to you if somebody sold me something? Who the fuck are you?"

"Name's Foley. Ray Foley.."

This earned a shrug. Oscar Leroux looked around the shop, blew out a long, bored breath, looked at his watch.

"Yeah," Ray said. "I'm bored, too. Talk straight to me and maybe I'll go away and never come back. Willie Foy."

Oscar sniffed. "I know who he is. I did a little business with him once or twice. Nothing recent. He's not the kind of people I associate with."

Ray watched Oscar fidget. The big man looked around his shop, let his gaze rest on objects here and there and never made eye contact with Ray.

So you do remember this, Ray thought.

"It just seems to me that there can't be that many street rats like Willie Foy who came in lately with a statue. You get a lot of *works of art* in here?"

"You'd be surprised. That little bronze piece there is by a French sculptor."

"Come on, Oscar, be straight with me."

Oscar hesitated, made a show of folding his arms across his chest. "I'm in business here. This is not a charity."

"What?" Ray gave him a puzzled look.

Oscar held out a palm and pretended to scratch it, and Ray translated. He came up with two bucks.

"All right, Willie Foy did come in that one time. Like I said, we knew each other from before. In fact, I used him once or twice as a picker."

"A picker?"

"Yeah. You know, a guy that trolls the alleys, looks for stuff other people have tossed out, things with some value. And Foy has a good eye. You'd be surprised."

"So he came in with this statue. Greek-looking."

"He had a statue, said he found it in a junkyard. But I could tell."

"Tell what?"

"That it was stolen. Guys come in with something they stole, and they don't really look you in the eye. But word was already out, that this Morrison was murdered and a couple of the guys that pulled it off were already dead. And word was that one thing they took was a statue. So I didn't want anything to do with the thing he had. Besides what good would a thing like that be to me? I was bullshitting about this French thing. I don't know what it is. Now see that one?"

Oscar pointed to a beautifully painted statue of the Infant of Prague.

"That's a statue has some value to me. Your Catholic, especially your Polack, he'll pay for that statue. This thing Willie Foy had? Too hot, no value to me. And besides, what do I know about Greek statues, Greek art. I couldn't even tell him if it was real. For that you got to see Emery Pogue. And that's what I told him."

"And where would I find him?"

Oscar Leroux gave him a smart-guy smile. "In the river."

"What—he's dead?"

"No. He lives on a boat." Oscar Leroux shook his head. "What kind of life is that for a grown man? Look for him over by Diversey. Diversey and the river."

* * *

At the place where Diversey met the river, Ray did indeed find a houseboat, with two more moored just a few yards downriver. This boat was a small, tidy affair, with whitewashed sides and rails. A man sat on a small folding chair at the stern of this boat, himself a small and tidy man to match his boat. His face was deeply sunburnt and he wore glasses that gave him a fragile aspect, but he bounced up from his chair at Ray's approach.

"Well, company? That's a fine thing on a beautiful morning." When Ray stopped at the water's edge, the small man waved him ahead. "Come on board, don't be shy about it."

He held out a long-fingered hand and gave Ray a surprisingly forceful tug to help him get over the gap between boat and water.

"My name's Ray Foley."

"Emery Pogue," the small man said, and thrust the hand at Ray. They shook and Emery Pogue showed Ray to a three-legged stool.

"So what can I do for you?"

"Oscar Leroux told me to look you up."

"Oscar, yeah," Emery Pogue said. "Sort of an unpleasant man in his way. Short-tempered, suspicious, greedy. We're good friends."

Ray laughed. "I wanted to ask you about a statue."

"A statue. What kind of statue?"

"A statue somebody stole. And I wondered if they tried to get you to tell them about its, you know, value."

Emery Pogue blinked behind his glasses and studied Ray for a moment. "And would you be involved in the theft of this object?"

"No. But someone I know was."

"You wouldn't believe it to look at me, or my little boat here, but I look at a lot of what they call *objets d'art*. Can you describe the statue?"

"Not really. I never saw it. I'm told it looked like a Greek statue of a woman, about a foot-and-a-half high. She was wearing some kind of green gown wrapped around her."

"Well, if it was still painted, it wouldn't be Greek—not ancient Greek, you understand. What is your intention with this statue, then? To return it to its owner?"

"No, he's dead. Killed when his house was robbed. And several guys connected with the robbery are dead. I'm trying to find out why."

"And you think the statue is at the heart of it?"

"Maybe."

Emery turned for a moment to watch a man pass by in a rowboat. He waved and the man nodded.

"Here's what I can tell you, son. The item in question is a lovely piece, probably made in Belgium in the nineteen-twenties. It is an imitation of a French statuette made a century or so earlier. That is to say, it is a fake. Not worth anything but as a decorative object, a lovely choice. I told him I'd give him two bucks for it, which was a good price. But I was not interested in the papers."

"The papers?"

Emery grinned. "Yes. The bottom was hollowed out, and inside were papers, a sheaf of papers rolled very tight to fit them all in the tight space."

"What kind of papers?"

"If they'd been lined, I would have said ledger pages, but they weren't. Instead, they seemed to be a listing of notations of various kinds of transactions with initials and amounts and dates. That kind of thing. Of no use to me." He paused a moment and then said, "But perhaps useful or even important to someone. I guess he decided to hang onto it."

For a moment Ray said nothing.

Papers.

He shook his head: this would have been too complicated for a street rat like Willie Foy, too subtle. He was in over his head if this was about papers. Ray shook his head.

"He wouldn't be interested in papers. Just money."

"I think you're more interested in the man than the statue."

"I am."

"The man who brought this piece, this was a bony fellow, wiry, with silver hair and a receding hairline. A shifty fellow, I'd say. Does that sound like him?"

"Yes."

"He was surprised, too. About the papers. 'Maybe that's it,' he said. But he didn't say what 'it' was. He seemed perplexed. And uncomfortable."

"He didn't know what he had. And the papers make it a little more—"

"Complicated. And people are dead because of this?"

"Well, three guys are dead who were involved in this robbery. And I'm betting they're all dead because of this statue. Or these papers."

Emery Pogue nodded and Ray had the sense that the old man already knew about the killings.

"Friends of yours, the fellows who were killed," Emery Pogue said. "That's right, isn't it?"

"Yes."

"And the robbery, this would be the Morrison affair, I think."

"Right again." Ray got up. "Well, thanks for your help."

Emery Pogue looked away, then back at Ray, and it was clear he was holding something back.

"What?"

"Others are looking for this statue. Or so I am told."

"Anybody that's been here?"

"Yes. One fellow, a big, heavy-set man in a bad-fitting suit. My sense is that he was representing someone. He didn't seem to have a clear idea what was in the statue."

"So his boss is looking for the statue."

"That was my impression." Emery gave him a thoughtful look. "This statue is a dangerous thing, my young friend. You would do well to stay clear of it."

"I know."

As Ray stepped off the houseboat, the old man called out, "Life's full of trouble and much of it lives in the city. I recommend a life on the river."

Ray waved and walked up the path to the street, thinking about statues and ledgers and robbery gone wrong.

The daytime crowds were pouring into Riverview, already filling the great amusement park. Ray could see the Para-Chute ride and the roller coasters already in business. As he passed the big tavern on Clybourn called Liquor Town, a man emerged and grabbed him by his arm. Ray pulled away and found himself facing Butch Turner.

"I want to talk to you."

"Yeah? You put your hand on me again, you'll need a new one."

"Tough guy."

Butch tried on a sneer but he couldn't hide the nervous look in his eyes. Butch had a couple of inches on Ray, and maybe to make himself look bulkier, he wore a heavy coat despite the heat. It hung on him like a tent. His face was a red mass of broken capillaries and there was a partially healed cut along the side of his face.

"We're gonna talk about your friend."

"My friend," Ray said, tonelessly.

He told himself he had just fought a war, lost a good friend, and a big hoodlum was grabbing him in broad daylight in his own town. Ray fingered the single-blade knife in his pocket—his sole souvenir from the War—and then decided he wouldn't need it.

"I don't have time for you."

"Step inside here with me, you. We're gonna have a talk."

"I don't drink with big slobs. It would ruin my reputation."

Butch's hand shot out and grabbed Ray's arm.

"One more time, let go of my arm."

"Or you'll what?"

"I'll pop you right here in front of all your fans."

Turner squeezed Ray's bicep and Ray flexed it.

"You know what I could do to you, punk?"

"You mean like last time? Or at night, in an alley with three of your hoods to back you up? Yeah, sure, some damage. But here in the daylight, just you and me? I don't like your chances."

"You got a smart mouth."

"Everybody tells me that." Ray leaned forward and dropped his voice to a whisper. He gripped the other man's shoulder, found the muscle between shoulder and neck pinched hard, and he felt Turner pull away even as he let go of Ray's arm. Ray put a hand on his chest and shoved, and Butch Turner had to fight for his balance.

"Here's the thing, Butch. I just got back from four years of shit. I've seen things that would make you puke, and they shot me, twice. So I don't know what's in the cards for me here and maybe I'll just wind up blowing town like I did before. But I won't take any shit from bums and hoods."

Ray gave another push and Butch fell against the side of the tavern door.

As he walked away he heard Turner say, "Okay, real tough guy, soldier boy. Hey, your punk friend Walsh—"

Ray turned slowly. "He's dead. How come you're not?"

Butch blinked, looked as though he'd been pole-axed.

"Yeah, there goes your money. If I see you again, Butch, I'll drop you in the street."

Ray kept on walking and gradually became aware that he was being watched. So Butch had a guy with him.

All right, Ray thought. He turned and saw Max Silver walking on the opposite side of the street. Ray poked his chin at him. Silver nodded in the direction of the humbled Butch Turner, who was moving fast in the other direction. He laughed and gave Ray the OK sign. At the next corner he turned and went on his way.

For a moment Ray wondered what would bring the detective to Clybourn Avenue, and then it was obvious.

You're following me.

* * *

That night he stopped for a beer at a small tavern near his room, then went home. He was a block away from the rooming house when he had the sensation that someone was watching him. He shot a quick look over his shoulder and saw nothing but empty sidewalk for at least two blocks. He slowed down and watched the street for a moment, then resumed his walk. A minute later he caught movement from the corner of his eye. A dark figure was walking on the far side of Belmont, keeping pace with Ray. He wore a fedora pulled low over his left eye and a dark raincoat, and though he did not look up, it was clear to Ray that this man was following him. At the next corner Ray stopped for the light. His watcher did the same on the far side of the street. Then, just as the light changed, a streetcar pulled up to the curb and hid the other man from view. When the light changed, the streetcar moved off and the man was gone.

Where did you disappear to? And who the hell are you?

Second time makes it a tail, Ray thought. I've got a tail.

Chapter Nine

He knew where she lived and found excuses to pass by her place, all the while wondering what he'd say if she suddenly materialized. He told himself they were, after all, more or less acquainted by virtue of their street encounter a couple of days earlier. Eventually he got his chance. He was standing on the corner near her building when the young blond nurse emerged. She saw him but looked away quickly, as though interested in something else on the street. As Ray debated whether to try to catch her, she began to move faster. Ray put a little more energy into his walk and she seemed to slow down. Then he saw a quick movement and something fluttered from her purse. A handkerchief.

Ray stopped, startled. Then he grinned.

I thought that was something they only did in pictures.

Nonetheless, he began moving faster, swooped the handkerchief up in one quick motion and caught the girl before she reached the next corner.

"Here, Miss. You dropped this."

She affected surprise but couldn't conceal her amusement.

"Oh, did I?"

She looked down at her purse as though trying to find holes. Then she took it, brushing Ray's hand.

"Thanks."

She squinted.

"I think—"

"Yeah, we met before. Sort of."

"Sure," she said, nodding now. "You helped me get that big creep off my back the other night."

"You were doing all right by yourself, as I recall."

She made a little shrug. "Maybe he would have tried to force the issue if you weren't around. Anyhow, thanks. You said your name is Ray, right?"

Ray nodded. She said, "And I'm—"

"—Hannah," Ray finished. "I remember."

Okay, what do I do with this now?

"Well," she said, looking up the street toward the corner.

You're losing this one, Foley.

"So I wonder—would you like to come out for a beer or a cup of coffee sometime?"

She made a small show of considering, nodded.

"Sure, why not?"

"And you can tell me where you learned to hit a guy with a shoe at twenty paces."

Now she laughed.

"Tonight?"

"I've got to work tomorrow."

"I won't keep you out late. How about seven?"

"All right." She gave him her address and she watched him write it in his notebook. She smiled. "So what else do you keep in there?"

"Things I want to make sure I don't forget."

Ray touched his finger to the brim of his new Dobbs hat and she gave him a little wave.

"See you," he said to her back.

He brought her to a small tavern on Kenmore and they took a table along the back wall.

"Beer?" he said, going to the bar.

"How about a highball?"

The farthest corner of the tavern was dominated by a huge jukebox so brightly lit that the wall glowed red and yellow. Hannah tilted her head and listened for a moment.

"I like this song. Jimmy Dorsey's orchestra. Bob Eberly. He's got a nice voice."

"I prefer the girl myself."

She smiled. "Helen O'Connell. You just like her because she's cute."

"Maybe."

She looked around. Toward the far end of the tavern two couples were dancing, and Hannah nodded approvingly. Someone dropped another nickel in the box and the couples waited awkwardly to see what came up next.

The gaudy jukebox gave them the opening bars of "Moonlight Serenade," and Hannah said simply, "Oh," and straightened up to watch the people on the floor.

"Glenn Miller."

"Do you dance, Ray?"

"A little," he said, but she was already on her feet, holding out her hand. She led him to the back where there were now four couples dancing, and they found a spot at the very edge of the impromptu dance floor. They fell into the steady rhythm of the song, the couples bumping into each other and smiling. An odd hush fell on the tavern as people listened to a sentimental ballad from the simpler time before the war. Hannah got closer and Ray could smell her hair, her perfume, he could feel her skin through the thin summer blouse. Then she put her cheek next to Ray's and he felt his face burning.

Jesus, Foley, it's like you never been close to a girl before.

His mouth was dry and he hoped his palms weren't wet.

When the song was over, the bartender and a couple of patrons at the bar clapped, and a faster number came on. Ray shook his head.

"I can't dance to this."

Hannah shrugged and they went back to the table.

"That was nice. I don't remember last time I—oh, yeah, I do. I danced with a soldier at the USO."

"I danced with a nurse at one of the army dance hall places. In Paris."

"Paris! You saw Paris."

"Yeah. I have to go back sometime when I have a little more, you know, knowledge of the world. To appreciate it."

"So you danced with a nurse? A pretty nurse?"

"Right about then, they were all pretty. This was right after I got out—"

He caught himself but she read the look.

"After you got out of the hospital."

"Right."

She nodded, smart enough to know what she could and couldn't ask. She cocked her head toward the box as a new song came on and said "Bunny Berrigan."

"My Ma liked Bunny Berrigan."

"And she's gone," Hannah said, and Ray would have said she knew this already.

"Just before the War."

They stayed for a few more songs, danced once, had a second drink, and Ray took Hannah home.

He took in her small but spotless apartment, the pictures on the wall, a bookshelf with several dozen books—a girl who liked to read.

He crossed her tiny living room and looked out the window. "So you stayed close to Poe Street after all."

"I always liked living around here. It's really the only neighborhood I know. You have to be comfortable in your neighborhood. I just wanted a nicer place, that's all. But Poe Street was spooky, the way the street bent at one end so you couldn't even see to the end of it. So if you were walking at night, somebody might be there, just around that little corner. How about you?"

"I've got a room over by Bissell and Armitage."

"Did you like living there? Poe Street?"

"It was our last place. We thought we were finally settled. And young kids like a place where they can roam around."

She smiled. "Like the river."

"Especially the river. We used to go down there looking for snakes and turtles. And there were rats down there. We used to throw rocks at them."

Hannah shuddered. "There always seems to be rats. Every place I've ever lived, there were rats."

"You're not from here."

"I was born here. We moved away when I was little. To Michigan, which is where I grew up. Flint, Michigan."

"What brought you back here?"

"I needed to start over in a place where—"

Ray nodded. "Where you knew your way around."

"No, where people didn't know me." She gave him a frank look and said, "I was seventeen and living with my drunken stepfather, and then– then as soon as I got loose from that, my life got complicated by another belligerent drunk. I left."

A girl with a whole life under her belt.

Ray wondered how all these girls ended up with assholes.

"And did you make the right move?" he asked.

She gave him a coy look. "So far, so good." Then she looked away and seemed to be remembering something. She looked back at Ray, shrugged and said, "Sometimes I wonder."

"Why?"

"Well, it seemed like a safe neighborhood until—what happened over there. The murder. And one night, just before that, I heard an argument in the street—"

"What? Drunks? They're everywhere."

"No, this was an older woman, maybe she was drunk. She was screeching at somebody and I heard him say something. He sounded like a young guy. I don't know why but I had the notion that this was a woman and her son. Then I didn't hear him anymore but she was still out there screaming."

She shook her head, then she smiled, straightened up, her body language informing him that this line of conversation was at a dead end.

"Would you like a cup of coffee?"

"Sure. Thanks."

Ray listened to her bustling around in the kitchen, heard metal on tin, the lid of a coffee pot being removed and realized he hadn't heard these sounds in years. More than that, he realized how long it had been since he had sat in a woman's place.

"It won't take long," she called out. "It's just a little pot."

"I don't have any other appointments," he said, and she laughed.

When the smell of coffee had filled the small flat, she came in with two cups and set them on the table in front of the couch, then sat down beside him. A few more inches, Ray noted, and they would be touching.

"Do you take cream and sugar?"

"I used to. I learned to drink it black overseas. There wasn't always a lot of choice."

She nodded. "Yeah. Where I was serving, we ran out of things."

Ray blinked. "You were in the service? Where'd you serve?"

She gave him a small smile, amused at his expression.

"All over the Pacific. On Guadalcanal, for a time. Then on a hospital ship."

"Did you ever—"

"See action? Yeah. We had snipers on a couple of the islands—it took a while to get Guadalcanal under control. And our ship, the hospital ship I was on, was strafed by Japanese planes twice. And we were at Leyte Gulf, you know about Leyte?"

"Kamikazes, yeah. You saw Kamikazes?"

She nodded. "One of them tried to hit us but one of our planes shot him down before he could reach us."

He shook his head. "So you saw the war."

"I enlisted before Pearl Harbor. A few weeks earlier and I might have been stationed in the Philippines when they attacked. I would have spent the war in a prisoner-of-war camp. Or I might have been dead. They killed some Australian nurses."

"So why did you join before Pearl?"

She shrugged. "Drink your coffee," she commanded. "Anyhow, I was bored with my life, I needed to change things, and I kept hearing that we would be in a war soon. Half the people you listened to said we'd never get involved in it, but I kept hearing we were getting ready, they were drafting guys and people were enlisting. So I joined the Navy."

She smiled at him and broke into the old song:

"I joined the Navy to see the world—
But what did I see?
I saw the sea."

"So you joined up and got shot at and almost got sunk by a Kamikaze."

"That was no big deal. The worst thing was the wounded, Ray. I was already a nurse before I went in, I'd seen stuff, a lot of it. But nothing in a regular hospital prepares you for what you're going to see in wartime. They brought guys in and I got so I could look at them in triage and tell before the doctors opened their mouths which guys weren't even going to survive the night, which guys they weren't even going to try to save. Guys blown open, guys missing arms and legs. Guys—no, *boys*, most of them—"

She stopped, turned away to compose herself.

"Sorry I got you started. I don't even talk about it. I talk about, you know, things I saw. I saw Sicily, where there were Roman ruins and everything. I was in North Africa, too, Africa! But if you ask me what Africa is like, I'd have to say it's a place full of Germans with guns."

She laughed now.

"And Paris, like I said. I liked Paris. I never saw anything like that before."

"Paris," she said, wiping her eyes with another of her small handkerchiefs.

Ray told himself she seemed to have no end of small white handkerchiefs.

"Yeah. That's a place my Ma always wanted to see. So I guess I saw it for her, I did all the things I thought she would do. I went to the parks, I walked along the Seine, I went to the Louvre."

"These are places I only read about in magazines. The Louvre!"

"A lot of it was empty. I guess when the Germans took France, the French hid the best stuff they had from their museums."

"Do you like art?"

"I liked the Louvre." He shrugged. "I can't say I always understood what I was looking at."

She sipped her coffee and watched him over the rim of her cup.

Ray looked at her and didn't know what to say next.

I been away in a war for four years and I don't know what to say to a girl? I'm tongue-tied, for God's sake?

He sipped his coffee, set it down, played with the cup on the saucer. Hannah bailed him out.

"So, Ray, all your traveling and you still wound up back here."

"I just never found anyplace else I wanted to stay. I liked a lot of it, but not enough to stay. I'm not saying I'm staying here forever. Just haven't made up my mind yet. How about you? You wanted to make changes but you came back."

"I always liked it here. I guess I made enough changes. Got rid of that other girl."

"Other girl?"

"Gladys McCoy. She's gone. I'm here."

He laughed and shook his head.

"I like Chicago," she said, "but lately it scares me a little."

"The Morrison thing."

"Yeah, that's one thing. I mean, it's a place I passed every day for years."

"You hear anything about it?"

"What do you mean?"

"About who did it? Hear anything like that?"

"No. I heard he surprised somebody robbing the house and they killed him."

She gave him a puzzled look.

"Why? Did you hear something else?"

He shrugged. "No. Except a couple of the guys were, you know, guys I knew from before the War. I can't see them killing anybody. But somebody killed them."

After a moment, she said, "These were your friends?"

"One in particular. His name was Eddy Walsh. We more or less grew up together. There was no reason to kill a kid like Eddy. It's something I need to find out about."

"Oh." A slight look of distress came into her eyes.

For the first time Ray understood that this was a young woman who lived alone, made her life in a big town far from her people, took her own chances, nobody to lean on. He tried to think of something to lighten the mood and once again Hannah beat him to it.

She set down her cup and said, "So what else have you been doing since you got back besides going to the movies? Looking for work?"

"No. I've been taking care of some personal things. And I look at the jobs in the papers. But I'm not really looking for work, not just yet. I've got some money left. Enough for a while. I don't know what I want to do yet, and for right now, I just want to see things, I just want to walk around and feel like a person living some kind of life. Part of me isn't completely convinced that I'm home, that all of that is over."

"It's over, Ray. When I came home, I spent a month doing nothing. I went up to Flint to visit my aunt and my grandmother, then I came back here and saw movies and went to museums. You ever been to any of the museums?"

"Sure. Science and Industry, and the Field Museum."

"Well, I went to all of them, especially the ones I'd never been to. Like the Art Institute."

Ray gave her an impressed look. "So you know about art?"

"No, not really. I mean I'm starting to learn the names of painters and types of art, but I don't know a lot about it. I used to draw when I was a girl. All the time I would draw."

"And you stopped?"

"I fool around with it once in awhile."

She looked off in the distance, a wistful smile on her lips.

"I bet you're pretty good."

She shrugged and took a sip of her coffee. Then she got up and went to a small table along the far wall and took a notebook from a drawer. She handed it to him.

Ray paged through it. On almost every page was a pencil drawing of a face. Girls in nurses' caps, a beat cop, a news vendor, a kid in a baseball cap.

"These are good."

He came to a page bearing a dark-complexioned man in a cap.

Ray tapped the picture.

"I know him. That's the old knife-sharpener. He's still around."

"I talked to him once while he sharpened a pair of scissors for me. He's a nice man."

Ray studied the face. She'd managed to capture the serenity in the eyes, the long life experience of the man. He flipped the page to the portrait of a woman: gaunt, disheveled, a distant look in her eyes.

"You're really good. You should—I don't know—could you sell these?"

"I doubt it. They're okay, I guess. Just something I do for fun. I turn on the radio and do faces."

"From memory?"

"Yeah, sometimes from memory. I've got a good memory." She smiled and Ray was surprised to see a flush across her face.

"What?"

"I remember you, Ray. From back before the War. We were neighbors."

"Yeah, well, I'll let you in on a little secret. I remember you from that time, I remember you with dark hair and your nurse's uniform. I didn't really know a lot of girls." Then he added, "And I saw you last week, I saw you there when they found Morrison."

Her smile died.

"Yes. I was there, I checked his signs, his pulse," she said, and waited to see where he would take this.

He looked at the cup to buy time, to put this train back on the rail.

"Anyway, myself, I haven't been up to much. I don't know for sure what I want to do with myself now." He nodded toward her bookshelf. "I read a bit, though, that's something I started in the Service—I just bought a bunch of books. The rest of my time, I'm just wandering around and trying to get used to everything. I still can't get used to calling Center Street *Armitage*."

She smiled now. "They seem to like to change street names."

"And I go to the beach down at North Avenue, just to walk around."

"And look at the girls, I bet."

"Maybe. But I was anxious to get to the beach."

"Why the beach?"

He smiled. "After Sicily and Normandy, I just wanted to experience a beach where nobody was shooting at me."

She shook her head. He tried to think of something else to say and gave up.

Hannah reached toward his ear, tilted her head slightly. "You got that over there."

"Yeah. Shell fragment."

"A slightly different angle and you would have been dead."

She frowned slightly, a look of distress came into her eyes.

"So many guys, young guys," she said quietly. Then she leaned over and touched his ear, gently, slowly, tracing the outline of his ear with a finger, and then the scar on his neck behind it.

He remembered kissing the young French girl, and dancing with the WAC in France after a couple of glasses of wine, and she'd put her hand on the back of his neck. And those had been the only times in five years that a woman had touched him. He felt the rapid beating of his heart, a pounding as though he was under fire once more, and he wondered if she could hear his heart. He looked at her and she was watching him, and smiling, a sly smile, he would have said.

"You know," he began and lost all track of where he'd been heading, and she leaned in toward him and now he thought he was on more familiar ground. He put his arm around her and they kissed. She pushed closer to him and he tried to open the top buttons of her blouse, tiny buttons that he could not navigate. She put her hand over his and stopped him. She leaned back and gave him an odd smile, and he could feel the blood rushing to his face.

"Don't look so disappointed," she said with a small laugh. "And don't believe everything you hear about nurses."

Ray smiled and hoped she couldn't read his mind.

She took the coffee cups back into the tiny kitchen and he listened to her washing the cups and saucers, and he drifted off. When he opened his eyes she was standing over him, smiling.

"Time to go, Ray Foley."

"Okay." He got to his feet and reached back for something to say, heard himself blurt out, "So I'll see you around."

"We'll see," she said.

At her door she gave him a quick kiss on the lips. He turned to leave and she stopped him.

His new hat.

"Try to collect yourself," she said, and he had to laugh. She put the hat on his head, adjusted it at an angle, gave it an approving glance and said good-night.

Ray walked for more than an hour before heading back to his room, thinking of the evening with Hannah, wondering if his luck had changed. When he took off his shirt he could smell her perfume.

* * *

Long after Ray had gone, Hannah Marcel sat in the dark in her flat and looked out the window. It hadn't been a steak at the Pump Room but it was nice just the same. A nice guy who understood the notion of limits, who kept his paws off her unless she wanted them on her. A gentleman. But there was something else about Ray Foley. For most of the evening he was hers, interested in everything she said, clearly happy just to be out with a girl. And then the talk had turned to the other things, to the Morrison murder and the other killings, and she'd seen a different look come into Ray's eyes. And even as they continued to talk she'd become aware that a part of him was somewhere else. That she'd lost him for a moment.

She thought about her evening and told herself even the nice ones would bear watching. She went to bed.

When Hannah left the hospital the next day Ray was waiting for her. She peeled off from a quartet of nurses who moved on toward Clark Street. He took her for coffee and when they were finished, she turned down his suggestion of a movie.

"I'm working a double tomorrow. I want to get home."

"The Century's right up the street."

"Another time, Ray."

"Friday?"

"I work."

"How about Sat—"

She gave him a slightly distressed look. "I've got something Saturday."

It struck him that he wasn't the only one interested in a certain blond nurse. He felt foolish.

To hide his discomfort, he said, "Not the guy you throw shoes at, I hope."

"No. And don't push, Ray." She gave him a look that said there was a point being made here.

"Right," he said, and bit back his impulse to keep asking until he found a day when she wasn't busy.

They parted at the corner, and just as Hannah was about to walk away, she paused, turned around and gave him a quick kiss on the cheek.

He watched her walk away in the tight white uniform and told himself he had no idea what to do next. He thought of the look she'd given him, and now he thought he understood that she was trying to keep a little distance between them. At least for now.

Chapter Ten

For three summers, Ray's father had worked as a mechanic at Riverview Park along with Willie Foy and Floyd Hennessey. A long time ago. Still, perhaps some of the grease monkeys who kept the coasters and Ferris wheel going would be able to tell him if they'd seen Willie Foy.

And so Ray rode the packed streetcar, got off and found himself in a mass of men in rolled up sleeves and women in summer dresses, all pushing toward the big painted wooden gates on Western Avenue.

Once inside, he made a long circuit of the midway, stopped here and there and watched the life of the park: the trained monkeys driving little cars in endless circles, a red -faced kid pulling at his girl's arm to get her into the dark tunnel of the Mill on the Floss, the shill in front of the sideshow promising miracles of nature inside, the dunk tank where a trio of black men muttered and questioned the manhood of the sweating, grunting whites who pelted baseballs at their targets, cursing in the fury to knock the mouthy black men into the water. And the screams: they screamed as the parachute ride dropped them, they screamed when the Bobs and the other big roller coasters dove down the rickety wooden hills, they screamed inside Aladdin's Castle as the shifting floors and trick mirrors played with the patrons' sense of reality. They wanted to be terrified, all of them, in this harmless and temporary way, all these people who had spent much of the last five years experiencing a more genuine and permanent sort of fear.

Ray stopped in front of the great staring face of Aladdin and the doorway into his raucous castle. The assault on his senses was overpowering. In the quick descent of dusk he could see the blue clouds of smoke, smelled cigars, sweat, perfume, beer, steamed hotdogs and fried burgers, and somehow, through it all he could smell cotton candy. He wondered if, after all these years he still had a kid's nose. Here was a place to forget the world. And yet the sights and smells recalled for him summer nights in what seemed another man's life.

In several places he managed to buttonhole the mechanics. Two of the older ones remembered his father. Ray shared a smoke with them and shot the breeze to no real purpose. No one had seen Willie Foy.

He was making his way out of Riverview, watching as a group of half a dozen young women fended off the advances of an equal number of young men. At the periphery of this scene, people watched and smiled as the girls rebuffed their would-be suitors. Two men walked by, one of them clearly drunk, the other attempting to keep him upright and moving. And then Ray saw a thin man in a dirty shirt slip out from behind a game booth and fall in behind them. This man kept his eyes on the men, moved closer, attention now on the drunk, on his back pocket.

A pickpocket. As he neared the drunk, Ray saw him bump into a woman. Not the slickest pickpocket on the street, Ray thought. Ray watched him close in on his mark, and then he recognized this man: Floyd Hennessey. And clearly not the corpse they found in the river.

At precisely that moment Floyd Hennessey stopped, his back to Ray, and he seemed to freeze. A quartet of sailors passed between them and when they moved on, so had Floyd Hennessey. At the very edge of the crowd Ray saw a face turn his way. They made eye contact and then Floyd Hennessey was gone.

All right, Floyd.

He likes the river, the Old Man had once said of Floyd Hennessey. *He just about lives there, fishes all day, sleeps on a boat. It's how he lives.* And so Ray would look for Floyd Hennessey along the river.

Emery Pogue had spoken to him of life on the river, and Ray soon learned that old Emery was not the only person living on a houseboat. Ray found a half dozen houseboats clustered along the river at Belmont, and single houseboats on a stretch of the river to the south. At each of these points on the river he climbed down to the water's edge and spoke with the city's hidden residents. Several of the houseboat people had nothing to say to him but the others proved more talkative, and one chatty gray-haired lady in a floppy hat gave him tea and suggested that he try the boatyards.

There were still three boatyards operating along the river and in each of them they knew Floyd Hennessey. The picture Ray began to form was of a man who had hit that place in life where he was no longer considered fit for anything but odd jobs and errands.

"You can't count on him showing up," the foreman at the first boatyard said.

At the third and largest of the boatyards he found a crew working to clear the propeller of an enormous sailboat. An improbable amount of rope had fouled the propeller.

The oldest of the men saw Ray looking at the rope. He shrugged.

"The guy fouls his prop on his own lines." He shook his head. "What can I do for you?"

"Floyd Hennessey. Know where I can find him?"

The foreman grinned. "In the slammer, in the alley, in a gin mill, sleeping it off under the tracks."

"That's a lot of places."

One of the workers turned. "You want to know where Floyd sleeps? In a rowboat."

The foreman nodded. "A dory, actually. Just a little half-wrecked dory he found. He ties up there near Belmont."

"By Riverview, then?"

"Yeah. There's a place where a big willow tree's leaning over the water, and he ties up there. At least that's where I saw him one time. Who says he's still there, though, you know? But I'd look up around that area."

* * *

That afternoon Ray found the willow, and back among the dense bushes that lined the riverbank, he found the dory, a small weathered boat covered by branches and a stained tarp. He took a breath and yanked the tarp off. The dory was empty. But now he knew where to find Floyd Hennessey, at least if Floyd was still alive.

At dusk Ray returned to the dory. It was nestled into a small nook in the riverbank and hidden from view by the huge dead trunk of a willow tree that stuck out into the water some twenty feet. For a time he stood silently and watched the small boat. The dory was wedged into the mud, its bow up on shore so that there was little rocking motion from the water, but close enough to the water that it could be slid into the river in seconds. Ray was conscious of the night noises of the river, the water slapping gently against the riverbank, the calls of a nighthawk overhead. In the distance he could hear the sounds of the great gaudy amusement park, the rumble of the roller coasters, a woman's distant scream, a man barking out some boast. It seemed another, distant world, sharing nothing in common with this place where people slept under bridges and on small boats.

From his vantage point Ray could see a figure bundled into the bottom of the dory, and he could see the handle of one of the short oars but nothing else. Slowly and patiently he moved around the massive tree trunk until he stood at the side of the boat and looked down at the man inside.

"Floyd. Floyd Hennessey. It's Ray Foley. I'm not here to cause you any trouble, Floyd. I just want to know about Willie Foy."

After a long moment's silence, Ray said, "Can you hear me, Floyd?"

The man in the bottom of the dory was silent, motionless. Ray peered over the side of the boat and studied him. He was about to speak again when it struck him that Floyd Hennessey was not breathing.

"Shit," he heard himself say, and he stepped over the side of the dory. It wobbled slightly but he righted himself and then reached over to pull back the blanket covering Floyd Hennessey. In the faint light he recognized Hennessey's haggard profile. Floyd lay with his mouth open, eyes half-closed, his cheeks sunken and covered in gray stubble. In Europe the men he'd seen with this look had all been starving. Ray shook his head and bent down to pull the blanket back the rest of the way.

He was bent over and so was off balance when the first kick caught him in the back of his leg. Ray fell to one side and the second kick found the underside of his jaw. Then Floyd Hennessey was at him, throwing punches hard, grunting with the effort and panting, and something else, a sort of growl. The boat slid beneath him and Ray fell against the side. He managed to grab hold of Floyd Hennessey's shirt and pull the man to him. He landed a punch of his own to Hennessey's temple and felt the other man lose his balance. Then they were both scrambling to get to their feet, both throwing punches, Ray attempting to grab onto Hennessey to hold him there.

"Wait!" he called out. "Talk to me, Floyd."

He tried to strengthen his hold on Hennessey's shirt and felt the material give way. Floyd Hennessey got off a quick, short punch that caught Ray just above the eye. Then Floyd lunged backward, lost his balance and went down. He rolled over and tried to get up but Ray was on him. He wrapped his arms around Hennessey, conscious of the other man's bony frame, all angles and points—and nails, as Hennessey squirmed to get at him, clawing at Ray's face. They rolled over and over on the dirt of the riverbank, and Ray hit his ear on the great hard knot of a tree root and inhaled dirt and the rank smell of Floyd Hennessey. Hennessey kneed him, bit into Ray's shoulder, tried to gouge his eye, to claw Ray's face, and all the while Ray used his size, his weight, his longer arms to hold on. Finally he threw Floyd Hennessey onto the ground and sat high on his back.

Ray listened to Floyd Hennessey breathing, gasping.

"C'mon, I can't breathe," Floyd said in a raspy voice, and Ray let him go. Ray sat back on his haunches and Floyd got up on one knee, seemed to wobble slightly, then sank back onto the ground. They sat across from each other on a bare patch of damp ground, both of them sucking in air and waiting, and in the distance Ray could hear music and the rumble of a truck moving by on Clybourn Avenue. The city was just a few yards away, Ray realized, but if one or the other of them was to die here by the river, the body wouldn't be found for days.

Floyd Hennessey sat there and glared at Ray and panted. He was filthy and covered with dirt, a red spot starting on his jaw, a small welt on one cheekbone.

Ray shifted his weight slightly and Floyd Hennessey came up with a blade, a shiv made long and slender from a kitchen knife. He got up on one knee in a half-crouch.

"Whaddya want with me?"

Ray held up a hand.

"No trouble. I want to talk, just talk."

In the fading light Floyd Hennessey squinted at him one-eyed. Ray was conscious of his own breathing, Hennessey's heavier panting, and in the distance the sounds of Riverview. He heard the great whoosh of a roller coaster and the voices of the riders. Somewhere close by he heard nighthawks.

Floyd Hennessey nodded once.

"You're Little Foley. Jem Foley's kid. I remember your old man."

Little Foley.

"Yeah. You started fighting before I could explain."

"A guy comes looking for you, you don't wait for no explanations. He might be a wrong guy and then you're fucked. You could still be a wrong guy for all I know."

"But I'm not. And we're just talking, like I said."

"So sit."

Ray frowned but did as he was told. Then he saw the strategy. If he sat on the ground while Floyd stayed in his crouch, he'd be a step slow if Floyd decided to bolt.

"Cops think you're dead, Floyd. They found a guy in the river with your discharge papers."

Floyd snorted. "It ain't hard to make 'em think you're dead, kid. I found a stiff under a bridge. Been dead a while. I just slipped my papers into his pocket and pushed him in the river."

He shrugged. "So what do you want with me?"

"I want to know about this thing you did with Willie Foy. The Morrison thing."

"What's that to you?"

"Eddy Walsh is dead. Did you know that?"

Floyd Hennessey blinked but said nothing. After a moment, he asked, "How?"

"Knifed."

"Poor fucking kid. Like Barney."

"Yeah, and Morrison, of course. And Jimmy Seeger."

For a long moment Floyd Hennessey was silent.

"Did you know Jimmy Seeger never made it out of the house?"

Floyd said nothing as he considered this, then shook his head.

"No. I didn't know what happened to anybody. We split up."

"So Jimmy and Barney and Eddy Walsh. All of them."

"He's still out there, then, that guy. Fuck."

"Do you know who?"

"Nah. No idea."

"What about Willie Foy?"

Floyd gave him a blank look.

"You mean, maybe Willie killed these guys? Nah, that's nuts. He's no killer." After a moment's thought, he added, "Not no more anyhow."

"You sure?"

"Not about much, kid, but I'm pretty sure about that."

"Who then? And for what?"

"All I know is we robbed a guy. Fucked it up, too. Made a lot of noise and got spooked and we run out without half the stuff we should of took."

"You took money."

Floyd shrugged. "A few hundred bucks. From a drawer. But that guy was made of money, he had safes, couple of 'em."

He held up two sun-browned fingers and gave Ray an incredulous look.

"And of course we couldn't do nothing with 'em. Too heavy to take out, and we couldn't open 'em. You know, we used to know a guy, Willie and me, this was a real yegg. Know what a yegg is?"

"A safecracker. A pro."

"That's what we needed. A guy to open those boxes. So instead we got a little money and silverware."

"And a statue. That's what I heard."

"From who?"

"Eddy Walsh. He stayed with me one night. He said you got a statue. And he said Willie went back in."

Floyd nodded.

"I think he was going back in for other stuff. Jewelry and stuff. And he comes out, running, and he says 'there's somebody in there, go.' There was something about the way he said it, put a scare into all of us, and he he's got this look in his eye like whatever he seen in there is some bad shit. And I'll tell you what, he never told me what he seen in there, but I think he maybe saw that guy get killed. And whoever did it, that guy saw us, maybe saw all of us. Maybe that's the reason he's after us."

"None of this makes any sense to me."

"It don't have to make sense. When a guy wants to kill somebody, it don't have to make sense."

"Did you see anything else that night?"

"In that house? Nothing." Floyd thought for a moment. "There was people around there, though. In the alley just up from that house. Two people standing by a garage. Man and a woman. We come running out of that place and they were looking at us."

"A bunch of guys running down the alley—why wouldn't they be looking at you?"

"I think they were watching that house. That's what I think."

"What did they look like?"

"I don't know, it was getting dark. The fella didn't have no hat."

"What about the woman?"

Floyd shrugged. "Who knows? Like I said, it was getting dark. I looked at 'em as we went by, to see if they were gonna do anything, call the cops or something like that. Big eyes, she had. That's all I remember. It was getting dark." Floyd shook his head.

"So where's Willie?"

"If he's smart, I guess he's layin' low somewhere. But he better watch his ass. This is a bad guy that's out there."

"I know."

"Nah, you don't know. So I'm gonna tell you. We all grew up together over on Goose Island, your old man and Willie and Barney and me, and let me tell you this, Barney Donlan was a tough sonofabitch. He was a boxer once, and he was a streetfighter, a good one, and the guy who took him got to him without any trouble and put a blade in his chest. So this is somebody special we're talking about. And when he comes for me, Foley, I want to be gone."

Ray looked over at the bushes where he could just see the bow of Floyd Hennessey's unique residence.

"You have a pretty good hiding place, though."

"Oh, yeah?" Floyd Hennessey gave Ray a long look. "You found me."

"Wasn't easy."

"But you found me." Floyd looked at his boat. "I keep moving it. I think I'm gonna just row my way up there to the south branch of the river and maybe keep on going. I figure if I leave town, this asshole won't bother with me. You know, you get out there on the South Branch, you can ride the current forever. It meets up with the canal and then the Des Plaines River, and then the Illinois, and from there you can get onto the Mississippi. And you can ride the big river all the way down to New Orleans."

Floyd gestured to the south. For a moment he stood there, looking off into space as though he could see his escape.

"Seems like a long voyage for a rowboat."

Floyd Hennessey shrugged. "It's been done. You just gotta be careful." He gazed at his boat and then at the river beyond. "I got to scrounge around, pick up some food." He squinted at Ray. "You wouldn't have a couple bucks would you? Help a guy out?"

After a moment Ray nodded and took out some cash. He pulled out two bucks and held it out. The money disappeared from Ray's hand as though the wind had sucked it out. He watched Floyd Hennessey tuck the bills in his shirt pocket.

"You rolling in dough, Foley?"

"No. But I've got a few bucks put by."

"You're a good egg, Kid. Anything else you got to say to me, Little Foley?"

"No."

"All right then. Next time you come looking for me, I'll be gone. Long gone." He nodded once and turned away.

As he left, Ray said to himself, *I hope that's true, Floyd.*

He stopped in a tavern on Clybourn and used the men's room mirror to assess his appearance. The shoulders of his shirt were covered with dirt, his knees were filthy, and Floyd Hennessey had left new marks on Ray's face: a small bruise along his jaw line and a couple of small scratches on one cheek.

He's a tough little sonofabitch, Ray's father had once said. *That Hennessey, he's a half-pint but he's tough. Fightin' him would be like being tied up in a sack with a wet cat.*

You were right about that, Pop.

Ray shook his head and told himself there was no percentage in fighting these old street guys.

He thought about what Floyd had said about his parents and Willie Foy. As he walked down the street, he recalled a certain conversation with his mother when Willie Foy spent the night on their couch.

"Why was Willie Foy here?"

His mother shrugged, her back to him.

"He needed a place to stay for the night."

"Why did he come here?"

She was looking out the window now, still showing him her back. He did not understand this, she always faced him when she spoke.

"Ah, well, he knew he'd be welcome here. But just for the one night."

"Is he your friend?"

She tilted her head to one side as though considering this.

"Well, we're cousins, like."

Cousins, like.

"Oh. I didn't know that."

Now she turned. "Not cousins like you and Thomas. Willie's father and my mother were cousins. They grew up together in Ireland."

"Is he my cousin?"

"Ah, I don't know how they figure these things. You're—related." She nodded and repeated, "Related, yes. But not like you and your real cousins."

"Why was he sick?"

"You heard that, did you?"

"He threw up."

"He drinks too much. There's the lesson for you. A grown man puking his guts out in the morning when other men are at work."

She turned then, asked him to bring over the baking soda and began telling him about the new bread recipe she was making, and he did not realize how completely she'd dropped the subject of Willie Foy.

Perhaps a month later he happened to see his mother on North Avenue. She had just emerged from the subway station. She was speaking to a man who had his back to Ray, but Ray recognized him: slim and sunburnt, with stooped shoulders and close-cropped gray hair: Willie Foy.

As he watched, he saw his mother shake her head and say something, then saw Willie Foy put his hand on her arm. She shook him off, said something short and sharp and walked past him. Ray watched Willie Foy staring after his mother.

The more he thought about it, it seemed that Willie Foy had always been around Poe Street, standing on the corner with two or three others like him, or walking up Clybourn with his head down and hands thrust into his pockets. But always there, in the background of everything. And now he'd managed to get two young guys killed with one of his schemes.

Chapter Eleven

Ray wore out shoe leather for four days looking for Willie Foy. Half the people he pressed for information had no idea where Willie was, and the other half lied to him, not out of any malice nor out of any intent to mislead Ray—they just refused to give up a guy who was, or had once been, one of their own. Their stonewalling gave Ray a little of what he needed: the evasiveness, the sudden stiffening of a back, refusal to look him in the eye, told him Willie was probably still around. But once in a while he struck gold.

On Clybourn, in front of the icehouse where just before the war a man had been killed in a fight over a woman, perched on a hydrant was a small man in a newsboy's cap and a tweed coat cut for his larger brother. His name was Maurice Fitzgibbon, but time was of the essence on the street so he went by Mo Fitz or, more commonly, Dandy. He had silver hair and huge tufts of eyebrow to match, and long years of sun and wind and the drink had given him red cheeks and a nose like a strawberry. He sat on his hydrant and grinned at the passing cars and pointed at the sky and shook his head in imaginary discourse and tried his best to reach the last row of the balcony, and Ray nearly burst out laughing at a performance he'd seen many times before. Dandy played drunk, stupid, absent-minded, slightly crazed and when the situation called for it—his own imminent peril, for example, or the threat of violence—he feigned full-throttle insanity, certain to terrify the sane and menacing alike.

"Ah, the young Foley himself, back from the wars," he called out, snapping out of his performance and clapping his hands. The brogue came and went like the weather, and Dandy could do voices, which gave him value in any con involving the telephone.

"Hello, Dandy. How're tricks?"

"Ah, you know how it is with the elderly. Your parts stop working and you get slower. Me, I'm losing me marbles one at a time. How about you, boyo? How has the great dark world been treating you?"

"I get by. Looking for work, mostly but I've got a few bucks so I'm not in any hurry."

"They're hiring at the brewery—Sieben's, that is. Well, maybe at the big one as well, the Meister Brau place."

"Good to know. And it would keep me close to the beer."

"Nothing wrong with that. Meself, I prefer the whiskey. 'Tis a family curse."

Dandy smiled and then tilted his head slightly.

"But I think you've got something else on your mind, lad."

"I do. Willie Foy. I'd like to find him. They used to tell me that you knew everything that happened on the street. Before it happened, sometimes. So can you tell me anything?"

"Oh, well, you know, I heard he had some business interests up north there, up by Wilson Avenue. And then I believe I heard he was running a small book over by Foster where the Swedes live."

"Dandy. I need to find him. No fairy stories."

The mask dropped and when Dandy spoke the brogue was gone as well. He leaned forward, his red hands on his knees.

"I'm no fella to be telling you your business, boyo, but this is deep shit you're wading into here, looking for that one. You don't want any part of this. I've told you what I've heard—"

"Yeah, sure, in that voice that says you've been talking to the Little People. It was pretty goddamn entertaining, Dandy, so I couldn't tell what to take seriously."

"This." He pointed at Ray. "This much and no more. Willie Foy, ever the master of the bad idea, the utterly fucked-up scheme, pulled one that exploded on him and got people killed. All right, that much you know. He's still around but he's trying to lay low. That's one thing. And for another, people have been looking for him."

"*People*? More than one? Who?"

"People, I don't know. A big fella in a baggy suit, is one of 'em. And cops, of course. Couple different ones, is what I heard. And there was talk of an item that was taken that night."

Dandy squinted at Ray with one eye.

"An item, huh? How about a statue?"

"Yeah, that's it. Seems people are looking for this statue, and somebody seen it. Near as I can make out, lad, they think Willie Foy might have it."

Ray pursed his lips, shook his head and played dumb. Dandy shrugged.

"Now, one other fellow there was, a well-dressed young man. Polite, I'm told. And the person that told me about him said he'd give you the chills."

Ray considered this. A young man, well-dressed and chilling.

"But Willie Foy?"

"Him, I've got nothing on, young Foley. But if he's here in town, he's layin' low. He knows they're lookin' for 'im."

"Laying low."

"He was always good at that, Son. Because there was always a reason."

"All right, Dandy."

Dandy said, "Could you help a fella out? I find myself short of funds."

Ray dug into his pocket and came up with a couple of bucks. He handed the money to Dandy, who winked.

"Ah, you're a good lad. I thank you."

At this rate, Ray thought, I'll be needing a job sooner than I thought.

As Ray walked away, Dandy slowed him down.

"Seems to me I recall in the old days, when he was broke, which y'understand was a chronic condition with Willie Foy, he used to flop in the storeroom over at the Mohawk. A long time ago, this was."

"That's useful. Thanks, Dandy."

"Don't mention it."

* * *

When it seemed the four walls of his room were about to suffocate him, he walked to the lake, sat on a bench and watched the swimmers. He stayed long after the beach had closed, watched an old man digging through the sand for dropped coins. While at certain times he was consumed by the need to avenge Eddy Walsh, there were moments when he saw himself as others might, a rootless ex-soldier who hadn't found anything to do with himself. He wondered if his involvement in this Morrison trouble was simply a strategy to keep from admitting that he had no idea where he belonged. It struck him now that perhaps there was no place for him in Chicago, that the best move might be to leave town, find a new city, start over where no one knew him.

But who knew him now? Ray realized that if he were to die here on the beach, his death might pass unnoticed. An image came to him now of the young nurse, smart, sure of herself, good-looking. Certainly she could do better than an unemployed ex-GI.

Sometime after midnight, Ray left the beach and began the long walk to his room.

The War had taught him to pay attention to sudden movement, a new noise, a change in the light, and now he had something—a man moving behind him and making an effort to go unnoticed. Soft, careful footsteps, and they were gaining on him. Ray slowed down and the footsteps came to a stop. He moved on and so did the man following him.

Ray made it to the corner and turned onto the next side street, then paused. The street lights were out, and the thick canopy of trees put the entire street in darkness. But if it was dark for him, it would be dark for the man behind him as well. He took half a dozen steps and spun round to face his pursuer. He'd expected to startle this man but what he saw was a dark figure, average height, slender, and coming for Ray fast.

Ray sidestepped and threw a quick left. It landed high on the side of this man's head, and he followed it with a right that never landed. He was telling himself this man was quick, very quick, when he felt something strike him in the stomach and heard two sounds almost simultaneously, his own grunt and the quick expulsion of breath from his attacker, and he understood that he'd been stabbed.

Instinctively Ray moved back several steps and the other man came at him, and now in the imperfect light Ray could see the wet blade of the knife. Then he thought he saw a second man emerge from the shadows. The man with the knife turned, froze, then was gone. Ray felt his knees weaken. He was aware of noises, people talking, a man's loud voice and a woman laughing, and he saw two people turn the corner. He was surprised to find himself settling onto the sidewalk. People seemed to be speaking to him.

"Hey, buddy, what's up? You got a load on? Look at this guy, Hon. Parking himself in the middle of the sidewalk."

"Dan, he's hurt. That's blood. Oh, Jesus."

A new voice now, someone from one of the houses wanting to know what was going on.

"You got a fella's been hurt here. Call an ambulance."

Ray tried to move up against a fence, to keep himself in a sitting position. He thought about getting to his feet.

"Honey, can you hear me?"

He blinked at tried to focus on her. He thought from her voice, her very sweet voice, that she must be the most beautiful woman in the world but he couldn't make out her face. Just that voice and her perfume, he liked her perfume. He nodded.

He said, "Stabbed."

"Okay, Sweetheart, help is one the way." To her gentleman friend, she said, "*Stabbed*, Dan. The poor guy."

The man called Dan crouched down beside him. Ray thought he smelled of Bay Rum.

"Here, buddy, we're gonna hold this against that—that place." He felt the man press something—a handkerchief, maybe—against the cut in his abdomen. He felt himself becoming sleepy in an odd way, and weak, as though he'd been sick a long time.

* * *

When he awoke, Ray found himself in a hospital bed. A white-haired man snored in the next bed. His skin felt tight across his stomach and he smelled the bleaching of the bedsheets. He moved slightly and a searing pain shot across his side. He moved his hand and touched a heavy layer of bandages. The view from his window gave him the back of a pair of buildings. As he craned to see better, a slight movement caught his eye. He turned his head and found Hannah Marcel standing in the doorway with an armful of towels and a look in her eye that said she was just as surprised as he was.

"*Ray.*"

"Hello."

"A stabbing victim in bed 2, they told me," she said, entering the room. "But I had no idea it was you." She laid down the towels and crossed the room, flicking back his bedsheet.

"Hey."

She smiled. "All of a sudden, you're modest. Guys get so silly in the hospital."

"Do we know how I'm doing?"

"Let's have a look."

She hesitated and he saw her studying the other scars on his shoulder and chest, but she said nothing. With a professional's touch, she peeled back a layer of covering tape, peeked under the gauze. He watched her eyes and they told him it was not a scratch.

A doctor stepped in, pale and thin with a preoccupied air. He bent over as Hannah showed him the wound.

"Coming along. Coming along nicely. The blade nicked a rib or we would have been telling sad stories about you, Mr. Foley."

Before Ray could say anything, the doctor spun on his heel and left the room. Hannah was watching him.

"So you got lucky, *Mr. Foley*. Some guys would have died from a wound like that. Did you get into a fight?"

"No. A guy jumped me."

"Do you know why?"

"Maybe."

She paused, gave him a measuring look.

"I don't suppose you've talked to the police about it."

"Not yet. But I don't think I will."

"Why would you not talk to them? Are you involved in—"

"This is something I'm going to handle on my own."

She pursed her lips, nodded as though assessing his response.

"So far you're doing a great job."

"Yeah? So what?"

"Tough guy. You know what, Ray? The town's full of them."

With that, she turned away and went about her business, stopping for a moment to check on the white-haired man in bed 1. She did not look back at Ray as she left.

* * *

Outside in the hall, Hannah stopped and thought about his knife wound—not quite deep enough to be a killing wound, but that was as she'd said, merely a matter of luck. Her impressions of Ray Foley were beginning to fall into place, forming familiar patterns. She had known other Ray Foleys, smart guys, tough guys, single-minded, certain of the rightness of the way they saw the world and convinced that they were damned near immortal. She remembered the look in his eye when he'd spoken of his friend Eddy Walsh, and a different look when he spoke of 'looking into' whoever had killed him.

You're dangerous, Ray Foley, and I have no time anymore for dangerous guys.

* * *

The old man in the first bed was snoring like a buzz saw and Ray was studying a cobweb in a high corner of the ceiling when a large dark shape filled the doorway and he knew he had a visitor.

Detective Carmody shuffled into the room, glanced at the old man and then at Ray. He shook his head.

"So here we are with Ray Foley again," Carmody said, and he wasn't amused.

Ray said nothing. He watched as Carmody sank with a sigh onto an empty bed. The bed groaned in sympathy.

"You know this is just stupidity, am I right?"

"What? Walking around by myself at night?"

"You know what I'm talking about. This was no mugging. If you saw the blood when they brought you in, you wouldn't think it was so funny."

"You were here when they—"

"That's right, I was here. So talk to me, Foley."

To buy time, Ray said, "Where's your partner?"

"In the cafeteria trying to kill time till lunch. He doesn't like you."

"Good."

"So what do you have for me?"

"I got jumped by a guy with a knife. All I know."

"A guy? What guy?"

"It was dark. He was wearing dark clothes and a hat pulled down over his eyes."

He remembered his assailant coming up out of a crouch, surprising him—taller than he'd looked.

"It was dark and it happened fast, so I can't say for sure. But a wiry guy, quick. He was really quick. And he knew how to handle a knife."

"Sound familiar to you?"

"Sure."

"And you don't see any connection between this and what happened with those other men?"

"I didn't say that. But I don't know what the connection would be. And there's still a chance this was just random, just a guy trying to mug me for a few bucks."

Carmody stared at Ray.

"A chance, yeah, but how likely is that, Foley?"

"Not very likely, I guess."

"So you've got this guy, you've drawn him out by what you're doing. And we know. We know you've been looking for this statue, you've been to see Bob the Book, Oscar Leroux, Emery Pogue, that half-wit Dandy, asking around about the guys who hit Morrison's place—yeah, Foley, we know what you've been up to, sticking your beak in all of this stuff that isn't your business."

"I think it is."

Carmody leaned forward, filling the space between the two beds. Ray heard the creaking of the springs.

"And I'm saying it isn't. It's police business and you're just a civilian. Stay out of this. I'd say you've had a couple of warnings now, and one of 'em was with a knife. What more do you need, Foley?"

"Tell me this, Detective. What would you do? And don't give me rules and regulations. If you had a friend, all your life, and somebody killed him and they were still out there—"

Carmody gave him an exasperated look.

"I don't know, all right? I don't know what I'd do. We're talking about you. I know you were friends—"

Ray shook his head. "Far back as I can remember, all the way back to, like second grade, we were together, and half the time I was pulling his ass out of trouble, beating guys off him. Just a few days ago I pulled a couple of punks off him in the alley over by Clybourn. And this one time—"

"You couldn't protect him. He got himself killed and you couldn't stop it."

"Yeah, something like that."

"But it's done. And now you've got to stay out of it."

Ray thought of the obvious responses but bit his tongue.

"All right," he said.

"Did you say something to me?"

"I said all right. Detective."

"Get better, Foley, and then leave this stuff alone. You didn't come back from overseas to get mixed up in this kind of thing. You don't need to die young, kid. All those guys you left back there, overseas, they didn't get a chance to have a life. You've got one."

Carmody studied him for a moment.

"Tell me this, Foley. When you were over there in all that shit, guys getting killed all around you—is this what you thought about coming back to? Spending your time like this, looking for a guy who's as likely to cut you open as look at you? Is that what you had in mind for yourself after all that?"

"No. Of course not. But I thought I'd be coming back to something different."

Carmody surprised him now by smiling.

"No, you thought you'd be picking up exactly where you left off, in that world. You'd come back and see people and maybe find a girl you had your eye on before, and you'd find a job the first ten minutes you were back, and everything would be hunky-dory. Because that's what you thought you were doing over there."

"I didn't know what I'd be coming back to."

"But not this."

"Who would expect to come back to this?" After a moment, Ray said, "That's how it was for you? After the first war?"

Carmody fished a pack of Camels out of his jacket, shook one out for Ray. Ray thought of the last time he'd seen Eddy, the two of them sharing a smoke.

"Nah. I'm quitting. Besides, I don't think you can smoke in here."

Carmody glanced at the old man in the other bed.

"He don't look like he cares." He held out the cigarette until Ray took it. "You can quit tomorrow."

Ray took the smoke and Carmody lit one for each of them. The cop blew out a long plume of smoke.

"Yeah, that's how it was for me. I thought I was picking up right where things left off. I had a certain girl in mind, and I thought I had a job. Well, the girl was married to a guy that came to town during the war, and the place I was going to work at had closed. I almost died twice over there. Once by a sniper's bullet and the other time with that flu, that Spanish Lady that killed millions of people. I made it through all of that, and when I came back I found I had to start over from scratch. Like you, Foley."

"So you became a cop."

"That's right. I became a cop. It's not for everybody, but—you know, it might just be for you. You've got a nose for trouble, it seems to me, and there's enough of that to go around in this town. You ought to think about that. But while you're at it—"

"I know, keep my nose out of this Morrison thing. Yeah. Well, I'll give that some thought."

"No, do more than that, Foley. I'll run you in, kid, I swear I will."

Ray almost said *For what?* but caught himself. There were a dozen things a smart old street cop could stick him with.

"I told you I'll stay out of it. Like you said, I'm not involved."

"Well, you are involved, as far as that goes. And as for this situation we're discussing, you're involved whether you want to be or not. Somebody tried to kill you, young Foley, so at least one person thinks you're involved. You see, we don't get to decide in life what things we're involved in. And in a philosophical sense, we are involved in all of it."

Ray laughed. "A philosopher cop."

"I like to read. I like to think about things. But it's time to show some sense about all this. You could just as easily have been killed by this character."

When Ray said nothing, Carmody said, "What if I was to tell you that someone else connected with that Morrison thing was killed recently. Same way as the others, stabbed to death."

Ray felt a sudden chill. "Who?"

"Woman named Opal Raines. That name mean anything to you?"

"No. Never met anybody named Opal."

He tried to sound casual but he knew the other shoe was about to drop.

"Used to be a pretty common name. You sure you don't recognize her?"

"No. Where did they find her?"

"Just around the corner from that Morrison place, in a basement on Maud Street. See, you live in a dangerous neighborhood, Foley."

"And you think she had something to do with Morrison?"

"Were not sure. But she was seen a couple times the week before Morrison was killed, standing outside his house and screaming at him, baying at the moon. Witnesses said she seemed to have some grudge, kept yelling that he was a phony, she knew all about him, she wasn't done with him yet. Et cetera."

"That's right. So I got somebody on the loose, killing people, Foley. If I'm right, and the same guy did this one, that's five people dead, and this guy's still out there.

Carmody squinted at Ray as if trying to get a clearer focus on him. He got slowly to his feet, grunting.

"You all right?"

"Ah, you know. Getting old. It takes me a little longer to get in and out of the car, as you no doubt noticed. And I've had some, you know, some health things, a little wrinkle here and there. No big deal, Foley, I'm just getting old."

"Some days I feel like I got older overnight," Ray said.

"Sure. But you're not old. The thing is, you get old without knowing, you don't realize.

Time passes and you don't know because you can't see it. You look back and years have gone by and it seems to you like nothing, like you were a young guy just a short time ago. You, Foley, you're a young guy. Live your life, enjoy life."

"Have adventures?"

"Nah. Fuck adventures. But travel, yeah, see the world."

"I just did. They shot me."

Carmody gave a short laugh. "That's good, Foley, keep your sense of humor. You know, that's what happened to me. I was too old for this war but I got in the last one, just in time to get shot."

Carmody patted his left shoulder. "My first time out of the state of Illinois and I get shot. No, forget adventures and thrills, young Foley. Travel, see the country. Find a nice girl and be happy."

"I'm trying."

Carmody squinted at him. "Doesn't look like it."

Hannah Marcel passed the room, looked in and saw Carmody's cigarette.

"I'll take that," she said, advancing on Carmody with her hand held out.

"Okay, no problem, miss," Carmody said.

She took the smoke between two fingers and walked out of the room, holding the cigarette like a diseased rodent. In the hall she shot Ray a look over her shoulder and it wasn't friendly.

"Tough little things, nurses," Carmody said. "So before I leave, let me bounce a couple names off you. See if they ring any bells. Passeau. Ever heard that name?"

"Pitcher on the Cubs. Right-hander. Pretty good, too."

"Yeah, besides old Claude."

"No."

"This Passeau was Mr. Cary Morrison's personal assistant. Whatever that is."

"What about him?"

"Well, I talked to him the night of the murder, but since then, this Passeau fella has sort of disappeared."

"So? If my boss got stabbed to death in his own house, I think I might cut out, too."

"Yeah, but this guy Passeau, he's gone underground. One day we're talking to him about his boss, and he's all busted up about it. The next day he's gone. Disappeared."

Carmody gave Ray a sly look.

"Or else—"

"Or else what?"

"Just something I might have heard. That maybe this is another one. Maybe this Passeau is dead, too."

"Or maybe he left town."

"Maybe. How about Lucas Orr? You know him."

"No. Who's he?"

"Personal chauffeur to the late Mr. Morrison. Chauffeur and all-around hard man from what I hear. Not a fellow to be messed with. Decorated in the first war. He's still here. The way I heard it, he wouldn't take his boss's murder sitting down."

"Interesting stuff."

"Yeah, ain't it, though? But the one I'd like to talk to sometime is this

Passeau. So if you ever hear anything about him, you give me a jingle."

When Carmody had left, Ray lay in his bed and acknowledged that what he'd said made sense. But Eddy Walsh had survived the War only to be killed, maybe for being in the wrong place at the wrong time, maybe over something as stupid as a statue. And maybe Carmody and his prune-faced partner would figure it all out, but Ray doubted it. And besides, it was now his own fight. The shadowy figure with the long knife had guaranteed that. If there had been any question about it.

A moment later Hannah Marcel walked by but did not look in his direction.

Chapter Twelve

That night when her shift ended Hannah went out with three other girls for a drink. Eventually she took a cab home and on an impulse she had the cabbie drop her off two blocks from her flat.

"Right here," she said, and directed him to pull over in front of what was left of the Morrison house.

"This place?"

"Yes."

"You know, a big shot gangster lived here. Somebody knifed him right in that house."

"Is that right?" she said. She paid him and got out of the cab.

He seemed to be watching for her reaction. He smiled but she ignored him. Then he put his cab in gear and took off. It struck her that she had seen this cabbie before, more than once.

When the cab was gone she stood for a moment and looked at the ruins. She'd seen the fire do its work but it was still a shock to see the great house hollowed out by the flames. A smoke-stained piece of police barrier tape fluttered from one side of what had been the doorway. For several minutes Hannah stood there, studying it. Then she went up the broken steps and stood at the entrance, telling herself she had once been inside this house, had gone down on one knee to check the lifeless Morrison for a pulse.

Now it was hard to believe this had been a mansion, its owner a figure of mystery. She hesitated at the doorway, looked out at the empty street and then she was inside. For a moment she stood at the doorway to what had been the living room, listening. In the imperfect light of the street lamps she picked her way through the darkened house, feeling both exhilarated and uneasy, like a child who has gone where she's been forbidden to go. A car moved by and she froze. Of course the site would have been looted soon after the fire, police barrier or no, picked clean of anything of the slightest value, anything even remotely useful. A Chicago tradition: neighbors swarming a recently vacated flat, and she was certain they'd swarmed Morrison's place, if only to get a souvenir of a celebrity. Here and there she saw traces of the man's life: part of a table, the torn cover of a notebook, a shard of mirror. Sections of the old carpet still remained, fire-stained and pungent, and a door lay in the center of a room, strangely untouched by the flames. They'd caught the fire before it moved to the front of the house, but she could see the charred remains of what had been the kitchen, all of it blackened.

A book lay on a side table by an enormous armchair, and she wondered what a man like this had been reading on the night of his death. Then she heard a noise from the back of the house. She froze again, this time held her breath, and she could hear the pulsing of her blood. Another sound and she began moving quietly back out of the room. Something in the rear of the house fell, something scampered.

Rats. Of course, rats, the city seemed to have more rats than people, and it took no great imagination to envision them taking over Morrison's huge house. But whether the noises were the rats or something more ominous, she understood the peril she'd put herself in. She hurried back out toward the front of the ruin, no longer careful where she stepped, tripping once and nearly turning her ankle on a brick. Then she was out on the street, under the yellow cone of the street light.

Her heart was beating fast and she could hear her own breathing. She took a moment to calm herself and then started to walk toward the bright lights on Clybourn. As she did so, she chanced to look across the street. The old playground was still there, and she wondered what the children who played there thought of the burnt-out mansion across the street, or if they even noticed it.

Then she saw the man on the bench. In the faint light in the playground, she could barely make him out: a man in dark clothes, in a small-brimmed fedora. Smoking, smoking and, she was certain, looking her way. She moved fast and then glanced quickly in his direction to see if he was getting up to follow her. He sat motionless and she saw the glow of his cigarette as he puffed at it. Then he turned toward her, tilted his head slightly as if considering her, considering his next movement. And then he was nodding, she was certain of it, just nodding in her direction. He flicked out his hand and she saw the orange arc as he tossed the cigarette. Hannah moved on fast, jammed her hand into her purse where she kept the razor—her single memento of her long-gone husband. She took out the razor and went on walking, faster and faster, telling herself this was the stupidest thing she'd done in years. When she reached the corner, she looked back, then across the street. There was no one behind her. She walked the remaining block to her flat, looking over her shoulder constantly and listening for the sounds of footsteps.

Inside, she locked her door, put the chain on, and made herself tea. She was slightly breathless, her heart beating fast, and she was surprised at herself.

For God's sake, she told herself. I've been shot at and they tried to blow up my ship. I'm not afraid of anything.

She thought of the man on the bench and now recalled a night several weeks before when a man had followed her part of the way down her street. She was sure he'd gotten off the streetcar when she had—*because* she had. But that wasn't it. She'd faced down creeps in the street before and this one was no different: she'd spun quickly on her heels and looked him in the eye.

Medium height, slim and well-dressed—and, at least in the waning twilight, handsome. A dark suit and hat, a tie. He met her eyes, frowned slightly and seemed to be staring at her intently, as though trying to place her. Hannah nodded almost imperceptibly. He touched the brim on his hat and nodded and she walked on, faster now, and had no doubt that the dapper stranger was still watching her. Then a car had come down the street. When she looked, the man was gone.

She thought again, as she had that night, that there was something familiar about the man who had followed her.

I've seen you before. I don't know where, but I've seen you.

She couldn't have said why she had gone to the Morrison house. Indulging an urge to revisit what she now thought of as her old life, perhaps. A darker life, Hannah would have said. She recalled it now as a solitary time, a lonely period of her life: a young girl recently arrived in town, escaping what she thought of as a dead-end life in a loveless marriage to a man who swore he would find her if she ever left him. A stranger in a big town, living in a tiny room on a street where she knew no one. Now she had a career, a few friends, a sense of who she was, a sense of her own worth—that was perhaps the greatest difference between Hannah Marcel and the young Gladys McCoy. Hannah believed she was worth something. Perhaps she'd gone to the Morrison place tonight just to remind herself that she had put that time behind her.

She thought a moment as she poured herself her tea. Men were the cause of so much of her trouble in life. At times the prospect of a life without a man in it was immensely appealing. But there were men in her life nonetheless: a couple of young doctors, one married and looking for a way out; and a red-haired young cop who she'd met in the emergency room. She thought about the married doctor, handsome and glib: in her old life as Gladys McCoy, she might have fallen for his line, for Gladys would have been grateful for the attention. The cop was cute and earnest but a little slow, and she didn't think he'd ever read a book. And of course there was trouble in the form of Ray Foley. In some ways the most appealing of the men she'd met. Honest, tough, good-looking but not overly aware of it. But she understood now that Ray might be a special kind of trouble. He'd already managed to get himself stabbed in the street. A boy who went into life's dark places, Ray Foley.

She sat at her kitchen table and turned on her radio. They were doing some kind of salute to poor Glenn Miller, who hadn't come back from the war. She sipped her tea and sat back, calm now, refusing to be afraid in her house. But she thought once more of the well-dressed man. She saw again the way he'd looked at her, the frown and then the stare: interested, maybe, then slightly hostile. And now it seemed to Hannah that just as she recalled him from somewhere, he remembered her. From some other place or time. Yes, that was it, he remembered her. Then Hannah thought of the dark figure smoking in the playground and watching her, and she shuddered.

* * *

In front of DeMars Grill on Ashland, Ray stopped and did a double take. Inside, there was a long counter, and behind it was a girl he recognized from the morning of Morrison's killing. He spent a moment pretending to look at the menu in the window, then went inside and took a stool at the near end of the counter.

"May I help you?"

She was small and pale and unsmiling, with straw-colored hair and blue eyes and a small mouth.

"Just a coke."

When she brought him his drink he pointed at her face and smiled.

"I've seen you before."

"I don't think so."

"I never forget a pretty girl."

She looked away, feigning irritation and blushing.

"It was the day that guy in the big house died. You were there."

He watched her struggle over what to say. Then she shrugged.

"Mr. Morrison, you mean. Yeah, I was there. I worked for him, you know." Then she added, "The poor man."

"Nasty stuff. Stabbed over money, is what I heard."

She shrugged and pursed her lips, unimpressed.

"That's what I heard, anyhow."

She looked him over. "So you were there that day, too."

"I live pretty close. Over on Armitage. So you worked for him?"

"I did. For almost a year. I think he liked me okay. He was a hard boss, though."

"Hard how?"

"If you didn't do things just right, he would fire you."

"Those rich guys can be hard to deal with. Say, my name's Ray, what's yours?"

"My name is Estelle but I should tell you right up front, I've got a boyfriend."

"Well, I'd be surprised if you didn't. I'm just trying to meet people, I'm just back from the service."

"Oh," she said, and her gaze took in the scar alongside his ear.

"So Morrison liked you but he didn't like other people who worked for him."

"Not the people who were there at the—you know, the end. There was Mary, the cook, and Bennie, who was kind of a houseboy, and Lucas." Her face became serious. "That was his driver, I never liked him, he made me kind of nervous the way he watched you." She flashed a sudden grin.

"And Mackal. His so-called bodyguard. Mackal the jackal, we called him. A jackal is this kind of African dog—"

"Right. What did this guy look like?"

"About your size but heavier. Dark hair. Smoked all the time."

Ray remembered the dark figure smoking behind a tree the morning of Morrison's death.

"Sounds like Morrison kept a full house, though."

"Yes, but he fired a couple of people before. He fired people a lot. He didn't trust anybody. He fired Hatch, and he fired Sophie. She was a maid. He thought she stole from him."

"You think she did?"

"I wouldn't put it past her." She gave Ray an appraising look. "You would like Sophie. Most fellas do. She's pretty. And she's tall, like you."

Sophie. Eddy Walsh had been chasing a girl by that name. Not a common name.

"Was that the girl you were talking to that day?"

"Yes. I don't even know why she was there. Like I said, he fired her about six months ago."

"Well, there were a lot of fire engines, a fire will draw people."

"I guess so." She shrugged again. "She always thought she was better than everybody else. She's working at Woolworth's now."

She looked away with a slight smile.

"Seems to me you found a job pretty quick."

"They would have hired me at Woolworth's, or Kresge's, even, but this is a better class of people."

Ray nodded and looked away, hoping to hide his amusement.

DeMars Grill. A diner. Better class of people.

"Tell me something, Estelle. That day of the, you know, the killing. I saw this young guy there," Ray said, improvising. "He seemed to be somebody. At least he acted like he was somebody. He tried to get in but the cops kept him out. Maybe that was this guy you mentioned, the one he fired—what was his name?"

"You mean Hatch?" She gave him an amused look. "Oh, no, you didn't see Hatch. Hatch is dead. Somebody robbed him and killed him and they threw the body in the river."

"Wow. So two people from that house are dead in just—"

"They didn't have anything to do with each other. This was way back in the Spring when they found Hatch."

"This guy was tall, blond hair, kind of good-looking, and he was telling people he worked for Morrison."

"That's Passeau. Geoffrey Passeau." She lifted the corner of her lip.

"Not your favorite."

"No. A very conceited guy."

"And he was what?"

"Mr. Morrison's assistant. Sort of."

"Like a butler or a valet?"

"No. He was more than that. He did things for Morrison, ran errands, made telephone calls, set things up. He was really smart, Passeau. I'll say that for him."

"He seemed pretty upset. I would have said it was genuine."

"Maybe he was upset, maybe he wasn't."

"So what kind of a guy was he? He seemed kind of a pretty boy."

Surprisingly, Estelle shuddered.

"I didn't like him. He gave me the creeps, always watching everybody. With those eyes. You see his eyes?"

Ray had not been close enough to see Passeau's eyes but nodded.

"I did. There was something odd about him. Yeah, maybe it was the eyes."

"Anyhow, I haven't seen him lately. He was a snob, too. I saw him once on the street and he pretended he didn't know me."

"Where was this?"

"He was coming out of some hamburger place on Sheffield." She started to say something else, then shook her head.

"Did he ever make a pass at you?"

She shrugged. "He made a pass at every girl, thought he was hot stuff. The one he was really after was Sophie."

"I see." A new question struck Ray. "A minute ago I think you were about to say something else. Maybe about this Hatch guy."

"Not about him. About Passeau."

"What about him?"

"Well, he acted funny after they found out about Hatch. He didn't seem bothered at all."

"What was so odd about that?"

"Him and Hatch were friends. They were always talking. One time I walked in on them

and they were talking very quietly, whispering almost, and they shut up when they saw me. I think they were planning something but Morrison fired Hatch and that was the end of it. But I think Passeau knew more about Hatch than he let on. He was a shifty guy."

"Violent guy?"

"I'm not saying nothing. I just know what I think."

She looked pointedly away, eyebrows raised, and Ray could almost imagine her doing the kid's thing, locking her lips with an imaginary key. Begging to be asked.

"You're thinking that maybe Passeau had something to do with what happened to Hatch."

"I never said nothing like that." She looked around the room with self-importance and Ray almost laughed. Then she met his eyes for just a moment longer than necessary.

"I'm just saying, if Passeau had any, you know, big ideas, Hatch would have known. That's what I think. I mean, if Passeau was planning to rob Morrison—"

She looked at Ray and shrugged.

A new wrinkle for Ray to consider: Passeau was involved somehow, this Hatch knew about it, maybe Passeau killed him to shut him up. A new wrinkle indeed.

"So this Passeau had a thing for Sophie."

"Yeah. I caught them in a back room of the house once, whispering and giggling like a couple little kids."

"That's interesting."

"But like I said, I haven't seen him around. I heard he might have left town. Good riddance."

Or he's dead, Ray thought.

"So you don't see any of those people now."

"Actually, I saw Bennie. The houseboy."

Ray remembered the young man in the white housecoat the morning they found Morrison, recalled the stricken look in the man's eyes.

Okay, I guess I know Bennie, too, a grown man with a boy's face.

"Where was this?"

"Up on Clark Street, by the ballpark. In that train yard place."

"Where the old boxcars are?"

"Yeah, he was sitting there in one of those boxcars. He didn't see me, though."

"Well, you've given me some information I didn't have, Estelle."

He drank the last of his coke and nodded as though the interview was finished. Then he gave it one last push.

"I always heard it was robbers that killed Morrison. What do you think?"

"No. I never believed that. He was careful about everything, you know? Too careful to have a bunch of robbers sneak up on him like that and kill him. He had guns all over the place. I heard there was a gun on the floor beside him when they found him. No, I think something else was going on."

Now she leaned forward and let her voice drop.

"He had enemies."

"What kind of enemies?"

"The kind rich people have who got their money the wrong way. *'Ill-gotten gain,'* my Ma used to say. It's poison. I think somebody planned it, came in and killed him and maybe made it look like a robbery. That's what I think. You know, there were people watching the house just before he got, you know—"

"People? What kind of people?"

"Well, one of them was this tall, skinny guy, old guy, sun-burned, baseball cap."

Ray looked away. She'd just described Willie Foy. He nodded and then met her eye.

"Anybody else?"

"This one guy, well-dressed fella in a nice suit and hat. I saw him across the street once, in the little park, watching the house. And another time, I'm sure I saw the same guy drive by in a nice car. Like a Cadillac. My boyfriend saw him, too. He said it was a LaSalle."

"Blue?"

She gave Ray a surprised look.

"Yeah. How'd you know that?"

"I think I've seen that car. There's not that many left. They stopped making them."

"A real nice-looking guy. Dark tan. Very distinguished. I think he knew Mr. Morrison."

"What makes you say that?"

"One time I came late to work and he was coming out of the house. And he had this look on his face, like he was having a good day. You know, like business and that. And a fancy car like that? You can bet he was a gangster."

"I think you're right about that. All right, Estelle, thanks."

He left change on the counter and went out.

Ray walked for more than an hour, thinking of all that Estelle had given him. There was where to find Sophie, first of all, and in the next day or so he would look her up. But she'd given him much more: the skinny guy in the cap was Willie Foy. The well-dressed man in the blue LaSalle was Max Silver.

Coming out of Morrison's house.

He knew him, Ray thought. He knew Morrison.

* * *

The next night he stopped at the big Woolworth's where his mother had taken him for lunch so many times in childhood. It was still noisy, crowded, the air heavy with the smells of popcorn, fried food, hot dogs steaming in a rotisserie, soap and cheap perfume. And it was full of women. He'd forgotten that part. As Ray made his way to the far side of the store he caught the look a couple of the young clerks gave him.

His waitress wore a name tag that identified her as *Peggy*. She seemed to be taking orders from an older girl whose tag read *Sophie*. She was tall, sullen, and good-looking, with dark hair and pale green eyes. As he nursed his coffee he watched her, and she caught him at it. She stared at him for a moment and then looked away. A couple of young guys, both drunk, stumbled up to the counter and she moved to wait on them. When she passed him, he leaned forward.

"Hello. It's Sophie, right?"

She shot him a look over her shoulder, frowned, said, "Yes" with a question mark in it.

"I'm sorry. My name's Ray. I was hoping we could talk for a minute."

She turned, wiped her hands on the apron, met his eyes. She gave him the once over. She had fair skin and a spray of freckles across her cheeks, and a plump lower lip you could bite into. Sophie seemed to read his thoughts. She relaxed a little, changed her pose, stuck out a hip.

Sure, Ray thought, *you've been watching how men react to you since you were 12.*

"About what?"

"I'm trying to get some information on something I think you're familiar with. The Morrison thing."

Ray waited for a heartbeat as she considered her answer.

"Who says I'm familiar with it?"

"A couple people. You worked for him, right?"

"Why do you want to know about that?"

"Let's just say I've got an interest in it."

"Why?"

"I'm just trying to find some things out."

She studied Ray's face.

"You've been in a fight."

"Couple guys mugged me. You roam around at night, it happens. Do you know where I could find any of the other people who worked for Morrison?"

Ray held his stare. Finally, she made an irritated shake of her head.

"Well, Mary, that was the cook—she found him, actually. She went back to Ireland. She was shocked by it all, you know?"

"Sure."

"And Lucas Orr, the driver, I don't know what became of him. He scared me, if you want to know the truth. He never said much, he always had a gun. None of us knew what he did in his free time. He didn't really talk to anyone."

"Do you think he ever had a grudge against his boss?"

Sophie gave him a wide-eyed look. "Lucas? No, he was like a watchdog, that fella. He was true blue and loyal. He'd never hurt Morrison."

"Maybe he'd hurt somebody who hurt Morrison."

"What do you mean by that?"

"You know there have been killings since that night, right? Some guys that the cops think were there that night. Three of them wound up dead."

"I don't know anything about that," Sophie said, but she turned away as she spoke.

"How about the guy that was his, ah, his assistant? His right-hand man?"

Now she faced him. "Passeau," she said, and shrugged. "That one. He's long gone. He lost his meal ticket. I didn't have anything to do with him."

"So you're the manager here."

She gave him a look from under her carefully penciled eyebrows.

"I'm the supervisor. The manager is a man. Always a man."

"That's the way it usually is."

She shrugged. "They think if you wear pants, it makes you smart."

"I bet you'd do all right."

She warmed up his coffee and came over to lean on the counter. He could smell her perfume.

He watched her and remembered what Floyd Hennessey had said, about the people they'd passed in the alley as they left Morrison's house. A tall guy and a girl with big eyes. He could imagine Eddy Walsh playing up to this girl, bragging and shooting off his mouth, probably intimating in some way that he knew something about her, about the night of the Morrison killing.

Sophie picked up a rag and wiped coffee stains from the counter, and Ray waited a few beats, then said, "And I'm pretty sure you knew a friend of mine."

"That so?"

"Eddy Walsh."

She was about to shake her head when Ray held up his hand.

"He told me about you. He was real interested in you, Sophie."

She froze and he saw her struggling to decide how much to say.

"Probably came here and pestered you every night, that's how he was."

"He seemed like a nice kid."

"He's dead, you know."

She blinked and bit her lip. She shook her head.

"No. What happened to him?"

"Somebody knifed him," Ray said slowly.

"For his money, probably."

"No."

She turned away slightly and Ray could see her trying to watch him from the corner of her eye.

"So you didn't hear about that."

"How would I?"

She went through the motions with the rag, wiping a place that she'd already cleaned.

"I don't know. Just wondering."

Ray took a last sip of his coffee, left half a buck, and nodded.

"I'll see you around, Sophie."

She shot him a quick, nervous look, nodded once.

When she left a half hour later, Ray watched her get into a cab. He hailed a Checker and had the cabbie follow Sophie's cab, all the way up Lincoln nearly to the Biograph Theater. Sophie's cab turned onto a side street and Ray told his cabbie to stop. He watched as Sophie got out and went into a rooming house.

"Your girl?" the cabbie said, watching Ray in the rearview mirror.

"Used to be. Before the War, this was. I'm just trying to see if she's got a fella now. Maybe I'm wasting my time."

The cabbie gave him a noncommittal shrug. Ray paid his fare and left.

In his room he sat by the window and watched the street. After a while he looked at the pages of his notebook, addresses and ideas jotted down, and told himself it was coming together.

* * *

The next day he stopped for a cup of coffee in a diner a few blocks from his room. He took a seat in a window booth which allowed him to watch the door and follow the street traffic at the same time. Directly across from this restaurant was a nearly identical one, different only in name, the sort of place that would serve breakfast all night and have the same Blue Plate Special. To his amusement, he saw Max Silver emerge from this restaurant. Silver paused at the curb, as if looking for a cab. Moments later, a familiar black Ford pulled in front of the fire hydrant and he watched Detective Carmody emerge. His partner got out from the passenger's side, moved around and took the driver's seat. Kessel said something to Carmody, gave an irritable shake of his head and drove off. As he left, Ray could see Kessel muttering to himself.

Carmody watched his partner drive off, then said something to Silver that made the detective laugh.

Carmody and Silver. Silver and Morrison.

Okay, everybody's in on the joke except me.

Chapter Thirteen

Ray stood on the corner, bouncing slightly on the balls of his feet and jingling the change in his pockets. The light changed and a dozen or so people made their way across the street toward him, and one of them was Max Silver.

Max Silver was looking his way but unfocused, he hadn't recognized Ray yet. Ray waited on the curb and then Silver saw him and gave Ray what passed for a smile.

"Come on, Foley, I'll buy you a cup of coffee."

Silver led Ray to a long, narrow diner on Halsted. They took a window booth and Silver flagged down a waitress, ordered two coffees and produced a pack of Luckies. They each lit up a smoke and Max Silver waited.

"So how've you been, Foley?"

"Okay so far."

Silver studied the marks on Ray's face. "But you've been in a fight."

"It's nothing."

"How about when you got yourself knifed—was that nothing?"

"How'd you hear about that?"

"I get my information from many sources. It's how I stay in business. How are you feeling?"

"The stitches still sting a little when I move too fast. But I'm okay."

"So, when you're not getting into fights or getting knifed, what else are you doing? Looking for work?"

"Everybody asks me that. Not yet, I've got money."

"Good for you, Foley. Take your time."

"So how's the detective racket?"

"I'm still getting the word out that I'm open for business."

"And you've already started following me."

"Not really."

"I've seen you three times now. I saw you drive by when I was talking to Carmody, after Eddy Walsh's wake."

"That doesn't mean I was following you."

"Just a coincidence, huh?"

Silver turned one hand in a noncommittal gesture.

"But you knew about Eddy Walsh. Your *sources* again, huh?"

"No, that was in the paper. Poor kid. Survives the War, comes back only to be killed in his hometown. Mugged for a few bucks." Silver sipped his coffee and watched Ray.

"You don't even believe that."

"I heard the wallet was gone."

"Big deal. You know what this is about. You know he was killed because of this Morrison thing."

"Who says?"

Ray drew smoke into his lungs and blew it out, then said, "I say. You didn't even know him, but you were there the night of his funeral, so you think so, too. You knew he was dead and how he was killed, and you think just like I do, that he was killed by the same one who killed those other guys and that he was killed for whatever happened that night."

"Suppose I do. Why would that surprise you?"

"It doesn't. It seems to me this thing means something to you. I don't know why—my guess, nobody's even paying you. But you just asked me why it's so important. Well, you think it's important. So—why is that?"

For a moment Silver said nothing. He tapped his fingers against the edge of the table and Ray realized with satisfaction that the detective was uncomfortable. Then Silver shook his head.

"I'm not interested in going into ancient history with you here. I have my own reasons—"

Ray stopped him with a raised hand.

"And I don't need to know your reasons. How about some information?"

"Why? What good will information do you?"

"It might give me something to go on."

"To go on? And do what?"

Max Silver frowned and watched him with just a trace of amusement, and Ray understood that this was the place where he was to be finessed by a more streetwise opponent.

"How can information help you?"

Outside a siren tore the air and Ray was aware of the clink of spoons in coffee cups at the booth behind them. Ray waited for a ten-count and then said, "A friend of mine is dead and I want to know why, and if I can do something about it, I'm going to do that. And I want to find Willie Foy."

Silver nodded. "Word is Willie Foy planned the robbery. So you hold him responsible." "And I think he's the one person who can tell me what happened."

"This kind of thing is not for you. You're a young guy, you ought to live your life now. Get a job, turn a dollar. Settle down."

"You sound like my Ma. Right now I don't think I'm accomplishing anything. I'm doing nothing, I have no purpose."

Silver stared out his window. He mouthed the word *purpose*. An odd look had come into his eyes, as though the talk had distressed him somehow. He looked back at Ray.

"You're right, Foley. Purpose. That's the thing, not just living day to day. You're a smart guy. So—first, tell me what you've been doing so far."

"I've been trying to track down Willie Foy. And a statue they took."

"A statue?"

A look of mild amusement came into the detective's eyes.

"Yeah. It might mean something. Who knows? And I've been asking around about Eddy, about who he'd been talking to."

Silver said nothing but looked around the room. The amusement had not left his face, and Ray had to wonder what was so funny about a statue.

Ray moved his coffee cup around on the table top, smearing the wet circles left by the cup.

"You've got a leaky cup," Silver pointed out.

"Yeah. I better drink faster."

He looked around, then at Silver.

The detective tilted his head slightly. "What is it?"

"Just checking to see if I've drawn anybody's attention. Seems I've got people following me these days."

Silver shrugged. "This surprises you?"

"I guess not."

"At least two that I've seen."

"Two, huh? So you are following me?"

"Not by design. So once or twice I've seen you on the street, thought I'd get an idea where you go, what you do with yourself."

"Why?"

"If we're working the same side of the street, I want to know a little about you. And if we're working opposites sides, I need to know that, too."

For a moment Ray considered this. The waitress came by and he pointed out the leak in his cup. She ran off to fetch a new cup of coffee.

"Okay, so tell me who's following me,"

"You mean besides that big hood I saw you with? No, this is a guy not used to it. He's a big guy—"

"Baggy suit?" Ray said, remembering Dandy's description.

"Yes. Round face. He's kind of pale, looks like he lives his life in an office. Not a pro, and not like you've been followed before. I don't think this one means you harm."

"How can you tell?"

Silver smiled. "How much time do you have? He jumps into a doorway every time you slow down, he runs to catch up when you start moving faster, he wears a straw porkpie hat that you can see a block away. If I had to make a guess, I'd say he's somebody's driver or something like that. This is not gang muscle we're talking about. He's kind of amusing, if you want to know the truth."

"Not to me."

"He thinks you know something. You ought to find out."

"Maybe I'll do that. Who's the other one?"

"Big guy, kind of slovenly, wears a black suit, black fedora. I think he worked for Morrison. Some kind of bodyguard."

"Did a great job for his boss, didn't he."

"He probably thinks you know something, too. All these people think you know something, Foley, because you've put yourself in it, right in the middle."

The waitress brought a new cup of coffee and Ray dressed it up with cream and sugar.

"That's okay with me."

"I enjoyed your performance the other day. When that big slob tried to put the arm on you. You made him nervous."

"Butch Turner. I pulled him off Eddy Walsh a couple weeks ago, something about a gambling debt."

"Big guy, no guts. I like how you handle yourself, Foley."

"Thanks."

He sipped his coffee and looked around the room, waiting for his moment. When he saw Silver look at his watch, he decided to play a hunch.

"There's something Carmody told me. I don't know how it fits in. He says a woman named Opal Raines was stabbed to death around the time Morrison was killed. Just around the corner on Maud. They found her in a basement."

Silver looked away for a moment, then shrugged. "That doesn't mean there's a connection."

"I guess people heard her screaming stuff at the big house, Morrison's house. And she was stabbed."

Max Silver nodded and raised his eyebrows.

"Was she. Well, that's a name I don't know," he said.

"I just thought I'd run it by you."

Silver signaled for the check, looked at it and gave the waitress a dollar.

"Keep it," he told her.

She smiled and thanked him.

"Yeah, I figured you for a big tipper."

"Doesn't hurt. These women don't make anything. All right, Foley," Silver said as he got to his feet.

"Listen. Here's my card again. I'm on Belmont between the VFW hall and the bakery. Drop in sometime and visit, and we'll talk about this thing. Right now, I've got to go. I have an actual client. To tell you the truth, I don't have much time nowadays for this other business."

"Good for you. And thanks for the coffee."

When Silver had gone, Ray sat and sipped his coffee and stared idly at the detective's card. He thought of Silver's reaction at Opal Raines's name. For just a second, Max Silver had looked away. The name meant something to him. And Ray didn't believe for a moment Max Silver's comment that he had no time "for this business."

Yeah, Mr. Silver, I'll be around to visit you sometime.

* * *

Ray leaned against the wrought iron fence and studied what was left of the great house: part of the roof had collapsed, the walls now smoke-blackened. The police had put up barrier tape but it had come loose and now fluttered in the wind. Morrison's well-tended lawn was being overtaken by weeds, some of them more than a foot high, and the small tree closest to the house was scorched black. A dead place.

From the corner of his eye he caught movement, someone coming his way. Ray turned and encountered one more sight from his pre-War past: trudging along the street, pushing his heavy cart before him, the old knife sharpener. Once, in that far-off summer before the War, Ray had on an odd impulse given half his Popsicle to this man. As he walked, the old man called out his services.

"Knife sharpen, scissors sharpen. Everything sharpen. Kitchen knife like new, scissors like new."

The man paused and took off his hat, wiped his forehead with his sleeve in a gesture Ray remembered from that long-ago last meeting. A woman came out with a pair of long kitchen knives and the old man nodded, smiled, said something. He splashed water on the sharpening wheel from a bottle on his cart, sat on his stool and worked the foot pedal, running the blade against the stone. At the first sparks, the woman took a sudden step back, spooked. He said something to her and she laughed. In a few minutes he had sharpened both her knives. She handed him some change and went on her way, and the knife sharpener put the coins in a small leather pouch that hung from his belt.

Another woman came out with a knife and a big scissors, an older woman. More comfortable with him than the earlier woman, she spoke to the knife-sharpener and Ray saw him nod and smile and say something. When he was finished sharpening her things, she left and he stood there for a moment as though catching his breath. Then he seemed to notice Ray.

For several seconds he stared as if trying to place Ray's face. Then he smiled and nodded.

"Hello. I know you. I remember you. You give me ice-cream thing. Long time ago."

Ray came forward, offering his hand, and the knife sharpener engulfed it in his big sun-darkened paw.

"And you're still here," Ray said.

"I'm everyplace," the knife-sharpener said, and grinned, taking ten years off his face.

Ray nodded toward the mansion. "We're here but the big house is gone. And the man in it."

"Yes." The man studied the ruins for a moment. "Somebody kills the man and burns his house. Angry man did this, I think. People are angry at this man. I see angry people watching this house sometime."

"Who? Who was watching the house?"

"One time, woman, screaming woman, make angry fists at the house."

"Young or old?"

"Old, maybe like me. Not like you. But I saw a boy, young man, I mean. One night I walk by here and this young man stares at the house. He sits there," the old man said, pointing across the street to the playground. "He sits and smokes but I can see his eyes when I walk by, he doesn't even see me. He watches the house. No, this is angry place."

Ray looked at the house. "Before the War, when I was a young guy, I used to stare at it and try to imagine what kind of life went on inside. I had the idea whoever lived here had a better life, a different kind of life."

"Different, maybe, not better. Big house, big money, I think big troubles." Then he looked at Ray and smiled.

"'*When I was young guy*' you say. You are still young. Still a young man. Older now, yes." He made an odd little gesture as if drawing a circle around Ray's eyes. "You see life, I think, bad things. The War. But you are still young man. You have much time for forget these bad things. To have a good life."

"You think you ever forget it?"

The knife sharpener looked off into the distance, wiped his forehead and face with a wrinkled blue bandanna. For a moment he said nothing, and Ray wondered what dark moments in his life the old man was remembering now.

"Not all, no," he said. "But some. You can think about things that are good, you can have life."

Ray's glance took in the old man's clothes, his face tanned from working in the sun, his fingers dark with the oil of his machine and thick from years of hard work, and the irony of this small lecture was not lost on him. He looked around the street and when his gaze returned to the old knife sharpener, he saw that the man was studying him.

"Maybe you're right."

"I think I am right. About this. You can have a good life."

"I hope you have a good life," Ray said on impulse.

The old man shrugged. "It is all right. I have wife, I have place to live, I have my job. I can still walk and push this—this thing. And I can still push the pedals and sharpen the knife." And now he smiled. "And I got no boss."

Ray nodded. "Well, I don't have a job yet, but I'm working on it."

The old man smiled and patted Ray on the shoulder. "Good. And maybe sometime I buy you an ice cream. Okay?"

"That sounds good."

The knife sharpener moved away, pushing his heavy contraption and calling out "Knife sharpen, scissors sharpen" in his strong voice.

Chapter Fourteen

The following night Ray left a sandwich shop and realized he was being followed by someone new to the task.

From the edge of his vision Ray had seen the man duck clumsily into a doorway and so he was not surprised when the man stepped out in front of him. He was a large moon-faced man in a baggy blue suit, a nice suit, Ray would have said, and perched on his large head he had a tiny straw porkpie hat with a dark blue band. Oddly narrow shoulders and a substantial gut. He recalled Max Silver's account amused account of one of the men following him.

Okay, so that was you.

The man in the baggy suit blocked Ray's way and held up the palm of a large hand and said, "Hold on a minute."

He squinted at Ray, small eyes in a flat white face. They looked like raisins in a pie.

Ray sidestepped him and was nearly past him when he grabbed the collar of Ray's jacket. Ray looked at the man's hand and then looked him in the eye. Then he grabbed the man's tie and tugged at it, pulling the big man slightly off balance.

"Hey, take it easy on the tie, kid. I've got somebody that wants to talk to you."

"Too bad. I've got appointments. Get out of my way."

"Like I said—"

"Did you hear me? I've got places to be."

The big man stepped back, smiling. But he blinked. Just once but Ray caught it.

The other man forced the smile a little.

"You're not in my weight class, kid."

"No. But you'd be slow. And you picked a fight in the middle of the day on a busy street so I know you're stupid. Slow and stupid. I like my chances."

The big man was nodding. "A smart ass. A punk. And it looks like somebody already kicked your ass."

Ray blinked.

Four years in combat and a big slug can call me a punk?

Ray felt the sudden surge of temper, told himself to hold it in. He let go of the man's tie.

"Let me by."

A couple of passersby had noted the tension, the facial expressions. They slowed down to see if a fight was about to happen. Others stopped and soon the two men had drawn a small crowd.

"Now we've got an audience. Is that what you want?"

The big man let go of Ray's jacket. Up ahead, a man emerged from a long dark sedan, shaking his head. He managed to look both disgusted and troubled.

"No. Jerry. Let's go."

The big man turned and shrugged. The other man shook his head. He was a man of average height, well-dressed and barbered and handsome, with thinning hair. He quickly hid the hair under a gray hat. He adjusted his hat and shrugged to settle his jacket on his shoulders.

The man looked from Ray to the big man called Jerry.

"Give him a card."

The big man drew a business card from inside his suit coat and handed it to Ray.

"It's about this business, you know what I mean. Just give me a ring. We'll talk." He nodded. "It will be to your advantage."

Ray took the card without looking at it. The bystanders began to move on, but he heard one of them say, "Bernie Moore, that was Bernie Moore."

The man called Jerry took a couple of shuffling steps backward, still watching Ray, clearly still interested in pursuing the conversation. He pointed a finger at Ray and the other man barked out his name one more time. Jerry turned and went to the car, pouring himself with difficulty into the front seat. The other man looked at Ray once more and got into the back seat.

Ray looked at the card, which announced that the man he'd just seen was a United States congressman.

It was an elegant card, to suit the elegant-looking man it introduced you to, embossed on fine stock. Ray turned the card over in his hand. There was a number on the back of the card, local, a Buckingham phone number and an office on Western Avenue not far from Riverview. He looked at United States Congressman Bernard Moore's name again and said "Big deal." But he liked the card. He thought he might invest a few bucks sometime in a nice set of business cards if he ever got something to put on them.

Later when he thought the politician had stewed in his own juices for long enough, Ray made the call. Jerry answered.

"We'll pick you up by your place."

"My place? How do you know my place?"

"How do you think?"

Of course, Ray thought. *You're the guy that was tailing me on Armitage. At least one of them.*

"We'll meet somewhere else," he said.

"No, we'll pick you up and he'll talk to you in the car."

"In the car? We're going to talk in his car? Like in the pictures? Who's your boss, George Raft?"

"It's more comfortable for him."

"I'm not interested in his comfort, to tell you the truth."

"Come on, it's worth a few bucks to you and it won't take much of your time."

"I don't like to meet strange men in their cars. I get so nervous."

Jerry made an exasperated noise in the back of his throat and Ray nearly laughed.

"This is a United States Congressman. We're talking about a man of some importance."

Jerry breathed heavily into the phone, clearly undone by Ray's intransigence. Ray told himself it was probably time to stop jerking Jerry's chain.

"All right. When?"

"Seven."

"All right. And we pull up somewhere there's a crowd. Or I walk."

"For Christ's sake, this is not some hoodlum." Jerry sighed, then said, "All right."

* * *

When Ray emerged from the rooming house the long sleek car was waiting at the curb.

Jerry emerged from the front seat and held the rear door open for Ray to get in. As Ray settled himself on the leather seat, the congressman extended his hand even as he slid away from Ray.

"Bernie Moore," he said, and pumped Ray's hand with vigor. Then he clapped the other hand onto Ray's, as if they were old friends separated by the years.

"Ray Foley."

"Oh, I know who you are. You're an interesting young man. You spent most of your life

in this general area, you served in North Africa and the European Theater, bronze star, Purple Hearts, rank of sergeant when you came out. And now you're doing business of some sort with a private detective named Max Silver."

Ray looked away to hide his surprise. It was one thing to feel that you were being followed on the street, but entirely something else to know someone—someone with connections and influence—was digging into your whole life.

The congressman gave a nervous laugh.

"I know, it makes you uncomfortable for a stranger to know about your life. But it's not a big deal, Ray. Companies do this all the time when they hire a new man, they want to know who they're getting, if he's got a past, if he's carrying any baggage, you see?"

"Are you hiring me?"

The congressman tried on some coyness. "That could happen, son. You never know. A man in my position, with my, ah, plans and aspirations, can use people, especially a resourceful man. And I know you to be that, a resourceful man."

"Okay, so, since you know so much about me, what is it that you want with me? I mean, why am I here?"

"Information, for starters. I need some information."

"About?"

"A couple of things. A fellow named Willie Foy, for starters."

"You're talking to the wrong guy."

"You've been looking for him."

"So?"

"So are we." The congressman winced. "That sounded bad. I'd like to talk to him."

"What would a congressman want with a guy like Willie Foy?"

"I think you know."

Ray pretended to think for a moment and then held up one finger.

"That Morrison thing, that's it."

The congressman colored slightly, shot a quick glance at his driver.

"Why would you connect that business with me?"

"Because everybody on God's earth knows Willie pulled a job there that night, everybody's looking for him. The cops, you—yeah, I've already heard about your man here following me. And asking about a certain statue. That's it, isn't it? The statue. You want the statue. What for?"

Congressman Moore shifted in the seat again.

"I'm not in a position to explain."

From the front seat, Jerry added, "Shouldn't have to explain to this guy."

"Take it easy, Jerry. No. I have an interest in something that might have come into Mr. Foy's possession, or that he may have knowledge of. There are unusual circumstances involved as well."

Ray sat back and watched the congressman and marveled at this man's ability to construct a sentence that never actually came to a direct point. These people had a gift,. Ray could only sit and marvel.

"I'm slow, sir. Give that to me in plain English."

Congressman Moore gave him a quick look of irritation, then sighed.

"Jerry, give us a couple of smokes here."

Jerry produced two cigarettes and a silver lighter. Ray noted the quick, sure movements, the deft handling of the lighter as he flicked it and lit his boss's cigarette.

Maybe you're faster than I gave you credit for, Ray thought.

Jerry lit Ray's smoke and Ray nodded.

"Here's the thing, Ray, here it is in a nutshell. You're right, it's connected with Morrison but not with his killing, not at all, that has nothing to do with me and I have no interest in it other than curiosity about who pulled it off. And maybe it was this Foy, who knows? But the issue is that Cary Morrison had something in his possession that belonged to me. And when all the dust had settled, it wasn't in the house."

"How do you know?"

The congressman gave a little shrug, looked pleased with himself. "I am not without influence on the police department. They looked on my behalf. It wasn't there. And then I—"

Moore broke off and looked uneasy.

You and your boy went in and rooted around there yourself.

"So, let me see if I understand. You need this statue, is that it? Or is it what's inside the statue. I'm told there were papers inside, some kind of documents. Kind of a funny place to keep important papers if you ask me. Who does that?"

"Morrison had documents—" Here Congressman Moore made a little wave with one hand. "—pertaining to my business."

"And he kept these documents in the statue. I get it. But why would a guy like Morrison—who I assume was some kind of hood—have papers *'pertaining to your business'?*"

Now Bernie Moore was actually blushing. He made another of his little shrugs, tried on one explanation, then shot a quick look at Jerry, who was clearly no help at all. To buy time he tugged at one lapel to straighten it, squeezed the knot of his tie, cleared his throat.

"I'm not at liberty to discuss these things in any more detail. You understand my position, as a public servant."

Oh, I do, Ray thought.

"Sure. I get it. Some things you can't talk about. Fair enough. But I haven't seen Willie Foy. I think word's gotten around that I'm looking for him, and right now I think I'm the last guy he'd want to run into."

Bernie Moore started to speak again and Ray stopped him with an upraised hand.

"Maybe Willie Foy still has this thing but I doubt it. I think as soon as he found out he couldn't get anything for it, he tossed it. Papers and all."

"Perhaps. But the statue has never surfaced. Nor have the papers. So I have reason to believe it is still at large."

"I thought only people could be at large."

Congressman Moore gave Ray a look that said the interview was experiencing a premature death. When he spoke again, it was in what Ray presumed to be his congressional voice, normally reserved for icy debate in the House.

"I'm interested in the return of this item, or in any information on the whereabouts of Willy Foy. For which I am willing to pay, and I pay generously for proper service."

Jerry chose this moment to rouse himself.

"You should see him tip."

The congressman fought a grimace as he reached inside his coat for his billfold. He withdrew two twenty-dollar bills and handed them to Ray.

"For your time and your trouble."

Ray looked at the money for a moment.

"Forty seems like a lot. As far as I know, I'm not working for you. But—"

He reached forward and took one of the bills and held it up.

"—I'll take this just for the irritation of being tailed. Maybe now old Jerry here won't need to follow me home."

He put the bill in his shirt pocket and climbed out of the car. He nodded to the congressman and left.

* * *

Ray sat in his room and wrote down in a dime notebook all the places where Willie Foy would be known, where he might stop for a shot and a beer or to put the arm on somebody for a loan. There was, of course, Liquor Town over on Clybourn, and a place called Hal's on Sheffield down the block from the Mulligan school, and a nameless gin mill on North Avenue up the street from the brewery and several others. No one in any of the taverns had seen Willie Foy, but in two places the bartender told him he wasn't the first guy to come in looking for him. The descriptions were puzzling: one bartender described a handsome, well-dressed man in his twenties and the other spoke of a genial young guy in a flannel shirt and baseball cap, but in each case the man had used almost exactly the same words:

"I'm looking for an old friend of mine named Willie Foy."

Ray thought about this smiling young man and wondered if he had already made this man's acquaintance on a dark street.

Now he recalled his meeting with the old street hustler named Dandy, who had mentioned the Mohawk as a place where Willie Foy had flopped in the old days. Ray knew the place—more than once his mother had sent him there to find his father—as she'd sent him to so many saloons, sometimes just to locate him, sometimes to drag him home. The Mohawk was a low-ceilinged dugout of a saloon under a drug store with a huge sign for Ben Bay Cigars—the Old Man might as well have been drinking in a cave.

Ray wasn't even certain the Mohawk still existed. It was worth a try. Anything was worth a try. The Mohawk was still there, a short walk from Lincoln Park. Inside it was dark as a witch's heart, and time had stopped here. It smelled of spilled liquor and the orange cleaning compound used to clean up spills in all the world's taverns, and Artie Shaw was on the jukebox playing "Begin the Beguine," and for just a moment he expected to find the Old Man and Willie Foy at a back table, nursing a couple of beers. Ray had a short glass of beer and asked about Willie but the bartender was young and had no idea who Willie Foy might be. An old guy at the far bend in the bar gave Ray a quick look at the mention of Willie's name and then began counting his change on the bar.

Ray watched the old-timer and could read his thought: not enough money for one more beer. The old man eyed the bartender and then shot a sly look Ray's way. Ray moved down the bar with his glass.

"How's it going?"

"Pretty fair," the old man said. "Willie Foy, you mentioned."

"That's right. Old friend of my family's."

"Haven't seen him."

Ray laughed. "Thanks, that's helpful."

Now the old man tried on a shy smile. "You think I'm an old asshole."

"No."

"So—does Willie owe you money? Seems he owes everybody money."

"Not to me. I don't gamble or anything like that."

"Ah. So you know about Willie's 'business.'"

"I do. But like I said, this isn't about money."

"Thing is, you're not the only one come in here asking about Willie Foy."

"Who else?"

"A young fella like you. Well dressed, suit coat and a good hat. Very polite and well spoken. I didn't like him."

Ray smiled. "Why not?"

"His eyes. Didn't like his eyes. He had this way about him, smiling and being polite and all but looking around with these hard eyes. He looked my way and I didn't like it. He had business, this fella, and nothing else was important. And he leaned over the bar when he talked to the bartender—another guy, not this kid here today."

"Can you describe him? Well dressed, you said."

"Young, like I said—of course, everybody seems young to me, he coulda been forty. Dark hair from what I could see. Said Willie Foy was an old friend. Sounded like a load of shit to me."

"Can I stand you to a drink?"

The old man grinned. "I wouldn't say no."

Ray looked at the empty shot glass and the small beer glass beside it, caught the bartender's eye and made a circling motion over the glasses. He sat with the old man for a time and they talked about the current fortunes of the Cubs—in third place and struggling to make their way back to the World Series—and the Sox—in fifth and treading water, and then he finished his beer, left change on the bar for the bartender and got up to leave.

"One other thing I can tell you, young man. This other fella we were discussing, he had a habit I noticed. When the bartender talked to him, he bit on the inside of his lip, kinda chewing on his lip. A real—what's the word I'm looking for? Intense, that's it. A real intense kid. Not like you. Not a guy that could sit still and enjoy a nice shot and a beer."

Ray patted the old man on the shoulder and thanked him.

As Ray was leaving, the old man held up a finger.

"I just had a thought."

"First one of the day?"

The old man smiled. "About Willie Foy. He used to have a woman, you know. Somebody he was seeing. This was over on Larrabee there, above a cigar shop. Brown, her name was. Ellen or Alice. One or the other."

"All right, thanks."

As Ray left he tossed a buck on the bar and signaled the bartender to give the old man another beer.

Chapter Fifteen

he building on Larrabee had been thrown together hastily in the first days after the Chicago Fire and nobody had touched it since. It leaned slightly to the south as if following the sun or good weather. The cigar shop on the ground floor was long gone but the tin sign for Ben Bey Cigars still ran the width of the building above the shop, and the door and windows were boarded up. From a window on the second floor, a shake blew in and out with the breeze. Next to the doorway leading upstairs was a tin mailbox with the name *E. Brown* printed in pencil above it.

Ray pushed open the warped door and went up a narrow, creaking staircase the smelled of rotting wood and damp plaster. A door opened and a woman appeared suddenly at the landing, as though she'd materialized out of the air. In one had she held a cigarette and in the other a cleaver.

She was slim, with dark eyes and brown hair beginning to go gray. Ray had pictured a woman Willie Foy's age but this was a younger woman. No kid, though: you could read her life in the lines in her face and the shrewd gaze in those eyes, and Ray tried not to pay attention to the cleaver.

"Hello, Ma'am, my name is Ray Foley—"

"What do you want, coming up here?"

Ray froze in mid-step.

"I'm looking for Willie Foy."

He thought about adding more to that but decided that brevity was his best choice in the circumstances.

"For Chrissake, why would he be here? He wouldn't be here, fella. He's not welcome here," she said, and Ray saw her fingers close tightly on the handle of the cleaver. She took a sudden puff of her cigarette and Ray saw that she was uneasy. Not frightened, it would take more to scare this woman, but uncomfortable.

"I'm sorry to bother you."

She studied Ray for a moment and then said, "What do you want him for?"

"He pulled off a robbery a couple of weeks ago and I think he got two friends of mine killed."

"So what happens if you find him? You going to kill him, or what? You don't seem the type."

"I'd like to think I'm through with killing. But I'd feel a lot better if I kicked his ass for him, and maybe let the cops know where he is."

A faint trace of amusement came into her eyes. She seemed to relax.

"I just made a pot of tea. Come on in."

Ray started to step backward, feeling for the step below, and she surprised him by laughing. An odd laugh that didn't quite match her battle-hardened face, girlish, with perhaps a slight edge.

"Come on, Foley—is that what you said your name was? I won't hurt you. I'm not crazy," she added, pointedly. "A cup of tea and then you're on your way."

He followed her into her flat, which smelled of old plaster and things fried in lard—and a faint aroma that he knew from his mother, lavender.

The woman had managed to create a small island of order in the wreck of a building. It was clean, tidy, and what appeared to be three rooms were packed with an odd assortment of old furniture. On three walls he saw framed prints, all landscapes.

She brought in tea on a tray, with cookies on a small plate. She caught Ray's look.

"My mother told me no matter what happens in your life and what kind of place you find yourself living in, if a visitor comes in, invited or not, you give them something to drink."

"My Ma said that, too."

"Irish?"

"Yeah. Brown's not Irish—so that's—"

"A married name. And Brown—well, he's another story."

She punctuated this with a sniff that said Mr. Brown was unworthy of discussion.

"My name is Ellen, by the way. Have a cookie, they're fresh-made from the bakery where I work."

Ray bit into a cookie and held it up.

"They're good."

She nodded.

"So. You want to know about Willie Foy. Well, as I said, he's not welcome here. Some mistakes you make over and over again until you get wise. Willie Foy is one of my mistakes" She looked away and shook her head. "He kept coming back into my life, you see. Life is like that sometimes—people keep coming back into it, popping up long after you thought they were gone from it for good. Willie is no good, you see. He's poison because he seems harmless, not violent or cruel or anything like that. Sometimes he was cocky and had his good ideas, and other times he would talk nonsense like he thought it was Gospel. And one time he came here and he had people looking for him." She glanced at Ray. "Serious people and they weren't looking to kick his ass.

"You know, I met him when I was just a girl. Seventeen years old, and Willie Foy was a man of the world, and he had that Irish brogue and the pretty blue eyes, and he could talk a monkey out of a tree."

"I talked to him once or twice when I was a kid. That brogue seemed to go in and out."

"He lost it long ago but he puts it on when he thinks it will do him some good."

She gave Ray an odd look, her head tilted to one side.

"You talked to him when you were a kid. Where was this?"

"He knew my folks. We lived over on Evergreen, basement flat under the tracks. He was a friend of my father's. My Ma, too, I guess, although I think he wore out his welcome with her."

"Your people, what were their names?"

"My dad was James Foley. People called him Jem."

"And your mother?"

"Her name was Betty."

Ray watched her face and thought he saw the faintest hint of recognition.

"You knew my mother."

"No, just to—I knew who she was. The way you know people you've never met when you all know the same people."

She smiled, uneasy, and for a moment she seemed confused. Then she changed track.

"Willie Foy." She shook her head. "Twice I made the mistake of taking up with him." She caught the doubtful look in Ray's eyes.

"Young people look at older people and you think we always looked like this. I was young once, not bad to look at," she said.

You're not bad now, Ray thought but held his tongue.

"You should have seen Willie Foy back then. He was such a handsome boy. Jet black hair and those big blue eyes, and always grinning about something. This was before the war—the first one. I always thought of that as our war because it came along when we were young people. Kids, really. But I knew Willie before the War, he was only in the country a couple of years at that point. And we had an understanding, you might say. Then he went off to France."

She paused and took a sip of her tea, and a distant look came into her eyes. Ray wondered if she had decided she'd said enough. Then she looked at him.

"When he came back, he looked the same, no scars you could see except one across his forearm. But he wasn't the same. He was always looking past you when he talked, like he was only half listening to himself or to you, like he was only half there.

"We lived together. The first time, I told myself I was his common law wife. To make myself think it was legitimate."

She gave Ray a frank look and a small shrug.

"And each time he left. The last time, he left in the middle of the night without saying a word to me. And he went through my pocketbook and took all my money." She made a small snorting sound. "And he stole a chunk of ham from my icebox. My money and my supper. A fine piece of work is Willie Foy."

She leaned forward and fixed Ray with a look until he met her eyes.

"Willie Foy has a gift for making trouble for the people around him, serious trouble sometimes. And I'm sure sorry about your friends, but I'm not surprised. Here's the thing, though, young Mr. Foley. If you go looking for Willie Foy with blood in your eye, take care you don't let him bring that kind of trouble on you. You said you hoped you were through with all that. You were in the service," she added, pointed at the scar below his ear. "Seems that one there could have killed you. Maybe there's a reason it didn't. Don't let Willie Foy bring you down to his level. He's no good."

Ray nodded. "I won't. But I'm going to find him, I've got to do that."

Now she frowned. "Here's the other thing about Willie. He's not what he seems."

"Meaning what?"

"A lot of people never took him seriously. He seemed like just a bum, a grifter. But he's dangerous. He can use a knife. I'm pretty sure one night he killed a man with a knife. A guy jumped him over by Seward Park, and Willie knifed him. A long time ago, this was."

"I'll remember that."

When he looked at her, she seemed preoccupied. She was looking at him through a sort of squint.

"Where did you say your people lived? On Evergreen?"

"Well, my ma and I lived on Poe Street. And before that, over on Evergreen. And before that, Alaska Street, and before that—"

They both laughed at this familiar moving pattern of the Depression.

She nodded. "I lived eleven different places during the Depression. There's no shame in that. You said your mother's name was Betty?"

"Right."

"Yeah, I think I knew her for a time. We both worked at Goldblatt's up on Lincoln."

"Yeah, she worked there."

Ray smiled at this unexpected connection with his mother's early life.

"I don't think I ever knew your father."

"Jem, they called him. Jem Foley." Ray thought a moment, looked away. "Can't say I knew him either. He never had much time for me. Then one day he was gone. And maybe Willie's long gone. A friend of his told me that."

"Which friend?"

"Floyd Hennessey."

She shook her head. "God almighty. Names from a long time ago. Yeah, I suppose he might be gone. But he always came back, Ray Foley. He always had a reason."

"You?"

She snorted. "Oh, I might have been his reason once." She gave Ray a serious look. "But he had other women. There was always a woman."

Ray sipped his tea and saw that she was studying him. She nodded and then a new thought seemed to strike her. Ray waited for her to speak but she looked away and said nothing more. He set down the cup, thanked her for the tea and took another cookie. She looked at him and seemed to be making up her mind about something.

"Alice Condon."

"Who is that?"

"The poor woman Willie Foy took up with some time ago. I don't know if they're still together. She lives on Sedgewick, above a grocery store. There's a drug store on the corner. Maybe 2100 Sedgewick. Around there."

"All right. Thanks."

"Come on back sometime and let me know how you made out."

"I'll do that."

He stood up and she gave him a quick glance, an appraising glance, he would have said.

Keep your head, Foley.

As he left, he remembered the thoughtful look he'd noted when he mentioned his parents. He recalled his mother's reticence about Willie Foy, her reticence about so much in her life. And he wondered if he had another motive for finding Willie Foy.

* * *

As he walked up Clark Street he realized he was being followed. He ducked into a doorway and looked back up the street but saw nothing. A few moments later, where Lincoln Avenue met Clark Street, at the very edge of Lincoln Park, he looked across the street and saw Detective Carmody watching him. The detective beckoned him to cross. Up the street Ray could see Detective Kessel sitting in the car.

Detective Carmody turned to watch a pair of old men throwing horseshoes in the park a few yards from the street. Carmody seemed rapt by the horseshoe match. He shook his head and cackled, munched on what appeared to be a bag of peanuts and then said, "Come on and watch these two old-timers, Foley, you might learn something."

He turned and grinned at Ray.

"Sit down, son."

Ray sat down at the far end. Carmody eyed him, looking pleased with himself.

"So you like horseshoes, Detective?"

"Yeah, I like horseshoes. Used to come up here and throw a few shoes in the old days. What I really like, though, is watching guys who've mastered their thing, whatever it is. Look at these two. They look like a couple hoboes."

Ray studied the two old men and had to agree: a couple of sweaty-looking men in their fifties, in baggy shirts. One had holes in the knees of his pants.

"I've seen these two destroy a couple of young punks that were laughing at 'em. They bet these guys a sawbuck and the old guys were just hustling 'em. And the two punks refused to admit that they could be beaten by these two so they kept going double or nothing. It would have been painful to watch if it wasn't so funny."

He squinted at Ray with one eye and Ray knew there was a lesson coming.

"The true professional, Foley, is the guy you want to study."

"Like you?"

Carmody chuckled and managed to look both pleased and menacing.

"That's nice, Kid. I'll take it as a compliment."

"So how come you're here and your partner's in the car?"

Carmody watched one of the old horseshoe players toss a ringer and knock his friend's shoe off the peg.

"See that? An artist like Babe Ruth picking on a fat pitch and hitting it into the seats. Or Carl Hubbell tying a guy in knots with that screwball of his. Oh, Kessel? He's all right. His pride's hurt, that's all. And he's nursing a beaut of a shiner. Seems he got his lights put out by one Max Silver."

"He had a scrap with Silver?"

"Ah, you might call it that. We were out having a beer and we ran into Silver. My boy Kessel called Silver a name. You know, something disrespectful about his parentage, his being a Jew. And I guess Silver took what they call 'umbrage,' which is to say he was hacked off. And I guess he decked my guy."

"You guess? You weren't there?"

"Oh, bad luck, Foley—*bad ciss*, my old Irish grandma used to say, she used to wish *'bad ciss'* on people she didn't like. No, I didn't see it. I wasn't looking. I had something in my eye. The sun was in my face. I was tying my shoe. I dropped a quarter and had to pick it up. I was watching the pigeons."

"You don't like your partner much."

"You don't get to pick your partner. But you've got to look out for him, and he's got to look out for you. And if he doesn't, he's no partner."

"So Kessel called Silver a couple names and Silver put him on the deck?"

Carmody shrugged. "I don't think I was there."

Then he looked at Ray with a grimace.

"Who does that, Foley? He's a detective, a police officer, and he picks a meaningless fight with a guy that we don't have any beef with, at least so far. So Silver popped him one."

"But you didn't see it," Ray pointed out, grinning.

"Nah, I missed the whole thing. I look up and Kessel is on his ass and his eye looks like it grew a plum. That Silver, he's a tough Jew. People forget about the tough ones. Maxie Rosenbloom, Benny Leonard—best fighter I ever saw—both of 'em Jews. And you remember Barney Ross, right? Our own guy, world champion fighter from our own town. And a tough Jew."

He gave Ray a frank look.

"Yeah, a tough guy, that Silver, but I still wouldn't trust him."

"You don't trust anybody."

"Well, maybe you, Foley. Jury's still out, though. Here, have a peanut."

Ray reached into the bag and took a couple of peanuts, did the business of cracking open the shells and popping the peanuts into his mouth, and waited for Carmody's inevitable question now that Max Silver's name had come up.

"So what's your impression of this Silver?"

"I'm not sure. Are you?"

"I have my ideas. He might be a solid guy, he might not. He's got nerve, though."

"I know that. I saw him in action."

Carmody eyed him for a moment, then nodded. "Here's my interest, Foley. I've got a thing happened half a mile from the station house where I work. That's a little embarrassing by itself. But then I've got these other killings, and they're part of it. There's something happening here and I can't see the pattern so I can't see the person at, you know, the heart of it. I want to put this to bed. And I can see some of the people involved in it. You're one of them, Foley—take it easy, let me finish. And this Silver is involved in that case. I don't know why, and I don't know what he might have. There's something to this guy that he's holding back. But you know him. So tell me what you know."

"I don't know much. But I think he was already investigating Morrison at the time of the killing, that's how I read it. I don't know what his interest was. And now it seems important to him to find out who killed Morrison."

"So he doesn't make these half-assed burglars for the murder."

"No."

"And he's got some reason we don't know about for pursuing this Morrison thing."

"That's about it."

Carmody did the slow, thoughtful nod and then casually said, "What do you hear about Willie Foy?"

When Ray hesitated, Carmody looked him in the eye.

"I'm listening, Foley."

"I don't hear anything. But I hope I do."

"You're looking for him."

"I am."

"It's not your business."

"Maybe, maybe not."

"I'm telling you it's not your business. And here's something else to think about. You're not the only one nosing around in this."

"So I've got competition, huh?"

"If you want to call it that. There's other people interested in what happened to our friend Mr. Morrison. Maybe even out-of-town people. I'm giving you that one for free. You want to be careful. You want to play policeman, join the force. We could use you. New blood, that's the thing."

"I'll think about that."

"Okay, Kid." Carmody patted him on the leg. "You get anything that might even be remotely useful to me, especially about Willie Foy, you get on the horn. Bittersweet—"

"—0676, I remember."

"All right."

Carmody stood and brushed peanut detritus from his pants. He looked at the two horseshoe players for a moment.

"Artists, Foley. Artists."

Then he was gone.

Ray watched Carmody hobble over to the car and thought about his warning. *Out-of-town people.* What exactly did that mean?

* * *

He walked up Poe Street, past the place where they'd lived, and then he turned the corner and stopped a few houses away from Hannah Marcel's building. He stood for a couple of minutes on the corner and had a cigarette. When he was finished, he turned to go home and then stopped. A dark green

162

car had pulled up in front and he saw her get out. From what little he could see, the driver was well dressed, slightly older, thirties perhaps, and he was speaking to Hannah as she closed the car door. She said something, waved to him, smiled, and made her way to her door without turning around again. The well-dressed man stared after her and then drove off. Ray couldn't be sure but he thought the man was shaking his head.

She didn't ask you in, did she, Bud?

That was something, at least.

Chapter Sixteen

At nine the next morning the hall phone rang outside Ray's room and it was Max Silver.

"I'm outside. We should talk."

When Ray went out, still buttoning his shirt, Silver was leaning against the blue LaSalle, arms folded.

"Foley."

"What's on your mind?"

"Something I learned, maybe you've already heard this from Carmody. That's who I heard it from."

"So you guys are pals after all."

"We find each other useful. You might have a new problem. A complication named Harvey De Camp."

"Who's he?"

"A very bad man. He's a hired killer from Detroit, formerly in the employ of the Purples."

"The Purple Gang, huh? I thought they were gone."

"They are, he's not. And there's a good chance he's going to come looking for you."

Ray nodded. "Carmody said there was somebody new out there. He didn't tell me any names."

"You see, Foley, if Morrison had the kinds of connections we all thought he did, then it figures that his passing would be of interest to certain mobsters here and elsewhere. He was a mob banker, among other things. He seems to have had relatively few dealings with the Chicago mob, but he did business with the Purples and with gangsters in Kansas City, St. Louis, and Milwaukee. When he was killed, some of these people got nervous that maybe they now had to do business with somebody else, that their paper had been transferred to another person, they'd been compromised. In fact, inquiries were made right after Morrison was killed, but since nobody new came out of the woodwork to put the arm on these people, they seem to have let it drop. At least most of them did. Then word seems to have gotten out that somebody got hold of what Morrison had on these people. So that's apparently what De Camp is looking for."

Ray thought for a moment and Silver smiled.

"Come on, Foley. I know I've caught you before your cornflakes but you know what this is."

Now Ray grinned. "The statue!"

"Yes, it's just possible. Your statue. I'm not buying this statue business, Foley, but at least a couple of people seem to think it's the answer. Your friend the congressman and

Butch Turner, and now this hoodlum."

"So how is he a complication to me?"

"Your name has come up with enough frequency that he will have heard of you by now.

This guy is a professional. He will have been to some of the places you've gone, somebody is bound to have said, 'Yeah, a guy named Ray Foley was in here asking about all this stuff.'"

Ray bit back the impulse to say something smart.

"So what does this hard guy look like? How would I recognize him?"

Silver nodded. "That's what I want to hear. No more street-corner bravado. Okay.

De Camp is a short man, stocky, very tough. Dark hair and a pencil mustache. An elegant fellow: he's a very careful dresser. And hats: he's funny about hats. A white panama on a hot day, or a gray homburg. He was busted once and they found two guns on him, a straight-razor, and a knife strapped to his leg."

"Jesus." Ray shook his head. "I'm tired of people following me."

"You've asked a lot of questions in a lot of places. You've called attention to yourself, Foley. But listen to me, this De Camp has killed many people, including a few with his hands, and I wouldn't be comfortable with him looking for me."

A new thought struck Ray.

"How do we know he isn't?"

"Maybe he is. But as far as I know, my name hasn't come up. If it does, maybe I'll leave town for a while."

Ray looked him in the eye.

"Somehow I think it would take more than one hood from Detroit to send Max Silver packing."

Silver smiled and looked down. He frowned slightly, as though he'd just recalled something.

"Just be careful. This De Camp would not be a guy to challenge. No heroics."

"I'll keep that in mind."

"Watch your back, Foley. You've already gotten yourself stabbed once."

Ray watched Silver get into the La Salle and drive off. He thought about Silver's warning. Another man to think about, a man who used a knife. It struck him then that perhaps Silver had another motive. Perhaps it was intended to keep Ray looking over his shoulder, perhaps even to keep him off the street.

Nobody can keep me off the street, Mr. Silver.

Later in the morning he rode a streetcar north to the ballpark. The last time he'd been here, the neighborhood was jammed with fans heading into a doubleheader with the Braves. Ray had ridden the El with a half dozen of the other kids, Eddy Walsh among them, squeezing in among the thousands of men pushing their way in through the gates. The Cubs had won both games, on their way to a pennant and then a loss in the '35 Series to the Detroit Tigers. Now the Cubs were on a long West Coast road trip and the streets around the park were empty. Ray made a slow circuit around the ballpark and remembered those old days, a half dozen kids in ragged t-shirts roaming the streets endlessly.

Ray recalled a photo he'd seen overseas just before he headed home, of the great throng of people crowding into Cubs Park for the '45 Series—they'd lost that one, too, again to the Tigers. But right now you couldn't prove that a ballclub played here. It might have been a giant tomb.

On the west side of the ballpark he found what he'd come for. The railroad tracks that wound all the way through the North Side and shut down street traffic several times a day passed the ballpark, and one set of tracks ended in a siding right here a few yards away from the main gate to the park. Four boxcars stood on the siding tracks. Two were shut tight. The door to the third was slid part of the way open and two men sat in the opening, their legs dangling, and stared at the street. They were sun-browned, ragged, and unshaven, and Ray could smell them from six feet away.

Ray said, "Hello," and received the faintest of nods in response.

"I'm looking for a young guy, dark hair, name's Bennie."

One of the men looked away. The other pursed his lips and gave a slow shake of his head.

Ray looked around, feigned nonchalance, took out a smoke and lit it. For a few seconds he made a show of enjoying his smoke. He noted how they both tried to conceal their interest in the cigarette. He started to walk away, then stopped.

"Where are my manners, huh?"

He tossed the pack to one of the men and watched them light up. The older of the two, a thin man with nearly colorless blue eyes, said, "Thanks," and started to toss the smokes back.

"Keep them. So can you tell me where Bennie is?"

The other man shrugged. "Nope. He comes and goes. He's restless. Got no patience, got to be roaming around all the time. We told him to catch a freight with us, we'd show him how to get by."

"Ain't seen him lately, though," his companion said. He exhaled smoke and looked away.

Ray watched him. Something in the man's face told Ray there was more.

"Why do you think that is?"

The man gave him a frank look.

"I think he got spooked by something. Maybe you."

"No," the older man said. "It was another one." He turned to his companion. "It was that other one."

"What other one?" Ray asked.

"Fella he saw on the street. He was sitting with us and he saw somebody. It spooked him."

"Did he say why?"

"Just said he thought this fella was dead. *'He's supposed to be dead.'* All he said."

"Did you get a look at the guy?"

"Just from the back. Dressed nice. Good-looking suit, nice hat. Right after that, Bennie took off. I think he's layin' low. You know?"

"Yeah, I think I do."

"If I needed to find him, I'd look up there on Wilson Avenue. Flophouse by the elevated tracks."

"Thanks."

Ray hopped on the El and rode the train a couple of stops to Uptown. As the older man on the boxcar had said, the flop was near the tracks. Close enough that Ray could see, as soon as he came out onto the street, that Wilson Avenue was full of cops. He slipped into the doorway of a tavern. Two squad cars and a black Ford were parked in the street in front of the flophouse, and two uniformed cops were making passersby take the sidewalk on the far side of the street. Two men in suits came out of the building: Carmody and Kessel. A moment later, two morgue attendants came out carrying a stretcher. A dark-haired man lay on it, his sightless eyes looking skyward. Bennie.

Ray watched them load the body on an ambulance and then left without being seen

"He thought this fella was dead."

A man in a suit. Passeau. So Bennie had thought Passeau was dead, and he'd recognized him. And now Bennie was dead—and Ray wondered if he'd underestimated Passeau.

* * *

Night came in, hot and humid. With nothing better to do, Ray took the streetcar up to Marigold Gardens, just off Halsted not half a mile from the boxcar where he'd talked to Bennie, and watched a fight card, not because he was interested in small-time boxers but because this was something he'd done before the War. It struck him that the first time he'd come here, it had been with his father, on a summer night like this, a small, hot, crowded open-air venue. And like that earlier night, a dense blue cloud of cigar smoke hung over the ring and thousands of moths fluttered crazily over the bright ring lights. There were four preliminary bouts, most featuring young local fighters against a stable from St. Louis. Two young middleweights were the main event—mismatched as it turned out, with the local kid flattening the aging pug they'd set him up with. At some point Ray understood he was being watched. He scanned the faces around him, then the men directly across the ring from him, until he found the face he was looking for. The man made no attempt to conceal his interest in Ray, and as Ray met his gaze, he realized he had seen this man before: a tall man with unusually high cheekbones, black hair, dark eyes and prominent nose and a look that said he was not to be taken lightly. Then it came to him: Morrison's driver. They studied each other for a moment more and then the other man returned his attention to the final moments of the one-sided main event. At one point Ray saw him shake his head. He looked back at Ray, and Ray shrugged.

On the way home the driver passed Ray in a dark sedan, slowing down briefly to give him a look. Then he was gone.

Ray was a block from his room when a man approached him holding up one finger.

"Excuse me," the man began. "Do these streetcars run at night?"

"Sure."

The man shook his head. He was short and well-dressed, dark-haired, with a pencil mustache. He wore a gray homburg cocked low over his eyes that made him look like a tourist. "I've been waiting here for ten minutes."

"Yeah, they're slow sometimes."

He looked up the street and was about to point out a streetcar coming toward them when the man said, "Ray Foley, am I right?"

Ray turned to face him and suddenly understood who this was.

"What do you want?" he said, moving back a step just as the other man caught him high on the cheekbone with a punch.

Ray staggered, fell against the wall of a building, tried to right himself. The small dapper man came at him again, threw a combination. Ray ducked one punch and ran into the other. He felt a cut open above his eye. The stranger hit him again, high on the forehead. Ray shot out his left and felt it connect solidly. The man's hat fell to the ground. Ray sagged against the wall again.

The stranger nodded, said, "Not bad. I heard you had some backbone."

Ray touched the cut, looked at the blood on his fingers.

"What do you want?"

"Just information. I want to know the whereabouts of certain documents. And perhaps an object containing said documents."

"A statue?"

The man smiled. "There you go."

"I keep hearing about a statue, this statue that I've never seen. It's got nothing to do with me."

"How about Willie Foy? Do you know where I can find him?"

"He's dead."

"Not what I've heard."

"I don't care what you've heard."

The man came at him again, seemed to pause as a car went by, then grabbed Ray by the collar.

"Do you think this is some kind of game? Like we're on a playground shadow-boxing?"

Ray grabbed him by the throat and the man hit him in the face with a short, piston-like punch.

Ray squeezed the man's throat with both hands and now the smaller man grabbed him by the wrists. They were both sweating now and the other man tried to pull Ray's hands away. Then Ray felt an explosion of pain in his groin. He slid down onto the sidewalk and curled up. The stranger seemed poised to stomp on his face and then a passing cab slowed down and Ray's assailant ran off.

"Hey, guy, you all right?"

Ray pulled himself into a sitting position, nauseous from the attack.

"I'll make it."

The cabbie had stepped out of his car. Ray peered up at him and recognized him from their conversation the night of Morrison's killing.

"You sure? What did he want? Money?"

"That's it. Thanks."

Ray breathed slowly and waited a moment as the nausea subsided.

"You sure you're all right?"

"Yeah. You saved my bacon."

"Don't mention it," the cabbie said. "I'll be seeing you." He got into his cab, waved once, and drove off.

Ray stood for a moment, looking up the street and a nearby alley for his assailant.

He staggered to his rooming house and sank onto the steps. He leaned forward, elbows on his knees, and felt the blood coming down from his eye. He could still feel the effects of the dapper man's knee.

Should have seen that coming. Every kid in an alley fight knows to watch for the knee.

When he had been sitting this way for some time he heard a shoe scrape on the sidewalk. He looked up, wiping the blood from his eye.

A man stood in front of him, hovering so close that Ray knew he'd never make it to his feet before he was hit. This was a tall man, with close-cropped dark hair going gray, long arms, and big hands that hung at his side. Ray squinted and knew this face: Morrison's driver. The man peered down at him and Ray had the impression he'd been there for a while.

Jesus, what did I do to deserve all this attention?

"What did he want with you?"

"You saw?"

The tall man nodded. "Do you know that man?"

"No. But I think I know who he is. A hoodlum."

"What is his interest in you?" An odd manner of speaking, Ray thought, composed and cultured.

"What's that to you?"

"Answer my questions first. This is not a game."

"Everybody tells me that." After a moment, Ray said, "He thinks I've got something. Information, or an object that's got the information."

"Did he mention Morrison? I know you know who that is. I know who you are, Mr. Foley."

"How do you know that?"

A small smile now.

"I spend my time as you do, gathering information."

"You were following me."

"Not really. After all, we spent the evening together."

"Right. At Marigold Gardens."

"I still enjoy the fights. Not much of a card, though, was it."

"No. It was just something to do." Ray heard the rasp in his voice. His breath was still coming hard.

The tall man nodded. "It's exhausting, a beating. I fought as a young man."

Ray saw the look in the dark eyes and told himself he would not have wanted to face this man in a boxing ring or an alley.

"What do you want with me?"

"You're asking questions about something of importance to me. You're interested in Morrison's death. As I am."

Ray looked at him now with clear eyes: tall, trim, meticulous. He remembered this man with his hard eyes and high cheekbones. And on the morning of Morrison's death, he recalled seeing a man who looked very much like this one hanging back in the street, far from the crowd around the big house.

"You were his driver."

"That, among other things. He came to rely on me for many—tasks. He was my employer—"

Here the tall man seemed to fumble for words. For the first time, he did not seem composed.

"He did many things for me. Many kindnesses, though he was not known for that."

"So you know my name. What's yours?"

"Lucas Orr."

Ray nodded, held out a bloodied hand, then thought better of it. Lucas Orr drew a spotless handkerchief from his jacket pocket and handed it to him. Ray held it to his cut eye.

"This man, did he say anything of interest?"

"No, just that he wanted to know where this thing is, this statue."

Lucas Orr snorted. "The statue. He's a clown. Do they really think those papers—" He paused and Ray could see him considering the implications. "But if he's looking for things taken that night, then he doesn't know anything. Still, the people he works for may have been responsible. I'll have to ask him."

Ray shook his head, got to his feet.

"That would be a bad idea. This is a hired killer. A professional. You fool around with him and he'll—"

Lucas Orr held up his big hands.

"Do you see that man killing me?"

"He'd probably use a gun."

"*Guns*," Lucas Orr said, and sounded amused. "I have guns. In the War—my War, Mr. Foley, I fought. I was a trench runner, if you know what that was, people constantly shooting at me. And then for a time I was a rifleman of some expertise, what you would now call a sniper. I've experienced many things, Mr. Foley, and there is nothing that fellow can do to frighten me. These are street punks. This is a man who shoots people in the back of the head," Orr said with obvious distaste. "What is his name?"

"We weren't introduced, but I was told to watch out for a hood named Harvey De Camp."

Lucas Orr nodded. Ray offered him the handkerchief but Orr made a dismissive gesture.

"Okay, thanks."

"And you, Mr. Foley—do you know anything about this stupid statue?"

"No, just that people seem to want it."

"Morons, all of them."

"So you're not looking for it?"

"I'm looking for the man who killed Mr. Cary Morrison. He's still here, making a mess of his affairs. A crude fellow. I intend to find him."

"And what?"

Lucas Orr cocked an eyebrow. "What do you think? Mr. Morrison showed me kindness, I already told you that. There are certain obligations we have in life. Get that face looked after," he said. He gave Ray a long look and then walked to a gleaming blue sedan that reflected the street lights all along the length of its carefully polished exterior. A Ford Tudor Deluxe, Ray noted. Morrison had bought himself the very first post-war car out of Detroit.

Chapter Seventeen

In the morning light, Ray studied the latest damage to his face. A dark bruise was blooming on one cheekbone, and De Camp had indeed cut him at the very end of his left eyebrow, a short cut that looked worse than it was because of the clotting. He could still see the scratches from his encounters with Floyd Hennessey.

"God Almighty," he said.

He used hot water to cut away some of the dark, clotted blood over his eye and tried to convince himself that it didn't look so bad.

When he was shaved and dressed, he paused for a moment, considering his knife. He realized a blade would be useless if Harvey De Camp came after him again. Still, it was better than nothing. After all, he thought, a knife was the weapon of choice for the man who had put him in the hospital.

He stopped inside the El station on Armitage and bought a *Daily News* and a pack of gum. The vendor was a tiny old man who could barely reach over the rows of candy bars and peanuts to hand Ray his change. He was pale and as wrinkled as a raisin, but he was smiling. Ray smiled back.

Staying above water, Old Timer? Good for you.

Outside the station he nearly ran into another old man, this one trying with difficulty to pick up a nickel from the sidewalk.

"Here, pal, let me do that."

Ray bent over and picked up the nickel, then handed it to the old man. He nodded his thanks.

"You get so's you can't bend over no more," the old man said.

Ray nodded and walked away, thinking about the two old men. One was hanging on, making a living, probably right on the edge. The other one was picking up nickels from the sidewalk. He shot a look over his shoulder and saw the old man shuffling over to a trash can. For just a moment he had the odd idea that he knew this face from somewhere. He walked a few more steps, then looked back, and the old man had vanished.

He slowed down as he passed Hannah's building and stared up at her window for a moment, hoping to catch a glimpse of her, then told himself he might already have ruined his chances with this one. He started home, then a sound stopped him almost immediately, a foot scraping the sidewalk. From the edge of his vision he saw a man cross from the far side of the street, bearing down on him and moving fast. Ray spun round and saw Willie Foy. His right hand, kept low, held a long, thin knife.

Willie Foy froze, gave Ray a thunderstruck look.

"You," he said.

Well, now.

Ray took a step toward him and for a moment he thought he had him now, finally close enough to Willie Foy to grab him by his scrawny throat and squeeze. He paused, glanced at the knife. Then Willie took off. Ray gave chase, telling himself he ought to be able to catch a man Willie's age, but Willie Foy knew the alleys and gangways like a street rat, and as soon as the older man ducked between two houses, Ray knew he had lost him.

He stood there for a moment longer but knew there was no chance he'd see Willie Foy again on this night. As he headed home, he found himself wondering about the stunned look Willie had given him just before he ran.

Saturday blew in hot and muggy. The heat shimmered on the street and a hot south wind carried with it dust and grit and the rank smell of the Stockyards. At the corner, perhaps twenty yards away, an old man was picking a crumpled paper bag from the gutter. He peered into it, shook it out, then tossed it. As Ray watched, the old man shuffled over to the trash can on the corner and began rummaging through it, and now recognized him, the old man who'd had trouble picking a nickel off the sidewalk.

As though he could hear Ray's thought, the old man suddenly looked up. He stared at Ray, then burst into a smile. He nodded, tipped his ratty porkpie hat and, when Ray waved, went back to his work digging through the garbage.

Happy hunting, Pal, Ray thought.

As he walked up the street, it struck him that the little man on the corner had seemed to materialize from nowhere. He turned and saw that the old man was gone.

How'd you manage that?

* * *

Twice in the next couple of days Ray watched the flat above the grocery store for Willie Foy. The second day he gave up early and decided to head down to the lake. At North Avenue Beach he took off his shoes and socks, rolled up his pants and strode into the water. He bought a coke, sat and had a smoke, then started walking north, thinking about what he knew and what was left to learn. And then what to do with it?

A pair of nurses passed him and he thought of Hannah Marcel, and wondered if he'd used up his last chance with her.

He made his way from North Avenue to Fullerton and then along the rocks to a stretch of lakefront between Diversey and Belmont where a white building interrupted the view and he could see men standing inside a concrete circle and firing shotguns at clay pigeons. He watched for a while and then found himself a spot to sit a few yards from the gun club. He'd come down here as a boy, with Eddy and some of the others, making the day of it, roaming across miles of the lakefront until they returned home too tired to do anything. Back then, it seemed fun, shooting at these round clay targets with a shotgun. But Ray didn't think there'd ever come a time again when he'd be able to consider firing a gun a pastime or a hobby.

"I don't much care for the noise," said a voice to his left. "I'll tell you that."

Ray turned and stared.

The little old man he'd seen twice on the street was sitting three feet away. He'd managed once again to appear from nowhere.

"How long have you been there?"

"Couple minutes. You had things on your mind."

Ray frowned, looked back toward the water. Something was wrong here: the old man's facial expression was different, alert and watchful. His voice had changed as well, an odd confidence that belied the shabby clothes and battered felt hat that looked as if it had been through the war.

"Oscar Meyer built this place. Did you know that? The hot dog king. Interesting the things some men find amusing."

Ray found himself shaking his head.

"What's wrong, young Foley?"

Ray faced him. "Well, you know my name, for starters."

"I do. And I'll share mine. I'm Salvatore di Grassi."

The old man held out his hand and Ray could see no other option but to take it. A surprising hand, at that, a much bigger man's hand, and calloused. Ray looked him in the eye. Hard eyes to match the hand.

Salvatore di Grassi, Ray thought. God almighty. Sal Green. One of the old mob, a man who had survived the beer wars of the 20s, once an intimate of Capone and Frank Nitti and Paul Ricca and the others.

My life just got much more complicated.

"You're uncomfortable. I've made you uncomfortable, which was not my intent, but I thought we should talk, you know."

"So those other times, they were no coincidence. You were following me."

"Yes. And on other occasions as well."

"Why?"

"You came to my attention. Word reached me that people were interested in the Morrison killing, that you were one of them. You, the police, some kind of private detective. Other people. I just wanted to see what you were about, young man. I wanted to gauge your interest. But I think I understand you. A boy was killed, a soldier just back from overseas and he was killed, and you were at his funeral."

Ray gave the old man a long look and wondered what else he knew.

"Relax, young man. I don't know everything about you. I just needed to be reassured that your part in all this had nothing to do with me."

"Why would it?"

The old man gave him a wily smile.

"A certain—"

"—statue," Ray finished.

"That's it exactly."

"So Morrison had something on you, too. You were into him for money?"

For the first time, Sal Di Grassi looked annoyed.

"The hell you talking about, Kid? I'd never borrow money from that conceited bastard. I'd never *need* to borrow money. From him or anybody else. What do you take me for?"

Ray's gaze went unintentionally to the old man's shabby clothes. Di Grassi noticed and grinned.

"Yeah, yeah, I get it. I dress like somebody who just rode a freight into town. Well, partly this is so I could blend in while I watched you. But I got to say, these are more comfortable than my better clothes. And my associates will tell you that in my old age, I have developed eccentricities."

"And you can't bend over," Ray said, and grinned.

Di Grassi nodded and laughed. "That, too. But here's the situation, young man. You've been looking into this Morrison thing, and you've been asking about the statue. And you've attracted attention, you got a tail on you. Or two. Or twelve."

He winked.

"A congressman, one of them," Ray said.

"That asshole. The people we put in office in this country." He shook his head. "This is one reason why my people operate outside the normal sphere of things. You can't count on these crummy people we elect."

Di Grassi turned slightly to get a better look at Ray. He squinted and pointed to Ray's eye.

"Where'd you get that eye?"

"I guess you already know. He's one of yours."

"One of mine? One of mine what? Like, one of my cavalry? One of my evil henchmen?"

"Harvey de Camp."

Di Grassi made a farting sound with his mouth, said "Harvey de Camp.

Like I'd employ that guy. For one thing, he's not even Sicilian. De Camp is some kind of Dutch name. He's an outsider, is De Camp, and he's got his own reasons for being in town. And if he's not careful he's gonna get sent back to Detroit in a cardboard box." The old man snorted. "Mr. Harvey De Camp! Did he say what he wanted?"

Ray smiled. "Your famous statue."

The old man grinned and nodded. "I think all these people want the statue more than I do. I only really got interested in it because I heard you and some others were looking for it. So I thought maybe somebody had it and people wanted it. But I'm not so interested in it. You know what the statue is, right?"

"I guess it had Morrison's papers in it. His records of people who owed him money."

"That and other things. And most of it is in his own personal code, he had a high opinion of his intellect, thought nobody could figure out his secret code. Like you'd need—what do they call them? A decoder pin, like on *Captain Midnight.* Or *Little Orphan Annie!*"

Sal laughed and shook his head.

"And if somebody could make sense of Morrison's records?"

"I wouldn't be worried. I did business with him a couple of times. Lent him a certain sum one time and on another occasion I used one of his businesses as a sort of temporary investment."

Ray thought for a moment. "To hide where the money came from."

"Smart kid. Anyhow, there's nothing in any document Morrison kept that would bother me. But people looking for the statue, they might not know that. So it made me curious. But I don't worry about this congressman, or Harvey de Camp, or punks on the make, or this detective you seem to be friends with, or *Mister* Butch Turner. Or you. I don't think you want to cause me trouble."

Di Grassi smiled and tilted his head slightly, as though inviting Ray to confirm or deny the old man's speculation.

"I'm only interested in one thing. I want the guy who killed Morrison because he killed a friend of mine. More than one, if you want to know the truth."

"I understand that, Mr. Foley. And I wish you good luck with that. I've enjoyed our talk."

With that, Salvatore Di Grassi patted Ray on the shoulder and got to his feet with a grunt.

"Old age, kid. That's the thing to be afraid of."

"I think people are trying to keep me from getting there."

Di Grassi laughed. Ray looked out at the water, and when he looked back, the old man had disappeared. Ray shook his head.

How the hell does he do that?

Chapter Eighteen

On each of the next three nights Ray stood across from the Woolworth's watching to see if someone showed up to meet Sophie. The third night proved the charm. Ray was waiting in a doorway up the street when the big Woolworth's closed. He saw Sophie take off her apron and hairnet, and then watched as she used a phone booth just inside the front door. When she emerged from the store, she looked frustrated. Instead of hailing a cab, she began walking up Lincoln, toward Belmont, and Ray followed on the opposite side of the street. Half a block from the intersection, she stopped in front of a tavern. A man emerged, a tall man in a straw fedora.

Ray watched them speak for a moment, and then Sophie put her face into the man's, quivering with anger, said something quickly, then turned and walked on toward the corner.

The man watched her for a moment, then looked around to see if anyone had witnessed this scene, and Ray saw his face. Geoffrey Passeau. For a moment Passeau stood there, hands in his pockets. Then he flagged a cab and was gone.

So he's here, not dead and not far.

* * *

Two days of scouring the North side gave him nothing, and then he struck gold. A streetcar moved through the intersection, and when it passed, he was looking at Geoffrey Passeau. He was amused when Passeau paused momentarily to examine himself in a store window.

He wore a gray hat and a pale gray summer weight suit and Ray recalled what the old street guy in the boxcar had said about the well-dressed man who had spooked Bennie. Passeau tugged at his lapel, straightened his hat, then began walking east on Diversey. Ray gave him a half block start, then followed. At one point he ducked into a doorway as Passeau turned and scanned the street behind him.

Ray thought back to the night of the Morrison killing and concentrated on what he'd seen of Geoffrey Passeau. He remembered Passeau trying to shoulder his way through the crowd, through the cops blocking the doorway, calling attention to himself. He saw Passeau's face, the odd expression in the eyes, a mixture of fear, excitement, urgency. But not surprise.

Ray nodded.

That's it, he thought.

He wasn't surprised. He already knew.

Ray followed him all the way to Clark Street. Passeau stopped in front of the massive Greek façade of the Century Theater and pretended to be studying the movie posters while nervously shooting glances up the street. Ray ducked into a coffee shop across the street and took a table by the window.

"Just coffee," he told the young waitress.

A dark figure moved just inside a cigar store next to the theater. He appeared to be watching Passeau. Finally the man in the store came out—Mackal, the bodyguard. He called out to Passeau, startling him, and smiled. Passeau began speaking to him earnestly, and Ray saw Mackal take the younger man by his arm and drag him into a doorway.

They stood at the mouth of the alley, faces close, and spoke—or argued. Of the two, Passeau was more agitated, waving his arms as he spoke. For his part, Mackal puffed at a cigarette, made curt responses to whatever Passeau was saying, and appeared calm and in control. At one point he merely shook his head and smiled.

Finally, Passeau asked a question and Mackal responded by raising his eyebrows and rubbing his thumb and finger together. Passeau leaned forward, red-faced, and put a finger up to Mackal's face. The older man just put his fingers on Passeau's chest and pushed him. Passeau looked down at Mackal's hand and then slowly met the other man's eyes. Something in Mackal's face changed and he backed away. He smiled and said something, tossed his smoke to the pavement and ground it out with his heel. When he left, he had a contented look on his face.

Money, Ray told himself. They have a connection and it's money.

As Ray watched, Passeau stared after Mackal as though frozen. Then he made a long, slow nod, a man who had made a decision. Then with a final look in the other man's direction, he turned and walked away. There was an oddly preoccupied look on Passeau's face.

Ray finished his coffee and thought about the scene between Mackal and Passeau. A brief meeting about money that ended with Mackal apparently believing he'd accomplished something. But he hadn't seen Passeau's face watching him. Ray had, and he no longer had trouble envisioning the pretty boy handling a knife. When he went outside the diner, Passeau was climbing onto a streetcar.

* * *

Ray stood in front of the Morrison mansion and studied it as though it might give up some of its secrets. Though he'd heard nothing concrete, somehow the utter completeness of the destruction suggested intent. This was arson, and the notion grew in him now that this was connected with the killing, a final step. He looked around and saw no one on the street and, on an impulse, stepped over the police barrier tape and entered the building. Once inside, he was able to move a few feet to the right or the left but not much further into the building

He stepped over the broken concrete of the front stairs and turned to look once more at the wreck of Cary Morrison's house. A passing car got his attention, and he pretended to be looking for something in one of his pockets. When the car did not slow down, he took one last look at the building and moved on. A woman emerged from a house, nodded, and Ray tipped his hat.

He was crossing an alley half a block away when movement caught his eye. A few yards from the entrance, a man was peering into a trash can. As Ray watched him, the man leaned over and pushed the can away. He bent over and came up with what appeared to be a coin. He smiled to himself and stood up. For a moment he busied himself with cleaning off the coin. Then he seemed to notice Ray watching him and he gave a start. Ray recognized this prospector for urban gold as the simple kid he'd spoken to the day of the Morrison killing. He entered the alley.

The kid gave him a wary look and took a couple of awkward steps back. He looked around as though seeking an escape. Ray smiled and held up a hand.

"Wait. I just wanted to talk."

The boy continued backing away.

"We talked before," Ray said. "Remember?"

The boy narrowed his eyes and then seemed to recognize Ray.

"When they killed the rich guy in that big house. I remember. You were at Omaha Beach. That was D-Day. I was at Peleliu."

"Good memory." Ray nodded at the trash can. "Find anything good?"

The kid held up his coin.

"Found a dime."

He put it in his shirt pocket, patted the pocket.

"Got forty cent so far. Just today."

He was tanned but unshaven, slim, of medium height. His sport shirt was wrinkled, and the pocket where he kept his treasure was filthy from his constant fingering of his coins. He wore a sweat-stained Brooklyn Dodgers cap, the bill of the cap dark with his fingerprints. But the most striking thing about him was the eyes: dark, feverish, disturbed. The eyes made it hard to tell his age, and Ray decided that whether he was eighteen or twenty-eight, he was still a kid.

Then he gave Ray a sidelong look and a slow smile.

"That guy they killed that time, he was a gangster."

"No kidding."

The kid gave him a serious look. "That's what I heard. He was a gangster and the other gang killed him."

"A gangster, right here in my neighborhood."

"I watched his house. He had parties with a hundred people and a band, right inside the house there, a whole band."

The kid's eyes grew wide at this memory and Ray wondered what else he had noticed.

"Parties with a hundred people, but somebody still caught him off his guard," Ray said.

"Guys like that, they got enemies."

Ray pushed it. "I'll tell you what I heard. I heard they had help, whoever killed him. Somebody inside that house."

The kid studied Ray for a moment, his mouth open, then looked at the house again and something seemed to come to him.

"The young guy, I bet."

"What young guy?"

"The guy he was always arguing with. Young guy with nice clothes."

Passeau.

"I think I know who you mean."

"One night I seen him right out there on the street, across from the house, he was smoking a cigarette and watching the house. I was walking by, you know, and he noticed me and he gave me this look and then he pretended to be looking at a house behind him. But I seen him, he was watching that big house. Seemed funny to me 'cause I saw him with that rich guy all the time, I think he worked for him."

"I believe so."

"So why would he be standing out here watching the house? Y'see what I mean?"

"Yeah. I get it."

The kid looked at Ray.

"People been coming by to look at the place. Like it's a famous place."

"Oh, yeah? You mean besides me?"

The kid nodded. "I saw this girl walking around in there one night, a nurse. I could tell because of her uniform. Nice-looking, too."

Hannah? Ray wondered.

"All by herself," the kid said. He shook his head. "You live over here?"

"I've got a room not far away. You?"

The boy looked away, evasive.

"I got a place too."

You live in somebody's garage, Ray thought. *Or you sleep on a park bench.*

The boy smiled at Ray. Then he rolled up one sleeve and showed the long ridge of scar tissue on his arm. It began at the elbow joint and ran up toward his shoulder. Ray noted that the kid's arm was surprisingly muscular. A laborer at some point, this boy.

"That's some scar," Ray said.

"Don't hurt anymore. And I got this, too," he said, patting the bad leg. "I got a purple heart," he said with pride.

I've got a collection of them, Ray thought.

To the kid he said, "What's your name?"

"Ad."

"Ad?"

"That's short for Adrian. My name's Adrian."

"My name's Ray."

He offered his hand and the boy took it and squeezed it and pumped it up and down, grinning as though he'd never made a friend.

"All right, Ad. I'll see you around."

"You bet." He patted the coin-filled pocket again. "One day I found a ten-dollar bill. A sawbuck just layin' in the street!"

Ray nodded and walked away. He knew there were others like this young man whose war had shattered some delicate equilibrium and somehow stunted them. The boy called Adrian would stay this way all his life, childlike and simple until he died. He took a glance behind him. Adrian was probing the contents of the gutter with a stick. He seemed to find something of interest, put it in his shirt pocket and then limped off.

And he thought of what Adrian had told him, of a man who sounded like Passeau surreptitiously watching the Morrison house and later visiting its wreckage. He sounded, to Ray, like a man obsessed with Morrison.

He walked on and remembered the other thing Adrian had given him: Hannah, or someone very much like her, wandering the ruins of the Morrison mansion.

Why would she do that?

Chapter Nineteen

Max Silver's office was a second-floor walkup on Belmont between a bakery and a VFW post named for Colin Kelly, a bomber pilot killed three days after Pearl Harbor. At the top of a winding staircase that smelled of old wood and creaked beneath his feet, Ray found three offices sharing the corridor. He studied the names stenciled on the pebbled glass: *George Sauer Imports* and *Kotowski Enterprises*. The third door bore the legend *MAX SILVER INVESTIGATIVE SERVICES* in large letters.

When he pushed his way in, he found the outer office guarded by an attractive woman with red hair and delicate, arching eyebrows. She picked up the phone and said, "A client, Mr. Silver."

Silver appeared in the doorway of the inner office.

"It's okay, Audrey. Go back to 'Max.' It's not a client, this is Ray Foley."

Now she smiled, a playful smile, took in his damaged face and said, "The infamous Ray Foley," and Ray thought that, 30 or 35 or whatever she proved to be, this one was interesting.

"Infamous? Never thought of myself that way."

Silver said, "Audrey Corman, Ray Foley."

Ray tipped his hat.

Silver ushered Ray into the inner office. "Have a seat."

Ray watched Silver lower himself onto the chair with a slight wince.

"Leg still bothers you?"

"Only now and then. It's getting better. I've been walking a lot, that helps."

"I heard you've been boxing. You took a swing at that detective, Kessel."

"I guess I did. How'd you hear about that?"

"Carmody. He seemed to think it was funny."

"Detective Kessel called me a *sheeny gumshoe*. Gumshoe! Who talks like that? Somebody in a movie." Silver gave Ray a sardonic look. "And I took exception to the *'sheeny'* part."

"You're sensitive about that."

"About what names somebody calls me? Yeah. Aren't you? If somebody calls you a drunken mick bastard, do you like it?"

"No, but I don't drink much and I'm not actually a bastard."

For a moment it seemed Silver was unsure how to take this. Ray held up a hand.

"I know, I know, it's different. You're a—you're Jewish and there are names you won't be called."

"That's right. There are about a half dozen of them. Anyway, it's something I take seriously. But I'm not religious. I don't go to temple, haven't been since long before the war. Last time I went was with my mother, just to make her happy. She showed me off—*Look at my boy, look at the suit, he's got a dozen suits of clothes like this.'* And when they asked her where I'd been, she said, *'He's been away downtown on his business.'*"

Silver smiled and seemed to relax. "She didn't understand about my 'business,' so I told her it was like police work, that sometimes I helped the police with their investigations."

"Not so far from the truth."

"Close enough to satisfy her. She was just a simple old lady, my Ma."

"She's gone?"

"Yeah. While I was in the service. I got the letter right about the time we crossed into Germany. By then she'd been dead a month."

Silver pointed at Ray's face.

"You've been having adventures yourself."

"I took your advice and met Harvey De Camp."

Silver squinted. "He marked you up but you're alive so you got off easy."

"Cab driver interrupted him or I would have got worse."

"You'll have to watch yourself. He might be back."

"This time I know him. I won't let him get in the first punch."

Silver shook his head, irritated.

"Next time he won't use his fists. He's not looking for a fair fight."

"Well, I know him now. Oh, and I also made the acquaintance of a guy named Lucas Orr."

Silver brightened. "The chauffeur. Nice work."

"Actually, he found me. He sort of picked me up off the canvas after my short fight with De Camp."

Silver thought a moment and then pointed a finger at Ray. "That means he was following you."

"I don't know."

Ray lit a cigarette and looked around for an ashtray. Silver slid one across the desk, colorful and tin, bearing the legend, *WORLD'S FAIR 1933*.

"I told you before, you're drawing these people to you, Foley. De Camp and Lucas Orr. And these other people."

"Not my idea."

"It never is. You need to start watching your back. And you just out of the hospital."

Ray gave him an irritated shrug.

"How about you? Are you still following me?"

"You've involved yourself in this Morrison thing, Foley. I was involved already."

"So why is that?"

Silver shook his head, thought a moment, then looked at Ray.

"Foley, you looked me up—you've got something on your mind."

"I wanted to tell you what I have so far."

"So you've convinced yourself that we're actually on the same side."

"I guess so."

"I don't blame you for taking your time. It's good to trust people in life, but it's also good to be a little cautious."

"The world is teaching me caution. Besides, I have this feeling that this Morrison thing means more to me than to you."

"It's not the first thing I think about when I wake up in the morning."

Ray pointed to the pile of manila folders on Silver's desk.

"Are those all different jobs? Cases?"

"Like I told you, business has picked up. I might even need to hire an assistant." Silver looked off into the distance and said, "some kind of assistant. A kid, at least for legwork and things like that."

He seemed to be talking to himself.

"A lot of people need a detective, huh?"

"For the moment, anyhow. The War put people's lives on hold. For five years, things that needed resolution didn't get resolved because of the War. The guy who didn't trust his partner, well, he couldn't prove anything when the partner went off to the Pacific."

"And the guy who didn't trust his wife—"

"I don't do those. But a lot of people seem to have lost track of loved ones or friends. This gentleman—" Silver touched one of the folders. "—has lost track of his son. The boy came back from the service and a couple of weeks later he just disappeared. And one of these people is trying to find a childhood sweetheart. She's gone, nobody has seen or heard anything about her since just before the War. So, yes, I've got work."

Ray lit up a smoke and waited.

"But I'm interested in what you think you've got."

"I've seen Passeau, Morrison's right-hand man. Carmody's looking for him, too. But I've found him. And I saw him in what I think was a business meeting. He was talking to another one of Morrison's former people. Mackal, I think that was his name."

"George Mackal, Morrison's bodyguard. Some bodyguard."

"I wasn't close enough to hear anything, but I'm pretty sure it was about money. I think this Mackal was looking for money. And Passeau didn't look happy when he left."

"That's good."

"Why?"

"I think sooner or later one of them will do something stupid. So what else did your friend Carmody have to say about Passeau?"

"Not much. He let me pretty much read between the lines. He says Passeau disappeared for a while right after his boss was murdered. Seemed to think it was at least possible that Passeau himself was dead. But he's not."

"What's your best guess about Carmody?"

"I think he wants to make Passeau for the Morrison killing."

"And what do you think about that?"

After a moment's thought, Ray shook his head.

"I don't know what I think."

"Why not? He seems a little too refined to be a killer?"

Ray gave Silver a look and saw that the detective was amusing himself.

"No, I saw guys in the War who were pretty unlikely killers and they did things you wouldn't have thought they had in them. No, that's not it. It's not the Morrison thing—I think he could've done that. In fact, I like him for that one. But not the other ones. The guy who killed Barney Donlan and my two guys, he's not a guy like Passeau. Old Barney Donlan would have would have flattened this guy."

Silver nodded. "Well, sure—if the killer gave him a chance. Here's something to consider: we don't know a whole lot about Passeau. And as for his looks, remember Gene Tunney? Nobody thought he looked much like a fighter. They weren't sure until he beat Dempsey. Did Carmody have anything else for you?"

Ray smiled. "I think he likes me, but I think he's not sure he can trust me. He's got this way of looking at me—"

"That little squint with one eye?" Silver grinned. "Yeah, I know the look, he's used it on me a few times. He's not sure about me either."

"What else do you have?"

"Well, I know Morrison's houseboy was found dead in a flophouse up on Wilson."

Silver nodded but said nothing, and it struck Ray that the detective already knew.

"And I've found a couple of Morrison's maids. I've talked to both of them."

Silver raised his eyebrows in surprise but Ray pretended not to notice.

"See, I think somebody that worked for Morrison was in it."

"Actually killed him, you mean?"

"I don't know. I just think somebody in that house was in on it. They knew what was happening, at least. I think this Passeau was in on it, and maybe a girl named Sophie. This is somebody Morrison fired earlier. I think it's at least possible that Passeau killed another guy who worked for Morrison, a kid named Hatch. This would have been shortly before the Morrison killing, maybe because this Hatch knew what they were planning. I know Eddy Walsh found the one called Sophie and I know he tried to make time with her. And maybe he tried to put a little pressure on her, about what he'd figured out."

"So I was right that Walsh actually caused his own—"

"Let me finish. I talked to this Sophie about that night and it made her nervous. Ray leaned forward. "And now I know where to find Passeau. And I know that between them, Passeau and Sophie, they know what happened. I'm sure of it. They were right in the middle of it."

Silver considered all of this. "So you think it was the two of them?"

"No. I mean, I don't know. But this guy Passeau, he's—it all revolves around him."

Silver looked away, and for a few moments stared out the side window of the office. His face tightened into a squint as he considered Ray's theory. He shook his head but said nothing.

When he looked back at Ray his facial expression was interested, non-committal.

"Has either of these girls said anything that would directly implicate Passeau?"

"No. One of them, a maid named Estelle, think he's a creep. And she told me about another guy Morrison fired, named Hatch. They found him in the river, and Estelle sort of wondered out loud if Passeau was involved."

Silver looked away and just said, "Hatch, huh? Another one."

"The older one, Sophie, she's the one that I think knows the most. There's something between her and Passeau. She knows something. A lot, maybe. And look, I know the problem: we've been going at this from different angles. You've been working with the idea that somebody from Morrison's past killed him, and I was trying to track down Willie Foy and this cockamamie statue. But I now think this was Morrison's people. I think they killed him, or if it wasn't them, they knew about it, which means they know who did it."

Now Silver smiled. "You've done some good work on all this stuff, Foley—"

I know some things you don't know, friend, Ray thought.

"And I'm sure you know things no one else does yet," Silver said, and Ray wondered if he read minds. He looked away.

"So tell me, Foley. Are you going to give any of this to Carmody?"

Ray smiled. "Sure thing. But not yet. I've still got some ideas to work out."

Silver nodded and thought for a moment.

"But I think you came here for a specific reason. You had that look when you came in."

"So there's a look, huh?"

"There's a look for just about everything. You have to watch faces, watch eyes. You'll pick it up eventually. It's just a matter of experience."

Ray shrugged, slightly embarrassed. "Maybe you're right."

"Everybody has to learn. So—Passeau, Willie Foy, this statue—how does this all hang together?"

"I'm not sure yet."

"Do you think Passeau and Willie Foy know each other?"

Ray blinked. "That never really occurred to me."

"And this statue?" Silver said and shook his head. "Why a statue?"

"If it's worth money, it might be what all this is about."

Silver pursed his lips, folded his arms and leaned back. He squinted and Ray was reminded of his high school principal, who always showed his skepticism with a squint.

"Okay, you've got my attention. Tell me what you have. Or what you think you have."

"They took a statue. Willie Foy did. He went back for a statue, and there's something about it, it has some kind of value. People are looking for it."

"What people?"

"That De Camp, for one. And a Congressman named Bernie Moore, he braced me on the street the other night. I don't know how he knew me, but he did. He asked about Willie Foy, and he's been having his assistant follow me. He wants the statue, too."

"So what do you think is the big deal about this statue? Is it solid gold? Is this the Maltese Falcon?"

"It's hollow. There's something in it that these guys want. Papers."

"What do you think that might be?" Silver asked, in precisely the voice that said he knew the answer.

"I think Morrison had something on these people, and probably more than just them. And he kept it hidden in a statue." Silver said nothing for a moment.

"So what do you think?" Ray said, blowing out smoke.

"I think you're onto something, but it's not the right thing."

"Meaning what?"

"Meaning maybe there is a statue—I mean, if so many people talk about it, it has to exist. Or it did. But this situation, all of this is not about a statue. This is not about a *thing*. All these murders, they're not about a statue. This kind of violence never is, that's a creation of the pictures, old stories. This is about something else. People don't kill for a thing, Foley. Here, right here on the desk," Silver said, and nodded toward the folded up *Daily News* on the desk. "Look at your newspaper, it's full of killing. Find me one where the guy that got killed was killed because he had a diamond or a gold statue or a painting. Even where there is some 'thing' involved, the killing wasn't about the thing but the feelings of the two people over it. The thing itself was just the last straw."

He shook his head, looked out the window again and said, "No, Foley, this isn't about a statue. I don't doubt that these characters are looking for a statue or some papers that could cause them trouble, but all these deaths—" Hel looked away again and seemed to be considering something.

"Here's the thing, Foley. Remember the first one killed in all of this? The guy they found in that alley not far from Morrison's house. His name was Webb."

"Right. Carmody told me. What about him?"

"He was a private investigator from Seattle. I think he was looking for Morrison. One of many over the years. Foley, if you were a man of violence, and you wanted something from these poor bastards—"

He leaned forward and dropped his voice.

"—what would the corpses look like?"

Ray blinked. "I don't get it."

"You've got a number of men killed the same way, with a long slender blade. A couple of them died from a single thrust."

"So he knew what he was doing. So what?"

"No, that's not what I mean. He killed them fast. If he's looking for something, at least for information on its whereabouts, does he do that? There wasn't a mark on any of these guys except for knife wounds. No, he wasn't interested in questioning them or beating them into telling him anything. He just wanted them dead, all of them. And you? Did the man who stabbed you ask you about a statue? He followed these men, found them, and killed them, and that is all he wanted to do."

Ray took a long puff on his smoke and thought. "All right. I see that. It's not about the goddamn statue."

"I'm not saying the statue isn't in it, involved in it somehow. But it's not the main thing. That's storybook stuff. And there's one other thing here, Foley. Now he's following you, managed to put you in the hospital."

"We don't know it was the same guy."

"Come on, Foley, you think it was."

"But none of this has anything to do with me."

"That's not true anymore, if it ever was. You've been looking for this man, trying to figure this thing out. And now he knows."

"How? How would he know?"

"That I don't know. Do this. Retrace your steps. Somewhere along the line you talked to somebody or did something that alerted him, told him maybe you were getting close."

Silver gave him a wry smile.

"And that's the one positive thing you can take from all this: you're getting close to something."

Silver leaned back in the chair. Ray watched him for a moment and then decided to push.

"How about letting me in on something, Mr. Silver."

"Such as what?"

"I know why I'm involved in all of this. This guy killed my friends and now he's after me, so I'm in the soup whether I want to be or not. But I don't know how you figure in all this. What's your interest?"

"I already told you, I've got other things on my plate now."

"But you were interested. For a long time. I don't think you've let it go, not entirely."

Ray watched Silver wrestle with what to say, how much to tell. "You see, old cases are like old habits: they die hard. Years back, I worked a case that involved Morrison."

"Here?"

"No. In Detroit. We looked into something connected to Morrison."

"*We?*"

"I was with the Holtz Agency then. I worked for a man named Charlie Holtz."

Silver gave him a small smile.

"Charlie Holtz taught me the detective business. He taught me everything I know. Anyhow, I worked that case." Silver looked out the window. "I never finished it, never closed it out, that's all."

"Somehow I doubt it. I think there's more to it, a lot more."

Silver shook his head, forced a smile, said, "Not really."

"Now how about giving it to me straight."

"Give you what, exactly?"

"You pick. Tell me what you know about Morrison, or tell me about why this is still important to you if he's dead."

"I told you, it's not. I've got no time for—"

"Yeah, I heard all that. That's a story."

Silver gave him a frank look.

"I guess you'd say we're both interested for the same reasons. We both feel connected to it personally, maybe even feel a little guilty. Somebody—all these men—people—died because of all this, and we didn't."

Ray heard the sudden change from *men* to *people* but said nothing.

"Wouldn't you say that's why you keep at this? Because your friends—especially one friend—died and you could have been killed yourself, but you weren't. You feel bad. It's like the War, Foley. You know about that. Some of your buddies never made it back from France or Germany. But you survived all of that. I'm the same, I got back and half the guys in my unit are still buried over there. Eight of them that first day on the beach in Normandy."

"All right, so I feel bad about Eddy. And maybe I'm a little guilty about the old man's part in this, that he got these other guys killed. So what's your involvement?"

"Let me tell you a story. There was a fellow in Seattle."

"Seattle again."

"Yes, this is a young man, early days of Prohibition, he's just back from France and

down on his luck. He gets involved in the local gangs, moves east a little bit, now he's in Montana, running liquor down from Canada, he starts to make a buck here and there, pretty soon he's got a nice piece of whatever action they've got there. Then he's got a bigger piece. He moves down to Denver, and now he's got money to work with."

"This is Morrison."

"Yes and no. It's the guy we know as Morrison. I don't even know what his name was originally. I know he shows up in Denver in the twenties and he's using 'Clarke.' And maybe another name as well. He's got a wife, couple of kids, and he's prospering, not actually in the local mob but starting a pattern, of making himself useful to them, even essential. Next thing we can find out about him, he's disappeared from Denver, something happened, a raid on a liquor warehouse and a cop got killed, a partner is left holding the bag. There might have been other factors as well, but he disappears and word goes out that he's dead. But no, he's still alive and well, and he reappears a little bit later in Toronto. Now he's calling himself Morgan. Then he's in Detroit. He's still not a big shot but he's doing well for himself, kind of a middleman to various mobsters. And always careful to keep his distance, his independence. Along the way he marries again. Another family." After a moment, he added, "A wife and a kid."

Ray caught the hesitation and took a shot. "And she was your client, you and Charlie Holtz."

"No, no." Silver looked away for a moment, as though unable to meet Ray's eyes. "Our client was someone who had done business with Morrison. That case just fell through. Charlie was killed in a robbery attempt and the client pulled out."

Silver paused, gave a slight shake of his head. He seemed to be trying to decide something. Finally he looked at Ray.

"But I did have a client later, a woman who hired me to look into Morrison. Her name was Gibbs. She had—another connection to Morrison that I'd rather not go into."

"Where is she now?"

"She's long dead. This was years ago."

"What did you do for her?"

"I was hired to look into Morrison's background for her, try to piece together his wanderings and his various identities. And I did. Much of what I know about Morrison I learned while working for her."

"What happened to her, this lady?"

Max Silver picked up a letter opener, set it down, touched a pen on the desk blotter. For a moment it seemed that Ray had lost him. Then he seemed to snap out of it.

"You see, Foley, these killings aren't really because of that night. They go back further. It's nothing to do with robbery. Or with a lost statue, if you don't mind my saying so."

"But people are still looking for it."

"Clearly. But they're not killing for it. Our killer is not interested in statues. He might be the only one who's not interested in this statue."

He looked off in the distance and squinted, and Ray thought he recognized this look, this moment. He pointed a finger at Max Silver.

"You've got something. You've got a hunch."

"More like a theory."

"Well, I've got nothing so I'm all ears."

"I think Morrison was personal for this killer. I think he had no interest in Morrison's money or anything in that house, including your infamous statue."

"Personal how?"

"Personal in the way people carry around old injuries, old scores. Personal that way."

"And all these men he's killed?"

"They got in the way. They were there that night."

Ray thought of what Floyd Hennessey had told him.

"I think Willie Foy saw him."

Silver nodded.

"And the other one, the kid who was killed there."

"Yes. But Eddy never saw him. And I don't think Barney Donlan did, either."

"Doesn't matter. This man doesn't know whether they saw him or not."

"And he jumped me because he thinks I know him?"

Max Silver gave him an odd, almost amused look.

"Or because he thinks you will eventually. I think maybe you've taken him by surprise."

"Good."

"No, not necessarily. You want answers to all of it. I understand that much. It's hard to let a thing go once you've gotten involved in it. Believe me, I do understand that."

Silver looked out the window again and nodded slowly, and Ray wondered what it was about the Morrison case that still rankled Max Silver.

He looked back at Ray.

"But you need to protect yourself. You need to restrain yourself. You're personally involved in something and that could get you killed because your involvement will cloud your judgment."

"So what would you do?"

"If I were you? I'd leave it alone."

"Why? You're not leaving it alone."

"Yes, I am. I'm still interested, I'm still curious. But I'm not letting it take over my life.

I've got other business to take care of."

He indicated the papers on his desk.

"I have actual clients, paying me money. Let the cops work it out, Foley. Maybe something will come to light eventually."

Ray listened and understood the difference: *If I were you* meant sage advice for Ray. But he had no doubt the detective would be at this like a dog worrying at an old bone.

On an impulse he said, "So you have business coming in, you're set."

"How about you, Foley? Is life starting to come together for you?"

"I don't know."

Ray thought of Hannah Marcel.

I thought I had something going with a girl.

As though reading his mind, Silver said, "I saw you the other day up on Halsted talking to a nice-looking young woman. A nurse?"

"You get around, don't you? Yeah. A tough kid. Lives on her own. She went overseas. Like us. Tough little dame."

Silver winced. "*Dame*? You shouldn't call them that. Or *broads* or *tomatoes*. It's not respectful."

Ray bristled. "You teaching me manners now?"

"Just trying to help you out, kid. Women like a gentleman."

"I'll keep that in mind." After a moment, he added, "I don't know much about being a gentleman. I still feel like the guy who left town in '41."

"Part of it is class, you'll pick that up. Part of it is consideration, thinking about the other person, whether it's a woman you're interested in or just a guy you meet on the street. You do what's right in those situations. And part of it is how you think about yourself. A gentleman has confidence that he knows how to act."

Ray shook his head. "No, I don't have that yet."

"It comes with experience. Like I said, you'll pick it up—at least you will if you make the effort. And it will pay off. People take a gentleman seriously. And you want that, you want to be taken seriously."

That would be a first in my life, Ray thought. *But yeah, that's what I want.*

Ray stood and they shook hands.

"Stay out of trouble, Foley. Don't add another killing to all this."

"And I'm supposed to worry about that? After what I've seen?"

"Fair enough. Although it seems to me after what you've been through, after surviving all of that overseas, you'd try not to put yourself in harm's way."

"I want to know about this. I want to know what happened to get these guys killed. I want to know why Eddy Walsh is dead. I want to know what you know. I've got no family to worry about me, I've got nothing better to do. I have enough money to take care of myself for now." Ray smiled. "Hey, the government just told us we can have twenty bucks a week for—"

Silver nodded. "Money to help us readjust."

"And I'm not afraid of any of this. I want to find out what happened and I'm not afraid of trouble, not anymore."

"That was a nice little speech. Here's what I can do—actually, I've already told you a lot of what I know. But if I hear anything, I'll let you know."

Ray took a piece of paper from Silver's desk and wrote down his number. He shrugged.

"It's the hall phone outside my room. They'll take a message if I'm not there."

Silver took the paper from him and stuck it in the corner of his blotter.

"Watch your back, Foley."

But Ray had gone almost a block before he realized that the detective had not really told him why he was still interested in the Morrison business—or what happened to the woman.

I'm not even sure that we're on the same side.

* * *

Hannah opened the door and he tried to read the look on her face as one mood—surprised and glad to see him—was quickly replaced by discomfort.

"Hello, Ray."

"It's a nice night out. I was wondering if you'd like to go out for a walk. We could get a cup of coffee somewhere, or—"

He stopped, she was already cutting him off.

"I can't, Ray. I'm sorry."

"Oh, do you have company or something?"

Now she frowned and he understood that he'd pushed too far. As always.

"I just can't, Ray."

"Another time, maybe."

"I'll see you, Ray," she said, and was closing the door before she'd finished her sentence.

Chapter Twenty

When Ray went out for breakfast the next day, a familiar black Ford followed him up the street. At Clark Street, the Ford pulled up next to the fire hydrant and the driver climbed halfway out of the car.

"Morning, Foley." Carmody squinted at him against the sun. "Get in."

Ray opened the passenger side door and slid in.

"Isn't this where Kessel sits?"

"He's out with a bad back. That's this week's injury. Last time he had a sprained wrist. I told him, 'How're you gonna know when you're retired? You're already off all the time.'" He shook his head.

"So how's your friend the private eye?"

"You tell me, Sergeant. You've probably seen him more recently than I have."

Carmody gave him a sly look.

"More recently than yesterday—when you went to see him?"

"So we're buddies, like you and him."

Carmody blinked and looked away. Then he shrugged.

"You had breakfast yet? Come on, I've got a good place." He pulled out sharply into traffic, cutting off a cab. The cabbie leaned on his horn. Carmody laughed.

"It must be fun being a cop."

"You got to have a sense of humor about life, Foley. So Willie Foy? Found him yet?"

"No. But I know he's alive. That's something."

"I knew that much already. But you've seen him."

"On the street. He was looking at me."

"Did you chase him?"

"Yeah. Like chasing a rat in the alley."

Just past Fullerton Carmody pulled over across from a storage company decorated to look like an Egyptian temple, then led Ray into a tiny diner with a half dozen booths and perhaps ten stools at the counter. They took the back booth and Carmody waved to the hard-working man at the grill, who flipped pancakes, omelets and ham steaks with one hand, holding a cigar with the other.

"So you've got nothing for me? How about this Passeau?"

Ray thought a moment. Time to feed the bears.

"I think I saw him over on Clark Street."

Carmody was nodding, a sly smile on his face.

"Good kid. We found him, too. Yeah, he's still here. We picked him up for questioning."

"Anything?"

"Nah. We had to let him go."

Ray watched the old cop's eyes.

"But you're still watching him."

"It happens we are."

Carmody made eye-contact with the tough-looking little waitress and held up two fingers, then shifted in the chair, wincing slightly.

"What's wrong?"

Carmody shook his head. "Nah, nothing. Rheumatism. Old age. Arthritis. Gravity. Pick one of 'em."

"So why am I here? You're desperate for company at breakfast?"

"You know, Kid, you're a wise ass and somebody's gonna clip you one and hurt your feelings."

The cop flicked out a soft left hand that just grazed Ray's face, then had to lean back as the waitress set down the coffee, hard. She fixed him with The Look and all three of them understood who was in charge.

"Just fooling around, Hon," Carmody said.

"You just watch it, Buster, or I'll throw you out."

"Yes, Ma'am."

The waitress stalked away and Carmody stirred sugar into his coffee and looked chastened.

"I think she means it," Ray said.

"I know she does. Never screw around with a waitress, kid. They can poison you or have the cook come out after you with a cleaver. I've *seen* it," he said with a wide-eyed look. "Now, back to our nice conversation. I know you're still roaming around, poking your nose into this Morrison thing. Getting yourself stabbed didn't make an impression on you. So what do you know?"

"I know a cheap hood named Butch Turner thinks I know something or I have something. And a political guy, this guy tells me he represents 'a very important man, a member of the United States Congress,' and I thought, you know, how important can he be if he's got a guy like this as his leg man."

Carmody made a small flipping motion of his hand.

"Oh. You knew this already?"

"I know the good Congressman Moore has been interested in the Morrison thing from the get-go."

Ray pointed a finger at him.

"And you know he's been having me followed."

"Ah, we hear things, we see things. We're damn near omnipotent. Loosen up, kid."

"You want things from me but you don't like to share. That's about the size of it, huh?"

For a moment it seemed that Carmody had ceased to pay attention. He sipped his coffee, made a face, added more sugar, sipped again, looked around the diner. He shifted his weight in the booth, then put his hands together on the table and sniffed.

"So tell me about your, ah, arrangement with one Max Silver."

"I don't have any arrangement."

"I say different. You've talked to him—"

"I'm talking to you."

"Nah, you go to his office, that's a little more official. Seems like an arrangement to me."

"I'm trying to work him for information. And he wants whatever I find."

"I hope you'll include me in this sweet little network."

"If I ever find anything that makes sense, you'll hear about it. But—can I say something here without you taking a swing at me?"

"Go ahead."

"Eddy Walsh was my friend, he's dead and the other kid, Jimmy Seeger, and you don't have a thing. So I'll give you what I find, if I find anything. But I don't have a lot of faith that you guys are going to be able to do anything about all this."

Carmody watched his face for a moment, then made a small nod.

"Fair enough. I can't argue with you. I know how it must seem to you. But I can tell you this: we haven't given up on this Morrison thing for one minute. At least I haven't. I'm going to see this through to the end, whatever that takes. And you can bank that."

Carmody made a stiff nod, then said, "And just remember, I'm the cop, and you aren't."

The waitress came by with their food and Carmody smiled at her.

"Say, you doing anything later?"

"Knock it off, you," she said, but she was smiling as she moved away.

Carmody looked at Ray. "I like the tough little ones."

For a moment Carmody was busy cutting up his ham and buttering his toast. Then, with a mouth full of eggs, he looked at Ray.

"So do we understand each other?"

"I think so."

"Good," Carmody said. He pointed the fork at Ray for a moment but said nothing more.

* * *

Ray watched Sophie's rooming house for a while and then gave up. He was heading up Lincoln and hadn't gone more than a few paces when he noticed the three men coming after him, backlit, walking fast toward him. Ray took off, ran past the Biograph and ducked into an alley, then saw to his dismay that his path was blocked by a car moving slowly into a garage. He turned, looking for a gangway to slip into and saw that he was too late.

Butch Turner blocked the alley, flanked by two younger men. Ray shot a look over one shoulder but saw no one behind him.

"So, smart guy. Here we are again."

Butch Turner grinned. The kid on his left tried on a tough guy smile. The one on his right wasn't sure he wanted to be in on this. He would be the weak spot.

"What do you want, Butch?"

"I want your friend Willie Foy. Or you, maybe. Whichever one of you has what I want."

"And what would that be?"

"I think you know."

"I don't have time for riddles."

"I want what your friends took."

"You need a new set of silverware?"

"Don't be smart. You're looking for a fat lip. He took a certain thing from that house."

Ray shrugged and Butch looked flustered.

"A statue."

"So you're—what? An art collector now?"

"I want that statue."

"I've never seen any statue."

"You've been looking for it."

A small jolt now. Butch Turner had actually been tailing him—or figuring out where Ray had been.

"It keeps coming up in conversation. I want to know about it. Why anybody would want it. Tell me why you're interested in a statue."

"I don't have to tell you nothing. It's a thing I'm interested in."

"I haven't got it. I haven't seen Willie Foy, either. So as far as I can see, you should really be having this talk with him. Now get the hell out of my way."

Butch looked at his companions. "Oh, he's a hard case, this Foley."

It struck Ray that he could bolt, he might be able to slip by them, run back toward Lincoln, a busier street, well-lit, with street traffic and just maybe a cop car in the vicinity, but he'd had a long sleepless night, a woman had just shown him the door and there was something about Butch Turner and his two imitation hard guys that stuck in his craw. No, he wasn't running from these three small-time hoods.

"I think you need your ass kicked for you, you punk."

"Who's gonna do that, Butchie? You and Dempsey and Tunney here?"

"Get him," Butch said, and the two young ones moved toward him.

Ray moved back until he had a wall behind him. Butch's boys came at him, both of them ready to swing. Ray stepped to one side, caught one of them in the mouth and took a blow to his forehead. He threw punches at both of them and the one on the right backed away. Now he could trade with the other one. He caught the kid in the nose, ducked as the kid threw a roundhouse right and heard the kid grunt as his fist hit the brick wall behind him.

"Hurts like shit, doesn't it?"

Now Butch was coming for him and he'd have all three to fight, and this no longer seemed a good idea. From the very edge of his vision he saw a fourth figure. He was taking off his jacket and doing something else. Ray chanced a quick look and saw Max Silver. The detective had folded his sport coat and laid it carefully on a fence and was now removing his tie. Ray moved along the wall and waited to see which of his three assailants would throw the next punch. Butch Turner pawed at the air in front of Ray, and the kid on the left now caught Ray in the cheekbone.

Max Silver called out, "Hey, you, punk," and when Butch Turner turned, pasted him in the mouth with a straight right. He landed several more punches and Butch Turner stumbled backward, grabbing onto the corner of a garage to keep from going down. His lip was bloody. One of the kids saw what had happened and ran off. The other traded punches with Ray, took one over the eye that drew blood, turned and ran.

Max Silver stood a couple of feet from Butch Turner until the hoodlum moved off. Then Silver turned to Ray.

"You okay, Foley?"

"Yeah. What took you so long? What were you doing—changing into a costume?"

"That's a new jacket. And my tie—you can't fight in a tie, Foley."

"Why not?"

"Might as well hand a guy a rope and say, 'Strangle me.'" Silver peered at Ray's face. You did all right there. No new damage that I can see—just all the old stuff." He shook his head, amused. "So much old stuff. You're starting to look like an old-time pug."

"You were following me. That's how come you're here."

"Just wanted to see what you were up to, Foley. What was all that about?"

"He was asking about Willie Foy. And that statue."

Now Silver threw back his head and laughed.

"Oh, the famous statue."

"I don't know why that's funny."

"Take it easy, Foley. I've had a long week and I can use a laugh. Come on by the office and we'll talk."

"All right. And thanks. I guess it's a good thing you were tailing me."

"I wasn't really—I came out of a restaurant and there you were, walking up Lincoln. Then you turned up this street and you seemed to know where you were headed, so I decided to see if you had anything interesting going on."

Ray said nothing.

"Did you?"

"One of Morrison's maids lives up this street. I was thinking of knocking on her door, catching her off her guard."

"Not bad."

Ray shook his head. "Not sure which place is hers. I think I'll leave that for another time."

"Good. Nice place to pick a fight, by the way. This is the alley where they got Dillinger. See if you can make it home without incident."

"Very funny," Ray said, and started walking.

When he had gone a few paces, he heard Silver call out.

"What?"

"It seems to me you had a chance to run from these three punks and you decided not to. You trying to get hurt?"

"They irritated me."

Max Silver laughed again and went on his way, shaking his head.

Chapter Twenty-One

Geoffrey Passeau was coming out of a phone booth with a folded-up paper in his hand and a pen and the look of a man running out of chances. Ray followed Passeau for nearly 45 minutes, at one point seating himself in the back booth of a diner where Passeau ordered coffee and then used the corner phone to make three consecutive calls. The first two calls made him frustrated, the third call made him blanch. Ray told himself he was watching a man in trouble.

When he left the restaurant Passeau headed up Clark Street, stopping once to straighten his hat.

Still worried about how pretty he is. Ray shook his head.

As he followed Passeau, he thought of poor Bennie, then of the others, Eddy Walsh especially. It was still hard for Ray to imagine that this pretty boy was the killer, but it all fit, and when he found out where Passeau was hiding out, he'd put the arm on Sophie and get the rest of it.

At the next light, Passeau stopped, smoothed his lapels, took off his hat and fingered the brim, and something snapped in Ray. He stopped in the middle of the sidewalk just twenty yards from the other man.

Turn around. I want you to see me.

As though he'd heard Ray's thought, Geoffrey Passeau looked behind him and saw Ray. Ray smiled, nodded. He made a small gesture with finger and thumb.

You and me.

A startled look came over Passeau's face. For a moment it seemed he was frozen in place, and then he surprised Ray by darting out into traffic. He crossed the street to a burst of horns and shouted profanity, shot Ray a quick look over his shoulder, and then disappeared into the gangway between two shops.

Ray followed and was nearly hit by a streetcar. He found himself in a wide alley, and here Ray stopped and watched for movement.

Nothing.

On a hunch he crossed the alley and went through a narrow yard. When he came out onto the street, he caught a glimpse of Passeau just rounding the next corner, and Ray followed at a dead run. At the corner he stopped and peered cautiously up the street just in time to see Geoffrey Passeau crossing the street and heading north.

Ray waited, then followed Passeau to a rooming house halfway up the block. There were fine old buildings lining both sides of the street but this wasn't one of them. It was yellow brick, a five-story walk-up with a long narrow walkway running from the street to the alley. Ray could see a broken window that had been patched with a piece of cardboard. In most of the other windows he could see small fans, and on one windowsill the resident had set out a ketchup bottle.

Passeau around the back of the building. Ray gave him ten seconds and then followed. In the narrow dirt courtyard of the rooming house Ray snuck under the stairs and listened to Passeau's footsteps all the way to the top, it seemed. When Passeau slowed down, Ray moved out into the yard and looked up in time to see the other man opening a door on the fifth floor.

Rented room on the fifth floor of a walk-up that's seen better days, Ray thought. Hard times for our man Passeau.

But now Ray had him.

He crept up the back stairs, pausing several times to listen. When he reached the fifth-

floor landing, he stopped at Passeau's door and tried to decide how to play this. Something about Geoffrey Passeau had convinced him that, killer or not, Passeau was a man who lived in fear.

Best just to tear open the door and rush inside, and scare the living hell out of him.

Ray's hand had just touched the doorknob when he heard the voices. Passeau was not alone. He was arguing in an impassioned voice with another man. They seemed to be in the front of the flat so that Ray could not make out their words but he could hear their tone: Passeau was berating the other man for something, and the other speaker responded in a low monotone. Ray would have said this second speaker was calm, self-confident, and as he spoke, he seemed to evoke frustration in Passeau.

Mackal again? Ray wondered.

Ray stood, listened, told himself this was no fight for one man with a folding knife. Silently he backed down the stairs. At the foot of the staircase he stopped and listened. Then he left. On the street outside, two cars were parked—a black Ford sedan and a cab, a Yellow cab without its driver.

As he left, Ray reflected with some amusement on the fact that Geoffrey Passeau lived just a stone's throw from the Sheffield Street police station and Detective Sergeant Carmody.

You fellows ought to get together.

As he headed back to his room, he took the long way to go past Hannah's place, but there was no light on.

* * *

Ray was paging idly through the *Tribune* when a story caught his eye, an item on page four reporting the discovery of a body beneath the bridge at Division Street and the river. The deceased was identified as Harvey De Camp, a known associate of gangland figures in both Chicago and Detroit, dead from a single gunshot to the head. The story went on to say that De Camp was heavily armed, "with two handguns on his person and a third in the glove box of his automobile."

He thought of his conversation with Lucas Orr.

Three guns weren't enough, were they, Harvey?

When he crawled into bed, he told himself he'd found Passeau and now he was going to find Willie Foy.

* * *

At dusk Ray stood in a doorway, watching the building across the street, where Ellen Brown had said he might find Willie Foy's current woman, Alice Condon. This was a building in its death throes. The ground floor windows were boarded up and there were no names above the three mailboxes in the doorway. Curtains showed in the second floor windows, perhaps signs of life, but there were no lights on. He was on his second smoke when she emerged, carrying a canvas shopping bag and moving quickly. She glanced up and down the street, then shot a quick look up at her second-floor window. Ray watched her trudge up Halsted until the streetcar came, and then she was gone. But he'd seen her glance back up at her window. Someone was still there. Ray sank back into the doorway and told himself if he could wait for hours under a German bombardment in France, he could outlast the man on the second floor.

And so it was that when Willie Foy emerged from the building, Ray was ready. Willie scanned the street and headed in the direction the woman had gone. Ray hung back until Willie was a block away, then followed. Just past North Avenue, Willie Foy went into a small diner, and when he'd given his quarry time to settle in, Ray followed him.

In a moment that now seemed to Ray as inevitable as the coming of winter, he slid onto a stool next to Willie Foy. He thought his chest would burst. He felt the sudden urge to crash a blow to the side of Willie Foy's head but held back. The other man was dropping oyster crackers onto a bowl of chili, and for a moment he did not look up or acknowledge the man on his right. Up close, Willie Foy smelled of the street, woodsmoke, an unwashed body in dirty cotton. He looked darker, his skin browned by years on the road, endless days in the sun, and a gray fringe along his chin showed that he hadn't shaved in a week. He seemed smaller, thinner, and it was difficult to imagine him as dangerous. But Ray remembered the look in Willie's eye that night on Poe Street, and the many tales of Willie Foy the street fighter, Willie Foy and his knife.

A counterman came over and Ray said, "coffee."

Now Willie Foy froze with the spoon halfway to his mouth. The counterman poured Ray's coffee and stepped back warily, looking from one man to the other. Willie set the spoon down, looked straight ahead as though suddenly fascinated by the hot dogs steaming along a back counter, and Ray understood that Willie was calculating his chances.

"Don't try, Willie. I'll have you before you make the door."

Willie Foy turned slowly and stared for a moment.

"What the fuck is it you want with me? We got some beef I don't know about?"

"What do you think?"

"I got no idea. Why I'm asking."

Ray shrugged. "Eddy Walsh."

"Yeah, good kid. I heard he got killed."

"That was you."

"No, don't be goofy, I never killed that kid. I never killed—" Willie pursed his lips and shook his head slowly, and Ray wondered if he'd left the past part unfinished because it was so far from the truth.

I never killed anybody.

"He was a good kid, that Eddy. And that other boy, he was a good boy, too. Jimmy."

"And you got them both killed."

Willie stirred his chili, shaking his head, then gave Ray a frank look.

"I got no beef with you, kid."

"Then why were you following me? I saw you. I saw that look in your eye like you wanted a piece of me."

"You been following me. You been looking for me, asking about me. I was pretty steamed, I'll tell you that—you could've caused me a lot of trouble. I got people looking for me, and now you come around, like you were gonna lead them right to me."

"Lead who, Willie? Who's following you?"

"Well, cops for one, that big—"

"Carmody. Who else, Willie?"

"Well, him, and a big guy in a baggy suit—"

"He's a driver for a politician named Bernie Moore."

Willie gave him a quizzical look. "The hell does he want with me?"

"The statue."

"What statue?"

"The one you took from the Morrison house."

"For Christ's sake. That thing."

"Don't play dumb. This Bernie Moore wants it because it's got papers in it that are of interest to him. Another guy, too. Maybe you haven't made his acquaintance yet. A hoodlum from Detroit named Harvey De Camp."

Willie gaped at him, open-mouthed.

"For Chrissakes."

"Don't worry, that one's dead. But who else, Willie? Who's looking for you?"

"That guy's people, maybe. Or—"

"Or who?"

Willie mixed a few more crackers into his chili, took a spoonful, and then looked at Ray.

"You're a smart kid. I think maybe you already figured it out."

"Here's what I figured out. I think one of two things. The one is that you did all this. You killed Morrison and then you turned on all your guys. All of them."

Even as he said this, Ray considered Willie Foy, considered the likelihood that he could surprise or overpower all these dead men. And he couldn't see it.

Willie was already shaking his head. Ray stopped him with an upraised hand.

"Or two, Willie. There's a guy out there who did all this. He killed Barney, and Jimmy, and Eddy Walsh. And he's probably the one who killed Morrison. Now he wants you. Is that about the size of it?"

Willie nodded.

"Yeah. That's the one. He killed all of them. Almost got me that night."

"So tell me about that night."

"We burgled the place and everything went to Hell. It was dark and we thought the guy, that Morrison wasn't home. But he was, and there was somebody else there, too."

"What happened?"

"We broke in, took some stuff. There was a safe we couldn't open, so we took off. Then I went back, 'cause it didn't seem we'd got all that much. I went back."

"For the statue."

"Nah, for whatever I could pick up, anything. I found some cash in a drawer—and that's when I saw him, Morrison. I saw it all."

"You saw what?"

"I saw that guy Morrison go into a room and then he was backing out, and I saw why, this guy, young guy, was stabbing him. And they were in a dark room but I saw the look on both of their faces, sort of. Morrison looked kind of shocked and this guy, young guy, I could just see his eyes, he looked excited, like this was something big for him, something he'd waited for. Morrison was backing away and the other guy was stabbing him, over and over."

"You said *a young guy.*"

"From what I could see. A young guy. And nuts. It's not like I saw his face very clear but it was the way he went after Morrison, he was on him like a cat, and he made this noise, these sounds, kind of a grunt, like he was excited."

"And he saw you."

"I don't know. I guess. I got out of there fast as I could. He wasn't a big guy or anything, but you see a guy like that, you don't want no part of that. I took off."

"What did he look like?"

"Like I said, there wasn't much light in that room. Dressed in dark clothes. I got a glimpse of his face, real quick. I would have said he was just a kid. He was in shadow but I remember his eyes. Crazy eyes."

"Blond? Was he blond?"

"I couldn't say. I wish I could tell you more about that night. I'm sorry about those kids, your friends. I know you feel bad about them. About old

Barney, too." He thought for a moment. "I wonder if he got Floyd, that guy."

"No. I found Floyd down by the river. By now he's long gone."

Willie blinked and managed the beginnings of a smile.

"Good. I'm glad. I heard about those other guys." Willie gave Ray an odd look, then a look of admiration. "You found Floyd, you found me. You're pretty good."

"I've got time on my hands. So where's this statue now?"

"I hocked it. Little pawnshop over on Belmont Street. So now what? Are we square?"

Willie watched him, an oddly earnest look on his face. Ray studied him, an old man whose bones showed through his filthy clothes. A wreck of a man living on the streets whose scheme had gotten three other men killed, and Ray felt suddenly drained. Of energy, of anger, of the need to hold Willie Foy responsible.

"Yeah, I guess so."

Willie dug idly around in the chili bowl and shook his head.

"All those guys."

"Bad luck, Willie. You robbed the wrong guy on the wrong night. Just bad luck, Willie."

"Only kind I ever had."

"You've still got some. He hasn't caught you. Besides, my Ma used to say sometimes you made your own luck."

Willie stared off into space for a moment, then looked at Ray, an odd smile on his face.

"Your Ma was a good egg, kid. I knew your Ma. You know that, right?"

After a moment, Ray said, "Yeah, I knew that."

Willie looked away. "We were, you know, friends. Your old man, too."

Ray nodded.

Friends how, Willie?

He studied Willie Foy and other questions fought their way to the surface, questions unrelated to the Morrison killing, and he stopped himself.

"All these guys after you, Willie, Carmody, Butch Turner—but I think this one guy is the guy you were really worried about."

Willie nodded, looking down.

"Him, yeah. Him and you. I knew you were looking for me, boyo. I heard. The both of you were looking for me."

"Yes, well, I've got a feeling this fella's looking for me now."

Willie nodded. "I heard things."

"What things?"

"He found you one time."

"That's right. He got the better of me that time. I'm looking for a rematch."

Willie Foy gave him a wary look.

"So are we finished?"

"Yeah, we're finished." Ray took a final sip of his coffee. "All right, Willie. Watch your back. This guy is still out there."

Ray wrote down the phone number from the rooming house and handed it to Willie.

"You see him, you call me."

Ray nodded, got up and tossed a bill on the counter, pointed it out to the counterman and indicated Willie Foy's chili with a nod.

"You're a good egg, kid."

At the door he turned to see Willie Foy watching him. Willie waved. After a moment Ray nodded.

Outside the diner, Ray paused and lit a cigarette and told himself he'd solved nothing by finally running down Willie Foy. No, that wasn't true: Willie had clarified some things. Willie Foy was no killer, he was as upset about what had happened to the others as Ray was. The sudden image came to him of what Willie had seen, a man repeatedly stabbing Morrison in a bloody frenzy. He was looking for a madman. As the madman was looking for him.

He began to walk back up Halsted, thinking of what he knew and of what he needed to find out. A cab passed by, slowed down, the cabbie leaned out his window and waved, then pointed at Ray. Ray smiled in recognition, the young cabbie who'd picked him off the sidewalk just a couple of nights ago.

Third time, now, Ray thought.

He shook his head and waved the cabbie on. The cabbie hesitated, then drove on.

That night he sat at the table by his window and reflected on what he knew. He'd found Willie Foy and he thought he knew what had happened at Morrison's place, and why the killer thought he needed to kill Willie Foy and his burglars. And he understood that it was personal, what drove this faceless man to murder Morrison so savagely.

* * *

Ray was waiting outside the hospital when Hannah emerged with two other nurses. She slowed down when she saw him and for a moment he thought she might turn and walk in another direction. One of the other nurses, a short brunette, smiled at him and said something to Hannah. Hannah shrugged.

That's not a good sign, Ray thought, but the other two nurses peeled off and went on their way. Hannah walked slowly toward him. She did not smile nor did she seem hostile.

"Hello, Ray."

"Can I take you home?"

"No."

"How about a walk. We could walk over to the lagoon."

She hesitated, then shrugged.

"Tough shift, or is it me?"

"A little of both, if you want to know the truth."

Then she smiled.

They found a bench in the park facing the lagoon and made small talk about the flock of ducks a few feet out on the water. After a moment Ray ran out of things to say. Hannah was watching him, amused.

"Cat got your tongue?"

"I'm all out of things to say about ducks."

"Gotten yourself stabbed lately?"

"No. But not for lack of trying."

She tried to hide her amusement, then squinted.

"Is that a bruise around your eye?"

"Yeah, but not from a fight."

After a moment, he blurted out, "I was wondering if I could see you again."

"I don't know. I think you're trouble, Ray Foley. I think you look for it."

"I don't think that's true. It just seems to—"

"To follow you around? I think you make it easy. I think all guys who have seen combat have trouble adjusting to peacetime. The taverns are full of them. But I think maybe you got a little too fond of the action, Ray. I don't know if you go looking for trouble, but I think you want it. You want—adventures."

He stared at the water and realized that she was probably right.

"That cop, Carmody. He thinks I should become a cop."

"Maybe you should. But you'd probably just be reckless. So maybe that's not the best thing for you."

Before he could answer, a Good Humor man walked by, pushing his cart, and Ray flagged him down.

He bought two ice cream bars and handed Hannah one. They ate in silence and gradually he relaxed. It struck him that this was the first moment in some time that he had felt at peace. So this was all he needed? A girl and an ice cream bar.

Maybe.

"Maybe what?"

"I didn't realize I said anything. I was thinking maybe you're right."

"Well, that's a start."

To the east a gray mass was bringing a storm in, and Ray saw in the distance a faint flash of lightning.

"I think we might get rained on," he said.

"You're not done with all this stuff yet, are you?" she asked, as though he had not spoken.

"I don't really know."

She nodded and ate the last of her ice cream.

"That tells me you're not done."

"I'd like to see it through."

She got to her feet.

"You're not the Army anymore, you're not the Chicago Police. Thanks for the ice cream, Ray."

As he watched her walk away, he told himself he'd just done something stupid.

No, he thought. *What I've been doing, that's what's probably stupid, she's right. But I can't stop, not yet. I'm almost done, I'm almost there.*

* * *

"With your looks," the girl called Nancy had said, "you ought to be beating them off with sticks. Don't you like guys?"

Hannah had laughed it off but it was true that most of these other nurses now had boyfriends. Two were engaged, and Hannah was no longer certain she ever would be. She was several years older than most of the other nurses she worked with, several years older and far more experienced. None of them had ever been married, had ever been abused by a drunken husband — although Hannah suspected at least one of them was already getting batted around by her fiancé. And none of these girls had seen the War.

As for men, she had her chances, always. The persistent young doctor had taken her out for drinks, a handsome, confident man with small features, delicate hands, and the profoundly held conviction that all that was lacking in his life was a woman to have his children and run his house.

"That sounds like a servant," she'd said, and he'd given her a puzzled look.

The young cop had taken her out for a drink but had little to say, and she shut the door on that one.

Hannah stood for a moment in the center of her tiny flat and looked around her. It wasn't much, she would have admitted that, but it was hers, it was a start. As long as she had her own place she had a center, she was beholden to no one, needed help from no one. She had her independence, underwritten by this small flat. She looked at her sofa and remembered sitting there nestled against Ray Foley.

Was there a place for Ray here? Or in her life? Of that, she was unsure.

Charm was one thing, and she enjoyed his company on several levels, but there was something else that Ray brought with him, and that was a sort of dark aura, the faint scent of menace. It was not that she feared Ray or even entertained the possibility that he might do her harm, no, it was more that he carried with him that aura of trouble, like a man who has just walked through smoke.

She thought about their last evening together, saw the look change in his eyes as he turned the conversation to Morrison, the killing of his friend.

No, Ray was trouble, he sought it out, and men like that brought their trouble to those around them. She had come close to inviting him into her bed. Another complication that she'd dodged.

Too bad, she thought, and went to the stove to make herself some tea.

Chapter Twenty-Two

Whaen Ray went out to get some breakfast the next morning he saw flags hanging from the windows of several houses.

"Oh, for Christ's sake," he said aloud.

The papers had prepared him for this but it seemed to Ray that holidays were not part of his life, not real. In Ray's life, it was Thursday. To the rest of the Big Town, it was the 4th of July. In his time back, there had been moments when he felt as though he were standing on the wrong side of a wall of glass watching life happen. Here was another of those moments.

People with actual lives, he told himself, *celebrate holidays.*

Hot and sunny, and a sudden gust from the south nearly took off his hat. He wandered, killed time, bought a paper, thought of Hannah Marcel and told himself he'd ruined that.

And now he recalled his conversation with the street kid named Adrian: he'd seen a nurse wandering around the ruins of Morrison's house.

I wonder why.

Something to ask her, perhaps. A pretext to call on her again. He took off his hat and wiped the sweat from his forehead, then began walking toward the lake. At Belmont Harbor, not far from where he'd met Sal Di Grassi, Ray stopped to look at the boats at anchor. In the faint breeze he heard the metallic sound of the clips and brackets of the rigging as the ropes hit the metal masts. It made an odd, gentle tinkling noise.

Rich guys' toys, Ray thought.

At the far end of one row of yachts, motorboats, and sailboats, one stood out, more ship than boat, a huge black yacht with enormous masts, something out of an old story, and Ray wondered if a man would sail around the world in such a yacht.

He made his way past the flat white structure of the yacht club and continued to the rocks near the gun club. Someone was shooting, badly: he watched the black clay pigeons shoot out into the air, heard the report of the shotgun, and saw the clay pigeons fall unharmed into the lake.

Just west of the shooting range he passed a field where several dozen picnickers had gotten up a ballgame, an incompetent affair accompanied by hoots and hollers, women on the sidelines ridiculing the players, the players laughing at each other and themselves. Ray tried to remember the last time he'd stood on grass with a mitt and chased down a fly ball. He watched the game and the picnickers, the girls in summer dresses, and felt as though he were watching life at a distances.

At the far end of the field, another man intently watched the game. The man managed by his body language and his distance from any of the other people to demonstrate that he was not a part of this raucous gathering. He was in shirtsleeves and a light brown hat, a tanned, fit-looking man.

Max Silver.

Ray waited and when Silver began walking away, Ray followed. The detective made his way to the rocks along the lakefront, and when he found himself a spot between two groups of sunbathers, Silver sat down.

A moment later, Ray sat down beside him

"Foley."

For once Max Silver looked surprised.

"What brings you down here?"

"The water. Watching the people. Girls on beach towels. How about you?"

"I come down here sometimes to look at the boats in the harbor. On my good days it makes me want to buy one and take it around the world."

"And on your bad ones?"

"On my bad days, it reminds me of Normandy, I remember lying there on the beach and looking out at the fleet, those thousands of ships and landing craft, and wondering if I was going to live through the day."

Ray nodded but said nothing.

Silver squinted in the sun, studying Ray.

"I'll tell you what I think. I think you've let this thing, this Morrison business, take over your life. You have to make room in your life, let other things in."

"Like you?"

"Right, I'm no one to talk. But I'm right about this."

"Actually, I think you are. I think I want my life simplified. I want—"

"You want to see this finished. So do I."

"Yeah. It seems like it gets into every part of my life. You know, the last time I was here, I had company then, too. An old man named Salvatore Di Grassi."

"Sal Di Grassi?" Silver gave him a startled look. "Sal the Thinker. He spoke to you?"

"Yeah. Trying to find out who I was, I guess, and what I was doing asking around about Morrison." Ray turned to Silver with a smile. "And the famous statue."

Silver laughed, then shook his head.

"It's got nothing to do with those people, Foley."

"I know. I think I convinced him I wasn't interested in him or the statue. I think he was just curious. You know, he let me see him a couple of times, dressed like he was down on his luck."

"Like an old street guy, or a hobo, right? He's gone eccentric in his dotage."

"His what? Oh, his old age."

"Yes. Which doesn't mean he's not dangerous if he thought you could cause him trouble."

Silver watched the water lap against the rocks.

"So you're just walking?"

"Well, that, and watching the people. And thinking about a girl, actually."

"Let me know if that works for you," Silver said with a wry smile.

Ray looked at him. "How about you?"

"I've been coming down here since I was a boy. I lived in a rundown building on a street full of them. Ruble Street. Over by Maxwell Street, this was. What you probably know as Jewtown."

"I know it. My Ma took me down there for shoes and clothes. She always bought me a hot dog. The whole place smelled like onions. You grew up there?"

"I did. A whole neighborhood full of Jews. Benny Goodman was from my neighborhood. And Barney Ross, of course."

"Ever meet either of them?"

"I knew Benny to say hello to. And I fought Barney Ross. In the amateurs, this was."

"Really? How'd you do?" Ray asked, grinning.

Silver gave him a wry look.

"How do you think I did? He killed me."

Ray laughed. "It's something to tell people, at least."

Silver shrugged. "Anyway, this is where I came, back then, down to the lake, and then I'd walk north all the way up here to Belmont Harbor to put distance between me and that crowded place full of noise and smells and bodies. And don't get me wrong, I love that place. I still go up there on Sundays when the market is on. Saturdays sometimes, too. But this is where I come to clear my head, Foley."

"I can understand that."

They both lit cigarettes then, just to be doing something in the silence. They smoked and Ray watched a small sailboat perhaps a mile out. He tried to picture the dapper Max Silver as a poor kid from Jewtown. He shot a quick glance at Silver. The detective tapped ash from his smoke and stared at the cigarette, for once looking vulnerable. Ray turned to face the water and understood that this was his moment.

"So tell me about the lady."

"What lady?"

"The one you—the one that meant something to you back then. In Detroit. While you were trying to piece Morrison's story together."

"I never said she was in Detroit."

"But I think she was. I think she was the client you told me about."

For a moment Silver said nothing. He took a couple more puffs on his cigarette and then flicked it with his index finger out over the rocks and into the water. He patted his straw hat down in the growing breeze, and Ray was about to apologize when he spoke.

"Her name was Lorraine, and she was tall and a little on the thin side. Slender, I'd prefer to call her. She had dark hair and gray eyes, beautiful gray eyes. I've never seen anything like them. Not necessarily a woman who would draw attention walking down the street, but if you saw her up close, saw those eyes, you'd remember her. An elegant looking lady. She hired me."

Silver met Ray's eyes, nodded.

"Yeah. I got involved with my—with the client. Which then made the thing personal, which is always a mistake, always unprofessional. She hired me. She was the half-sister of a woman Morrison had left behind all those years ago out west. The sister was long dead but Lorraine wanted to track this man down, call him to account for what he'd done. And I also think she was trying to put together a picture for herself of what her sister's life was like."

He gave Ray a sudden look.

"I'll tell you something, Foley. You can't just leave one life and start another. You leave traces whether you know it or not. People try all the time but the past has a long reach. Anyhow. She hired me to find out things about Morrison. And we got—" Silver looked away, searched for the word, then said, "—involved. I lost focus. And in the middle of it I lost her as well. She was hit by a car. Killed instantly. She died in a town halfway across the continent from where she lived her whole life."

Ray waited for Silver to get this story back on track and then it hit him.

"You think it was Morrison."

Silver pursed his lips as though considering this for the first time.

"There's not a single piece of evidence that it was him. No reason at all to suspect it was anything but some drunk who got behind the wheel and killed a stranger. Happens all the time. But, yes, I think it was Morrison. Or somebody that he had do it."

For a moment Ray thought Silver was holding something back. He watched him and then said, "But Morrison's dead. If it was him, you can go out and get drunk and say 'thank you' to whoever killed him."

"No. It's like a story, Foley. All of this is part of the same story." He gave Ray a frank look. "You wanted to know about Opal Raines. She was his wife, first wife, that is. Now she's dead, too."

"His wife," Ray said, nodding slowly as he processed this latest information.

"One of several, Foley. He left a trail of broken lives in his wake and people are still dying because of him. It's not finished. So, come on, how likely is it that I'd just drop it all because Morrison is dead? I want to know what happened. And it seems to me the person—or persons—who killed Morrison—maybe they know something about it all. They're still out there. I'd just like to know for sure."

"So this is personal, too. You're doing the same thing. All over again." Silver turned and smiled.

"I never told you this, but one night, right after the Morrison killing, a guy followed me for about two blocks. He was good enough to stay in the shadows so I couldn't get a good look at him, but I knew he was there. So I kept walking and then I stopped and I caught him in mid-stride. I couldn't tell you much about him except that he was not tall, he wore dark clothes, and there was something agile and athletic about his movements. And I spread my feet and reached inside my coat and kept my hand there. And he froze. He couldn't tell whether I had a gun, so I helped him, I started walking toward him, fast, and he took off. But I think that was our man, our killer. So, yes, Foley, I've made it personal. I think I've got a couple of reasons."

"Not very professional."

"No, I guess not."

"See, I'm trying to learn how a detective operates."

"This isn't it."

Ray laughed and after a moment, Silver joined him. He patted Ray on the back.

"Enjoy your afternoon here, Foley. I'm moving on."

Ray watched Silver move off. He waited for a ten-count and then called out his question.

"You were never going to tell me, were you?"

Silver stopped and turned, slowly. "Tell you what?"

"About you and Morrison. You knew him. I know you were in his house."

Silver put both hands in his pants pockets and looked down at the ground. Then he nodded. He walked back toward Ray.

"The maids, one of the maids told you." He squinted at Ray. "You're getting pretty good at this."

"Maybe. So—do you want to tell me about that?"

Max Silver scratched the back of his head, patted the fedora back into place, shot a glance out at the water, and Ray realized with satisfaction that he'd caught the detective completely by surprised, perhaps even embarrassed him.

Finally Silver faced him. "Twice. I was there twice, Foley. The second time he wouldn't see me. That nervous little houseboy told me he was out. The first time, though, I got in to see him. I used a name from his past and his curiosity got the better of him. But it was pointless, Foley, a bonehead play, the result of impatience and impulsiveness." He pointed a finger in Ray's face. "Those are things that can ruin a case or get you killed. Anyhow, I threw indiscriminate questions at him, had the pleasure of seeing him squirm. I made up a case but I made it clear who my real quarry was. By the time I left, I'd made an enemy."

"Sounds like it was worth it."

"It would sound like that to you. Like I said, it was a pleasure to see him squirm. But I gained nothing by it, and I might even have put myself in harm's way. Without doing a single thing for my case. I'll see you around, Foley."

Ray watched the sailboats far out on the lake and admitted to himself that Max Silver had just made him feel sheepish. Still, he would have bet his last dollar that the detective still had cards he wasn't showing.

Then Ray smiled as the truth manifested itself. All along he'd told himself he was in a fight, against whoever had killed all these men, against people putting roadblocks in his way, and now Ray saw that all along he had been in another sort of fight, a competition, certainly. That was against Max

Silver, to answer all these many questions, find a killer. And it seemed to Ray that he had an edge, no matter how many hole cards Max Silver might have. For Ray had been there the morning they'd found Morrison, he'd seen them all, and he knew where all the players were.

I've got the edge, Mr. Silver.

* * *

Max Silver headed back toward the distant parking lot where he'd left his car, and now that his fencing with young Foley was finished, he felt the heat for the first time that day. He had been walking along the lakefront for hours, and his shirt stuck to his back like a wet hand. He thought about Ray Foley, the implacable Ray Foley. The surprising Ray Foley—the kid was smart and resourceful, impossible to stop. And, Max Silver had to admit, capable of tossing the occasional curve, an unpredictable young man.

What else do you know, kid?

His conversation with Foley brought things back to him. For a while as he walked, he recalled the old neighborhood off Maxwell Street, his block—as he'd told Foley, an entire street full of Jews. For a time, in childhood, he thought that this was the way of the world, Jews everywhere, a world full of Jews. Then they'd moved, and his new environs, his new school, had shown him the error of his thinking. School was where the young Max Silver had learned to fight. Learned perseverance as well, single-mindedness, and finally, hardest of all lessons, learned to control and channel his anger.

The visit to Morrison's house had been a rare exception, an aberration in the life of Max Silver, for it had been as he'd characterized it to Foley, a bonehead play, driven by his anger and a need for confrontation. And as he'd also admitted, a brief moment of satisfaction. He'd caught Morrison off his guard, entered his private fortress, forced him into a face-to-face meeting with a stranger whose ominous affect was magnified by the fact that Morrison had no idea who he was.

In fact, he'd frightened Morrison, and when he understood that simple fact, Max Silver had used the kinds of tricks he'd picked up over the years of his work on the street: facial expression, eye contact, a stiff and insincere smile, body language—he'd leaned forward into the small space between their chairs, imperceptibly but steadily, until his face was just a couple of feet from Morrison's, until he could smell the man's cologne, a dandy in a smoking jacket. Silver had almost laughed at the smoking jacket.

He'd gained entry to Morrison's home with a lie, and the lie had added to Morrison's confusion.

"You're working for someone named Opal Raines?" Morrison pursed his lips, shook his head, was about to deny knowledge, and then Silver had interrupted him.

"No, no, sir, there's some misunderstanding here. I'm not working for her, I'm looking for her."

Morrison blinked, fished a cigarette out of an enameled case, closed it, remembered too late to show his manners. He held out the case, his hand trembling slightly.

Silver shook his head.

"I don't know any Opal Raines. Why have you—"

"My information is that you know—or you knew Opal Raines."

"Who told you that?"

An innocent look. "Several people, sir. It seems to be common knowledge."

"You're mistaken. I've never heard of any Opal Raines. You have wasted your time."

"Well, I'm sorry to have wasted yours."

At that point Morrison had called in his driver, an imposing man, tall, dark-eyed, utterly self-assured.

"Lucas, have the car ready. The Bentley. I wish to go out."

Max Silver had no doubt Morrison had called in the impressive driver merely to show him that he was admirably protected.

He'd gotten to his feet, tossed a business card on a small side table. The driver showed him out. At the door, Silver had touched the brim of his hat, wished them both a fine day, and gone on his way.

Max Silver remembered coming down the stairs of Morrison's house, his chest near to bursting with excitement, no, more than that, something like exultation.

There had been a moment in that curt, hostile interview when Silver knew he could have had both hands on Morrison's throat before the driver or anyone else could get to him. And a quick look in Morrison's cat's eyes had told him that Morrison knew this as well.

A fine moment, pointless, adolescent, but just to see the flash of fear across Morrison's face had been worth it.

Chapter Twenty-Three

Ray took a long way home, bought hot dogs from a bushy-haired man with a pushcart just outside the Zoo and ate on a bench. In the distance, he could hear the first firecrackers, small ones that suggested small kids having fun in an alley. He didn't mind those, he minded the big ones that sounded more like explosives and brought to mind the real thing, beachheads in Sicily and Normandy.

Up ahead of him on Fullerton, a familiar figure rooted around in a trash can on the corner, oblivious to the looks from passersby.

Ray watched him dig, saw him open a bag and sniff at the insides. Adrian tossed the bag and then picked up what appeared to be a half sandwich in waxed paper.

"Be careful with that stuff, Adrian."

The kid turned quickly and gave Ray a startled look, then smiled when he recognized him.

"Aw, I wouldn't eat that. I'm just looking at stuff. You know, people throw out—"

"I know. All kinds of good stuff."

Adrian nodded.

"Listen. I'm glad I ran into you. I need some information. It's worth a couple of bucks to me."

Adrian let the sandwich drop back into the trashcan.

"What kinda information?"

"Over there by the Morrison place—where you and I talked before. Ever see anybody over there behaving, you know, strange? Maybe the young guy we talked about, the one with the nice clothes. Or anybody else hanging around there. In that little park, maybe."

Adrian gave him a distressed look.

"I don't go there no more. I don't like it over there."

Adrian looked away, and Ray saw that there was more to this.

"Why not? Something happened?"

"There was this guy. He was following me. He came out of the little playground and give me a look. I just started walking, you know. And I look over my shoulder and he's still there. And one more time I look over my shoulder and he's gaining on me. So I took off. I ran. I'm pretty fast."

"Did you get a good look at him?"

"No. It was getting dark. He was my size, and he was pretty fast, too. I got outta there, Mr. Foley."

"Ray. Call me 'Ray.' Is that the only time you ever saw him?"

"I don't know. There was one other time it coulda been him. Walking around in that burned-out house."

"Here. Buy yourself a hamburger," Ray said, and gave Adrian the two dollars. Then he handed him a slip of paper with his phone number. "Call me at this number if you see that guy again."

"I won't see him. I'm not going there no more." He shook his head. "Nobody should go there. That's a bad place."

"Well, just give me a ring if you see him anywhere."

Adrian thought about this, nodded, then stuck the number and the two bucks in his shirt pocket.

"All right."

"Take it easy, Adrian."

Adrian nodded and walked away. As Ray watched, Adrian took the two dollars out as if to assure himself that it was still there, then tucked the money back in his pocket.

The small fan on the dresser blew the hot air around the room and the night breeze barely moved the thin curtains. In the distance he could hear the last die-hards setting off fireworks, and somewhere a siren cut through the night. Earlier he had spent a few minutes on a darkened side street watching the big fireworks display from Riverview. Hot, bored, restless, he went to the window and looked out onto the street.

It seemed to him that there was nothing so maddening as a hot night in a small airless room, when you knew there was a woman just a short walk away.

He poured himself a glass of water and told himself to think. He tried to fit what Max Silver had told him into what he already knew, cautioned himself that the death of a woman in Detroit might have nothing at all to do with Morrison. He got up and turned the fan so that it blew the warm air directly on him.

So what do I have?

Sophie and Passeau.

Ray wondered about that. Maybe it was too easy. He thought of the second voice in Passeau's room. Yeah, one more player, that was what this was about. One more player. Time to give it one more push and see what shook loose. He went out and headed for Passeau's place, emerging onto the street just in time to see a Checker cab moving off.

* * *

He returned to Passeau's rooming house and made his quiet way up the back stairs. For a moment, he stood outside the door and listened. Once again he heard voices, an argument, rapid fire back-and-forth, and then Ray understood he was listening to a radio broadcast, some sort of drama. He waited a moment longer, told himself he had no clear idea what he'd say to Passeau. He thought of the look he'd seen in Passeau's eyes when they'd seen each other and decided this was not a man who sought out confrontation.

I'll have an advantage, he thought. Maybe enough to make him sweat.

All right.

He knocked on the door. When there was no response, he knocked again. Nothing. He could still hear the radio and wondered if Passeau was somewhere in the room where the radio drowned out sound.

"Mr. Passeau?" he called out. "Geoffrey Passeau?"

238

After a couple of seconds, he turned the knob and the door opened. He stuck his head in.

"Geoffrey Passeau? My name is Ray Foley, and I think we should talk. I'm not here to cause you trouble."

Well, that part is a lie.

He stepped into the room, which proved to be a tiny suite, a bedroom with a small sitting room. There was a hotplate on a countertop with a small tin coffee pot on it. The coffee had boiled over and burned on the hotplate, but the overwhelming odor in the room was the smell of blood. And blood there was, a spray pattern across the table in the center of the room, blood spray along the wall, blood on the worn rug near the window. Passeau himself lay as he had fallen, sideways across a chair facing the window that overlooked Halsted, and he was dead. One arm hung down nearly to the floor where it had dripped blood from several gashes across the forearm and hand, for Mr. Geoffrey Passeau had died fighting. His throat was torn from one side to the other, a fatal wound in any case, but Ray peered at him and found the solitary wound he knew would be there, the single clean puncture into the heart by a master who'd done this now five times.

"Shit."

Passeau's chin rested on his chest and the odd green eyes stared off at the roof tops across the street.

Ray looked back the way he had come. There was no damage to the door, no sign of a struggle in the entryway to the small apartment: Passeau had let his killer in.

I don't understand, he told himself. Sophie, he thought, then discarded the notion. He looked around the room at the blood, the stark violence of the scene: no woman did this. A new idea struck him, a man driving by slowly, in a Checker cab.

For a moment he wondered what to do next. He leaned for a moment on the small radiator along the wall. Then he used the hall phone to call Carmody.

* * *

Carmody's face was blood red, the anger came off him in waves of heat. Ray wondered if he would explode.

"Tell me this. Tell me how it is that you show up at this guy's room. You're the one finds him dead and I told you, I told you, Foley, if you had anything on this asshole, you were to give it to me. The first guy into this room—this crime scene, Foley—should have been me."

"I didn't touch anything."

"That's small consolation. You and I are gonna talk about this, kid, and when we're done, you'll understand that I'm—that we're the police, these guys in the room and me, we're the ones that do this work for a living, and not much of a living at that. But it's what we do, and you've got nothing to do with it."

Ray's stomach was churning, and he could feel the eyes of the other cops on him.

"I'm sorry. I thought he was the guy. The one who killed Eddy Walsh."

Carmody gave him a long look, then shot a look over his shoulder at the uniforms in the room.

"That Walsh kid, that was this guy's friend." Carmody glared at him. "So now he's a *vigilante*."

Ray saw one cop nod his understanding. Another just shook his head.

"Mackal," Ray said.

Carmody frowned. "What?"

"George Mackal. Morrison's old bodyguard."

"We know about Mackal."

Carmody shot the other cops a look.

"So what do you want to tell me about Mackal?"

"I saw him arguing with Passeau. This could have been him."

"That would be a good tip, son, except your boy Mackal is dead. Want to guess how?"

"Somebody stabbed him," Ray said in a defeated voice.

"That's right. We found him in an alley. Had a surprised look on his face."

Carmody watched Ray, clearly pleased with the effects of his news.

The blood smell was getting to Ray now, the smell he'd never gotten used to in the War. He held a hand to his mouth and wondered if he would be sick in front of these men.

"Nasty smell, ain't it?" Carmody said. "Go on home, Foley. And you'll be hearing from me."

So what else is new?

As he made his way out of the building Ray lit up a cigarette, inhaled, blew smoke out through his nostrils, just to wipe out the smell of death.

I've screwed this up so bad.

* * *

He turned off the light and sank back onto the bed. As he dozed off, he remembered Adrian's description of a young man watching Morrison's house, and now another image came to him, from the old knife sharpener, a young man watching that house. An angry young man, he'd suggested.

He got up for a glass of water and then went back to bed. He woke sometime later, with no clear idea what time it was. In the distance he heard the ratcheting of the El train making its Diversey stop. Then nothing. He sat up and listened to the quiet. He had been dreaming, a series of dreams, one bleeding into another, first people following him in darkness, Harvey De Camp, then Sal Greene, and then he saw the dead faces of this Morrison thing—Eddy, Jimmy Seeger, Barney Donlan. He saw Willie Foy, briefly, watching him from the far side of a darkened street. Then he was sitting somewhere, facing Floyd Hennessey. In his dream Floyd was speaking to him, shaking his head, telling him he'd missed it.

What? Ray thought. What did I miss?

Probably a dozen things.

Now he remembered Floyd explaining how he'd taken himself out of harm's way.

"It ain't hard to make 'em think you're dead, Kid."

He began to see another way of looking at all of it—that it hadn't begun with the death of Morrison and all the ensuing carnage but with the death of a shadowy character named Hatch, dead before any of this took place

In his mind's eye he now saw the body floating in the river, another body identified as Hatch, a man now presumed dead and therefore free to come and go as long as he kept out of the sight of the people who knew him best. The more he considered this possibility, the more sense it made to Ray.

He thought of the man in the boxcar speaking about Bennie.

"He thought this fella was dead."

Not Passeau. Bennie thought he'd seen Hatch.

"Jesus," Ray said aloud.

Chapter Twenty-Four

He caught Sophie bending over to pour disinfectant into a sink.

"Hello, Sophie."

She jumped slightly, put her hand to her breast in a gesture that Ray found theatrical and slightly amusing.

"That's cute. Little scared girl. You kill people but you spook easily."

She gave him a long look. "What are you, goofy? What are you talking about?"

"Something I've been working on for what seems like a long time. Putting it all together. You know, about you and Passeau."

Sophie curled her lip.

"No, no, I know, you don't like him. I mean, who would? But you don't have to worry about him anymore because he's dead."

She froze and this time it wasn't an act.

"Dead how?"

"What you'd expect. He was stabbed to death. By the other guy."

She screwed her face into a frown of puzzlement but Ray had seen the sudden look of fear in her eyes.

She was in the middle of "What other guy—" when Ray threw the slider.

"Hatch." He said the name slowly, enunciating carefully. "Hatch."

She began shaking her head but he held up his hand.

"No. He's here. He's been seen. He's the guy that's been at the bottom of all of it, he killed Morrison and all these other people. Who knows why? No, that's a stupid question, Sophie, because I think you do. I think you've known all along. You're part of it. You've always been."

"You don't know what you're talking about."

"For once, I think I do. And I'm pretty sure you helped this creep kill Morrison, you were in on all of that."

Sophie looked around at the nearly empty counter. A man at the far end held up his cup for a refill and she went down to serve him. Then she killed time wiping down the counter and straightening the salt and pepper shakers. When she was ready to talk again she came down the counter and gave Ray a little smile.

"You talk a lot of nonsense. You just make things up and say them and watch people react. That's it, isn't it?"

"Part of it. But I'm not making anything up. And you know it. You were in this with Hatch and Passeau, the three of you."

Sophie bent over the sink, shaking her head. She grabbed a dish and ran a sponge over it. When she turned toward him again, the color had left her face. Ray smiled.

"I'll stop by again and we'll talk. But for now, tell your friend Hatch I said hello. I'm hoping to tell him face-to-face for once. We haven't been properly introduced."

Sophie straightened up, still holding the sponge, and gave him a look of pure malice.

"He knows you."

"That's good," Ray said, and left.

* * *

In the small hours of a long, hot night, Ray lay on top of his bed and tried to sleep

Eventually he got up and went to the windowsill. He opened a warm bottle of beer and drank half of it at one long swallow.

I've been walking all day, I ought to be able to sleep.

He leaned on the windowsill and studied the darkened street. His brief conversation with Sophie came back to him. He recalled the look in her eyes when he mentioned Hatch. Her reaction told him enough.

So I'm close, he thought.

Then he thought about what she'd said.

He knows you.

He replayed the moment again, then again. And this time he heard the slight emphasis on the last word.

He knows *you.*

Ray straightened and set down the beer. He heard Sophie's voice again and understood the part she'd left unsaid.

He knows you but you don't know him.

Ray shook his head in frustration.

He knows me. He's seen me. No, he's talked to me. So I should know him.

"I know him," he said aloud, "I've talked to him."

He leaned forward with both hands on the windowsill. Outside on the corner, an argument was developing, two men nose to nose and ready to go to it, and Ray paid them no heed, for he was seeing the faces, all the faces from Max Silver to a certain chauffeur, to Bernie Moore's hard-looking driver, and then he had it, he knew who Hatch had to be.

"Oh, Jesus!"

Ray hit the windowsill with both fists. And now a conversation with Hannah Marcel came back to him, of an overheard argument between a woman soon to be murdered and a young man Hannah took to be her son. Opal Raines and her son.

Now I know you, too, Hatch. I've got you.

This time when he lay back on the bed, sleep came to him, a fitful sleep but better than nothing.

In the morning, he woke early, far too early to accomplish anything. So he showered down the hall from his room and went out. He walked and found a paper, got a cup of coffee and a donut from a small restaurant and had breakfast on a bench.

Then he found a pay phone on the corner and called Silver.

"It's me, Ray Foley. I've got it."

"You think so?"

"Yeah, I do. You said Morrison left families behind, angry wives, kids."

"He did, more than once."

"Yeah, and I think you've been putting all that together, his history."

After a moment's silence, Silver said, "Yes, we've talked about his history."

"Not all of it. You didn't give it all to me."

"No? What did I leave out?"

"Opal Raines. The woman who was murdered."

"His wife, I told you that."

"And she had kids, am I right?"

"Yes. Two children."

"I bet you even know their names."

He heard Silver rooting around in a drawer.

"All right. Let's see: the girl's name was Greta. And the boy's name—"

Silver hesitated and Ray filled the blank for him.

"Adrian. His name was Adrian, right?"

"How'd you figure that?"

"I got lucky. I have to go. Got to meet a new friend."

As he hung up the phone Ray had the satisfaction of hearing Max Silver say, "Wait a minute, Ray—" with an off-balance note in his voice.

I beat you to this one, Mr. Silver.

* * *

The manager at Woolworth's told him Sophie had quit.

"She just called and said she was done. No notice or anything."

He gave Ray an aggrieved look as though Ray were somehow responsible.

As Ray stepped out into the street, he thought he knew what this meant. *She's leaving.*

Ray was leaning against a car outside Sophie's building when she emerged. She was carrying a green suitcase and a dark blue overnight bag.

"Morning, Sophie."

"I have nothing to say to you. Get out of my way. I have to catch a cab."

"Leaving town?"

"That's right."

"With Hatch? Or do we call him 'Adrian'? That's his name, after all."

She gave him a stunned look, then tried to walk around him. Ray shifted his feet and blocked her way.

"I've got nothing to do with him."

She set down the suitcases and tried on a dismissive look but Ray could see the fear underneath.

"Are you sure?"

She lost some of the color in her face, shook her head.

"I don't want anything to do with him."

"And you know he was Morrison's son."

Sophie sighed, looked past him. She seemed to be debating something with herself.

"They were both his sons," she said in a tired voice. Then she shot Ray a quick look, amused if only for a moment.

"Yeah, you think you know everything but you didn't know that. They were both his sons, Passeau and Jimmy Hatch. Half-brothers. They both tracked him down here. Geoff Passeau first and then Jimmy. They didn't even know about each other until they met here. So they met here and planned to kill Morrison on a night when the staff was off, and Jimmy Hatch did it."

For a moment Ray said nothing. Then he shook his head at all of it.

"So now he's killed his brother."

"Geoff Passeau was stupid. Geoff wanted money from him, with Geoff it was always about money. He was convinced Jimmy had somehow managed to get at Morrison's money that night. And Jimmy never even cared about the money."

"He killed all these people, his father and his mother. And a bunch of guys he didn't even know. Guys who never did a thing to him, didn't even know him."

Sophie gave him a frank look. She shrugged.

"They were there. They got in the way, they ruined what he had planned. He said he wanted it clean and they got in the way."

"Most of them couldn't even identify him, Sophie."

She gave him a little shake of her head, irritated.

"He wasn't afraid of that. He's not afraid of anything. He was angry that they interfered with his plan. He killed them all because he was angry. He wanted it clean. It's how he is."

"Who else has he killed, Sophie?"

Sophie tilted her head. "How much time you got?" She gave Ray an appraising look. "And now he's going to kill you because you came after him. You ought to get on the next bus out of town. He's going to kill you."

"We'll have to see about that. None of those other people had a fair chance."

Sophie looked him in the eye and raised one eyebrow. Ray smiled.

"And how about you, Sophie? What's he got planned for you?"

She gave him a hard little smile.

"I'll be gone before he misses me. If he ever does. I waited long enough for him. I never knew it would go this far."

Then she walked away and Ray saw a couple of men interrupt their conversation to watch her, a tall, sullen, good-looking girl. For a moment Ray could imagine her walking that way, all the way downtown to the bus station or the train depot and right out of town. He watched the two men and imagined calling out, *"She'd kill you in your sleep."*

In the late afternoon he sat on his bed and read the papers. He understood that he ought to be calling Carmody, perhaps Max Silver, but he knew he would not.

I want to see his face, I want to look him in the eye.

He thought of the moments when he'd encountered Adrian on the street and understood where this final meeting had to take place. For now, he lay back on his bed and closed his eyes.

* * *

At dusk Ray left his room and walked east, aimlessly at first to kill the time, then heading south, to keep his appointment. Somewhere on Halsted he understood that he had picked up a tail, but he kept walking as the light bled out of the sky. It was nearly eight when he reached Poe Street, aware now that the tail was closer. He paused momentarily in front of the old place and the man behind him slowed down. Ray lit a cigarette and blew out smoke, glanced overhead at a pair of nighthawks on the prowl, turned casually to look behind him, saw nothing. Then he moved on.

The block where Morrison's mansion once stood now looked oddly incomplete. The city had begun demolition of the house, hauling away the rubble, leaving a wide gap among the houses. After a moment, Ray crossed the street and stood in front of the ruins. As he stared at the remains of the house, he was certain that a dark shape had crossed the street half a block behind him. Then Ray turned, so that he was facing the playground. And there he was.

The man called Hatch was sitting on a bench, smoking, his legs crossed, and looking right at Ray.

Ray took a final puff on his cigarette, flipped it with his thumb and made a show of watching its high arc, then stepped off into the street to meet Hatch. He shot a quick glance up the street, then headed across, toward the playground.

In the fading light he could see Hatch, now sitting with his hands in his pockets, a well-dressed young man in a dark suit and hat. When he reached the far side of the street, Ray stopped under the cone of light from a streetlamp. Hatch got to his feet and stretched like a lazy cat. He slipped off the jacket, made a production of folding it, then placing it on the bench, and resting the hat on it. Then he came toward Ray, and Ray could see the knife held close to his leg.

With a slow, studied motion Ray brought out his own knife, held it up, noted with satisfaction that Hatch paused in mid-step, almost imperceptibly but it was there. Ray smiled, waved the knife back and forth.

Not used to facing a guy with a weapon, huh?

"Hello, Adrian," he called out.

The strange young man he knew as Adrian came forward, transformed now, a clean-cut young man in a good shirt. And with this new appearance came a new aura. The wide-eyed boy in the Dodger cap was gone, replaced by a clear-eyed, confident man with what Ray might have called a sardonic look in his eye. And of course the limp was gone.

When he was perhaps ten feet from Ray, Adrian slowed down and spread his feet, waving the knife slowly in front of him.

"I'll admit I'm impressed by the act, Adrian. You've got talent."

Adrian smiled and tilted his head as though acknowledging the compliment.

"If you dress like a bum, people don't even see your face. I almost got you that other time. You got a lot of luck."

"There was no reason to kill those guys, Adrian. You know that, I think."

Adrian blinked as though this thought was hard to process. He shrugged.

"The one guy saw, the old one. He saw me, took me by surprise. How do I know what he said to those other guys? So they're dead, a lot of bums. Big deal." Adrian gave him a half smile. "And now you're dead. Like all those other ones."

Ray shrugged. "None of them had a chance. You know what? I'm going to put you on the sidewalk and break your arms. Come on," he said. "I don't have all day."

A flash of anger in the eyes, then, and Adrian came at him, the knife held low in his left hand. He took a little side-step and Ray saw how he had been able to kill these men with a single thrust.

But Ray knew what was coming and took a side-step of his own and Adrian's blade caught cloth and nothing else.

They circled one another now, the scraping of their feet the only sound to break the night silence. Adrian came at Ray again, took a wide swipe this time, but Ray kept circling to his right and the blade missed him. Now Adrian changed direction and came forward, and Ray backed up suddenly. He felt something at his back, the fence around the playground, and moved too late to his left, and Adrian caught him this time along his side. In moments his shirt was soaked, and as Ray backed away it seemed that Adrian relaxed. Ray moved into the center of the sidewalk and waited.

Adrian paused just a moment before him, made a show of tossing the knife from his right hand to his left. He made a small feint one way, then another.

Ray recalled an older kid trying to teach him how to catch a runner in the open field.

Watch his body, his waist. He can fake with his feet or his head, but his body's only gonna go one way.

And so he watched Adrian run through his little moves and feints, watched Adrian's belt buckle, and when it moved to the left, Ray sidestepped. Adrian swiped at him with the knife and missed, and as he passed Ray, Ray swung his own knife behind him, swiped the blade hard across the side of Adrian's head and opened a great gash from his hairline down to his jaw.

Adrian stumbled, took a step back, mouth agape. He made a snarling sound, put his hand to the wound and looked at it, startled. Then he glared at Ray.

"You sonofabitch," he said in a low voice.

"Not going the way you thought, huh?"

Ray came forward and Adrian moved toward him, and now they threw caution aside and slashed at one another. Ray caught Adrian along the arm, felt a new cut open at the top of his shoulder. Adrian lunged at him again, making odd grunts of frustration. The smaller man's face was a mask of rage, the side of his head wet with blood, and now he grew careless. He swung his arm with the knife, caught nothing but air, and Ray drove a fist to the side of Adrian's head. Adrian staggered, made a last sweep with his knife, missed, and Ray landed a final punch under Adrian's chin. He stepped back, turned, and ran to the street, lurching drunkenly.

He turned one last time and raised the knife blade, muttering a threat that Ray could not hear. Then Adrian broke and ran, stumbling out into the center of the street. He spun around to look at Ray once more, pointed the knife his way and so he never saw the car.

A long black sedan bore down on Adrian, a Tudor Deluxe, Ray would have said, and the car never slowed down, not even when it struck him. The heavy thump of the collision carried through the night, and Adrian landed on the street with an audible crack. Somewhere a woman screamed. The driver of the sedan came to a stop perhaps fifty feet away. He backed up fast, stopped again, then moved off at an oddly sedate speed.

Somewhere behind them a window opened and a man's voice carried out into the night.

"What the hell's going on there?"

Ray could hear other voices overhead now. He felt a sharp pain along his ribs, and the pain worsened as the sweat reached the cut

People began to come out of the houses. A few feet away, a man in a robe was examining the body in the street.

"Got a knife in his hand," Ray heard him say.

The man looked back at Ray.

"I'm calling the cops."

"Do that. Ask for Detective Carmody."

* * *

Carmody and Kessel emerged from the car. As Kessel moved ahead to the body, Carmody came a few steps toward Ray, pointed at him and said, "Don't move."

Ray watched him limp over to where three uniformed cops and his partner were already standing over the dead man. He said something to one of the cops, who shook his head. Carmody squatted down beside the body, seemed to study the face.

Then he hitched up his pants and made his way back to Ray.

"I'm getting tired of these tricks, kid. I'm looking for that soft spot in the canvas now. Getting too old for all this shit." Carmody looked over at the body in the street. He sighed. "Still had that long blade in his hand. So let me guess who that is."

Ray nodded. "That's him. Name, Adrian Raines, near as I can figure. He was Morrison's son."

"You've known this for how long?"

"I just put it together."

"And you found him—how?"

"No. He found me. I think he's been tailing me."

"And?"

Ray looked him in the eye, then nodded at the dead man.

"He jumped me, he cut me. I think I got him, too."

"So how did he end up in a little flat pile in the street?"

"A guy ran him over. He ran out into the street, this car came tearing up the street, going real fast, never slowed down."

Carmody studied the street for a moment. One of the uniformed officers caught his eye, shook his head.

"So this guy's dead from a speeding car."

He made a show of looking up and down the street, then tipped back his hat and scratched his scalp.

"Funny. I wouldn't think a guy would be driving that fast on a short block like this. I don't suppose you got a look at the driver."

Ray shook his head. "It was dark and he was really going fast. I didn't see his face. Looked like a newer car, though. Dark, maybe blue. Could have been a Cadillac."

"That all you got?"

"That's it."

Carmody let out a sigh. He waved the ambulance attendants away from the dead man in the street and gestured at Ray. A gray-haired man emerged from a house across the street carrying a medical bag. He made straight for the body in the street.

Carmody watched him, then turned to Ray one last time.

"So you weren't following him here."

"No. Like I said, he jumped me."

The detective nodded once, rubbed his chin, looked up at the cloudless sky. Then he squinted at Ray.

"Tried to finish what he started, huh? Almost got you this time, Foley."

"Almost."

"And you don't have anything else for me?"

Ray thought a moment and then said, "There's a girl—I don't have it all figured out yet, but I think she knew him. Her name is Sophie Bivins and she works at the Woolworth's over by the YMCA. I talked to her a couple times. She worked for Morrison."

"And you just remembered her now."

"I just found her." Ray shrugged. "That's all I know."

Carmody gave him a long look and then walked away.

* * *

For several days Ray put off visiting Max Silver. Toward the end of the week, he stopped by Silver's office. Audrey gave him what he thought was an amused look. She looked over her shoulder, where they could both see into Silver's office. He was on the phone, apparently giving a report to a client. When he noticed Ray, he motioned him in, pointed at the chair, and Ray sat.

When he was finished, Silver set down the phone. It rang again immediately and he called out to Audrey to take a message. Then he sank back in his chair and eyed Ray without expression.

To fill the silence, Ray said, "I know what you're thinking—" but Silver stopped him with an upraised palm.

"Don't say that. It's stupid. People are always saying that. Nobody knows what other people are thinking. It'd be a different world if we did. I was wondering when I was going to see you, Foley. I've been forced to follow your adventures through the newspapers."

Here Ray thought he saw just a quick flash of anger.

"I'm sorry. I know you would have wanted to be in at the end. I just couldn't think about anything else."

Silver looked out the window.

"It doesn't really matter. It was Morrison who killed her, not this crazed punk. That's what the papers are calling him, by the way."

"If the shoe fits."

Now Silver turned and gave him an amused look.

"I had a short visit from our friend Carmody—who thinks you're nuts and has the odd notion that I have some influence over you. I told him you'd gone underground."

"Yeah, I've spent a lot of time in my room or just walking around—I just had to do some thinking."

"What do you think you're going to do?"

"I don't know. I guess if things don't pan out for me, I might leave town, try to start out someplace else."

Silver looked out the window again, pursed his lips, a man politely considering a dubious notion. After a moment, he nodded.

"Terrific idea. Go to another town so you can be one more guy among the ten thousand guys just back from overseas who don't have a job or a place." He gave Ray a frank look. "Does that make sense to you? Going someplace where you don't know anyone, where you'd have no resources, no connections?"

"Sometimes you need a fresh start."

"Well, it's your life. But you've shown me something, Foley. You're a smart guy, you're resourceful, you're persistent. You make connections and you've got good instincts. You're also a little reckless, you think you're the sheriff of the town, nobody else can be trusted to do anything."

"That's not entirely—"

"I'm not finished." The phone rang again and Silver indicated the telephone with a wave. Ray could hear Audrey taking the call.

"You see how it is? I've got a lot of business here, things are proceeding fast. I'm looking for someone to work with me."

"As a—what do you call them? An operative?"

"That's the formal term. You'd be a detective in my agency."

"Can I think about it?"

"Sure. Just ask yourself whether you're going to get a better offer or, more importantly, an offer to do something as interesting. People come to me in trouble and I see what I can do."

"Carmody told me once I should be a cop. I'm not sure he still thinks that."

"You might be good at that. But I don't know if I can see you working in harness. Come work for me and you wouldn't be on a clock, you wouldn't be tied to a desk. You could do worse, Ray."

Ray got to his feet. "You're probably right about that. I'll be in touch."

On the way out, Ray smiled at Audrey.

Just up the street from Silver's office, across the street from the big gray building of the Jahn school, he passed a resale shop. He glanced idly at the odds and ends in the long window and was about to cross the street when he stopped. In the far corner of the window he had spotted a statue. He squatted before the window to study it, a statue of a red-haired woman in a toga. A green toga.

"A Greek-looking statue of some sort, about a foot-and-a-half high. A woman with a sort of green dress wrapped around her."

Ray grinned, then went inside. A tiny, birdlike woman with white hair like spun glass smiled, wished him good morning and called out, "Two dollars for that statue, young man."

"You don't miss much, do you, ma'am?"

"It helps to pay attention to the world as it goes by."

She retrieved the statue from the window and let him examine it. He hefted it, feeling as though he'd run into an old friend. The base was sealed, though the statue made an odd sound when he rapped on the bottom with his knuckle. He looked up at the little woman and realized he was smiling.

"It pleases you."

"I know someone who'd really enjoy this. Do you have a phone book?"

She gave him a quizzical look, then fetched the fat phone directory. Ray paged through it, found the name he was looking for, and the address. He gave her the two dollars, plus a dollar to have it mailed to the name he gave her.

"A Congressman?" She peered at him as though she might be able to see through pretense and subterfuge, and when he smiled, she nodded. "A private joke, then."

"That's it exactly, Ma'am."

When he left the shop, the sun was shining in a cloudless sky, and Ray was grinning.

* * *

At the end of a long warm day, Ray bought himself dinner in a small restaurant and thought about Silver's offer. When he was finished, he stepped out onto the street and began walking, and he hadn't gone a dozen steps when he realized he was being followed—and not surreptitiously but openly.

I thought I was done with all this.

He slowed down and listened: the click-click of a man with cleats on his shoes coming rapidly toward him. Ray turned and sidestepped to avoid the expected blow but the other man just stopped.

Lucas Orr.

"Good evening, Foley."

"Mr. Orr. You want to speak to me? Or—" He shrugged.

Make your play and be done with it.

The other man smiled. A grim smile, Ray would have said, the smile of a fellow who had few occasions in his life for mirth.

"I'm not here to do violence. If I were—"

Ray smiled. "I'd be on the pavement already."

"More or less."

"What then? I don't mean to be impolite but what do you want from me?"

"Nothing. I wanted to say thank you."

"For what?"

"All the legwork. The rooting around in the dark, all of it. You found him, Hatch. And you led me to him." A thoughtful look crossed Orr's face.

"One night I thought I saw him, just a momentary flash of a familiar face. Then he was gone. And gradually I came to believe what I'd seen, that he was not dead, that he was here, and the cause of all of this. And I finally found him, thanks to you."

Ray blinked, shook his head slowly, uncomprehending. Then he smiled.

"Yeah, it occurred to me that might be you. In the car."

Lucas Orr shrugged. "A man ran out in front of a car. The car struck him. He was killed instantly."

Ray thought for a moment, recalling his last conversation with Lucas Orr. "You know, they found that hood Harvey De Camp down by the river with a slug in his head."

"So I heard."

"That was you."

"He followed me for a time, which was an annoyance but nothing important. Then he came after me. A stumblebum. There was a meeting. He did not survive it."

Lucas gave Ray a frank look.

Ray said, "Facing his opponent, he wasn't much. That wasn't his way."

Lucas Orr nodded and held out his big hand. They shook and he spun on his heel to walk away.

* * *

As far as anyone knew, Sophie Bivins made good her escape. She bought a bus ticket for St. Louis, but as far as anyone could tell, left the bus sometime before her destination. The more Ray considered this news, the more he realized he was hoping on some level that she would get away.

Epilogue

On a steamy Friday evening toward the end of August, Max Silver took Ray to a hotel on Clark Street to meet a client, one Richard Todhunter, a businessman trying to find his long-lost son.

When they left the meeting, they ran into Hannah Marcel, literally, for she bumped into Max Silver with an armload of packages.

"I'm so sorry," she said.

"It's all right, Miss," Silver said. "My fault."

Then she saw Ray. "Oh."

"Hello." He smiled, lost a moment to indecision, then remembered his manners.

"Hannah Marcel, this is Max Silver. I work for him now."

She nodded and smiled at Silver. "You're the detective."

"So is Ray, now."

"I guess that's good, since that's what he's been doing anyway."

Ray managed a stiff smile. He felt the blood rushing to his face.

Max Silver gave him a quick look, then said, "I've got to be somewhere. We'll talk later, Ray."

"Nice to meet you, Mr. Silver," Hannah said.

"It was my pleasure." Silver tipped his hat, then stepped out into the street.

"Mr. Silver?" Hannah said.

"Yes?"

She nodded toward Ray. "Will you keep him out of harm's way?"

"Ma'am, you don't know what you're asking."

When he'd left, Hannah turned back to Ray.

"New suit. Nice."

"Can I carry those boxes?"

"No, I'm a big girl."

"So. How've you been?"

"I'm fine," she said, and Ray caught the edge in her voice: *What do you expect me to be?*

"That's—well, that's good."

He caught a glint of amusement in the brown eyes.

"Well—" he began again.

"You'll have to tell me all about the detective business sometime," she said, and began to walk away.

When? How will I do that?

Ray said, "I was wondering—" but she held up a small hand and stopped him.

"I've got to go, Ray."

He watched her walk away with that quick-step little strut, a tough little girl who was through with Ray Foley and all the trouble he could bring her. Then, just as he began to turn away he caught the change in movement, she was slowing down. She shook her head, he saw her struggling to balance her packages as she fumbled with her purse.

She glanced over her shoulder at Ray, and then resumed her self-assured walk, and she'd gone perhaps a dozen steps when he saw the flash of white, a piece of cloth. A small, delicate ladies' handkerchief floating to the sidewalk.

Ray headed toward her, moving fast, and saw another man bearing down on the handkerchief.

"This one's mine, buddy," Ray said, and swooped down on the handker-chief. He raised it and saw that she was gone. He looked around and saw a blue and white cab on the far side of the street, and Hannah was getting in. She did not look back.

Ray held the handkerchief to his noise, smelled her perfume, other things—soap, maybe, makeup, the fascinating mixture of smells from the dark recesses of a woman's purse. Ray looked up the street where the cab was just turning the corner.

Does this mean anything?

He knew what she'd say: *You're the detective.*

He folded the handkerchief and tucked it in his shirt pocket, wondering as he did so if all his life to the end of his days women would be able to tie his mind in knots.

We're not through, he thought.

About the Author

Michael Raleigh is the author of ten previous novels. These include the coming-of-age novel *In the Castle Of The Flynns* (Sourcebooks 2002), the comic adventure *The Blue Moon Circus* (Sourcebooks 2003), and a five-book mystery series featuring private investigator Paul Whelan (St. Martin's Press). Most recently, Raleigh has published *The Conjurer's Boy* (Harvard Square Editions 2013), *Peerless Detective* (Diversion Books 2015), and *Murder in the Summer Of Love* (Epicenter 2021).

Michael lives in Chicago, where he teaches first year writing in the Honors Program at DePaul University.He has taught at DePaul since 2007 and in 2019 was named Distinguished Professor by the Honors Program. Prior to DePaul, he taught English and Chicago History at Truman Community College. He is married and has three grown children.

He has been a stock boy, a bartender, a microfiche maker, a bank-teller, fund-raiser and manager of social programs for the Salvation Army, and liaison officer for the Chicago Department of Human Services.

Michael is currently a member of the Mystery Writers of America and the Society of Midland Authors. When he is not writing or grading papers, Michael raises tomatoes, practices archery, watches English mysteries with his wife and works on his lock-picking skills.

AUTHOR WEBSITE:
  michaelraleighwriter.com

Also by Michael Raleigh

Death In Uptown (St. Martin's Press 1991)

A Body In Belmont Harbor (St. Martin's Press 1993)

The Maxwell Street Blues (St. Martin's Press 1994)

A Killer On Argyle Street (St. Martin's Press 1995)

The Riverview Murders (St. Martin's Press 1997)

In The Castle Of The Flynns (Sourcebooks 2002)

The Blue Moon Circus (Sourcebooks 2003)

The Conjurer's Boy (Harvard Square Editions 2013)

Peerless Detective (Diversion Books 2015)

Murder In The Summer Of Love (Epicenter/Coffeetown 2021)